Mary Atkins is the author of *A Journey of Creative Healing* and *Finding Your Voice: Ten Steps to Successful Public Speaking*. A Home Economist she is the Past President of the Australian Association of Food Professionals. Mary is also an award-winning speaker who currently travels the world lecturing on cruise ships.

LOSING YOU

MARY ATKINS

Losing You

First published 2013

Mary Atkins
Peregian Springs QLD 4573
Australia
Email: findingyourvoice@bigpond.com
Website: maryatkinsauthor.com

ISBN: 9780648192244
Internal design: Big Shed Creative Communications
Set in 12pt/16pt Minion Pro
Cover design: Big Shed Creative Communications
Cover images: iStock by Getty Images

Printed and bound by Kindle Direct Publishing

For my family, past and present

What you leave behind
is not what is engraved in stone monuments
but what is woven into the lives of others
Pericles

Prologue

· · · · · · · · · · ·

It was the summer of 1942 when Captain Frank Taylor was posted to an Officer Cadet Training Unit in a small town in Wales. His wife Lucy and young daughters were casualties of the Blitz. Homeless, they followed Frank to Wales and found lodgings with a teacher and his wife.

Their landlord, Evan Hughes, a pale moon faced man with small hands disproportionate to his large body, taught at the local primary school. In his spare time he was a part time air raid warden and butterfly collector. On the cream stucco walls in the hall of his home were the boxed and framed displays of his butterfly collection. His steel helmet stencilled with a large white 'W' hung on the oak hallstand close to the front door.

Being a teacher he was good with children especially with the timid four-year-old Kate who spent most of her young life viewing it from behind her mother's skirts. He showed the girls the balsa board where the dead butterflies were spread-eagled to dry out ready for mounting and the killing jar filled with cotton wool balls soaked in a mixture of ether and chloroform. He explained that once a butterfly is caught he would pinch it's thorax to stun it before popping it in the jar where it simply went to sleep peacefully, his lips squeezed a smile as he gave Kate a soft pinch to her tummy. Doing this, he added, stops them bashing their wings against the side of the jar trying to escape.

He took the girls out to a local hamlet where the fields spread out before them and butterflies rose in the air, their scale covered wings of glorious hues lifting them in the updraft as they sourced nectar. Eight-year-old Jane was way ahead of them excitedly swooping the large net whenever she saw a butterfly. Kate ran through the long grass grasping the handle of the gauze net held steady by Mr Hughes, her legs hardly keeping up with his pace. He shouted but she could not hear his words. She turned her head and his hand gripped her face pressing something over her nose and mouth. She jerked her head but was held fast. The smell scalded her nostrils and made her eyes water. She tried to push his hands away but his hold was firm. The odour, reminding her of her mother's nail polish remover filled her nostrils.

Mr Hughes voice echoed distantly. 'You be a good girl or I will tell your mother.'

She knew nothing more.

Chapter 1

• • • • • • • • • • •

A Summer's Day 1963

Greg Sinclair pinched his lips together as he attempted to tie a double Windsor knot in his red and blue tartan tie. The mirror fixture on the dressing table was broken and the oval mirror tilted forward, reflections of Greg's white short sleeve shirt and grey pants flashed before it settled on the image of the double bed and his wife Kate, her fair hair draped like a curtain over one shoulder feeding their two-week old son.

'Bugger,' he said as he righted the mirror and fiddled with the screw to tighten it.

Kate tried to recall what the local community nurse had told her, something about the baby's lower jaw taking a good chunk of breast and that his lips should curl outwards. Ben switched his head in frustration and whimpered, his lips pursing. She tried again and Ben took the nipple pulling it back and forth before letting out an almighty anguished howl.

Greg began again weaving the tie in and over but the

knitted fabric defied his efforts.

'Bloody bugger of a thing,' he said and opened the drawer of the dressing table and flipped through the contents until he found the blue and grey striped clip-on tie. He clipped it on behind the top button of his white shirt and adjusted the knot so it sat neatly under his collar.

'How you're doing Katie? He asked.

'Don't ask me. With Ally it was a disaster and now Ben. He's hungry and I'm in agony.'

'You can do it Katie,' he said as he crammed the drawer of the dressing table shut. The mirror slipped again reflecting a wall of white laminated wardrobe doors with fancy glass doorknobs and a cream shag pile carpet.

'I bet it would be a different story if it were your nipples going through the mangle.'

'Of course, you just need to persevere,' he said, and bent to kiss her forehead.

'Yes just like you persevered with your double thingamajig knot.'

'Now that's a different proposition Katie, breastfeeding is natural and a double Windsor knot,' his lips twitched, 'is not.'

Kate shook her head as he gazed down at her, his smile creasing his cheeks and sassy eyes. Ben gave another yowl, his head twitching to find a source of comfort.

Her nipples were gorged and throbbed like angry wasp stings. She wanted to cup her breasts with cool hands to soothe them. She draped the baby over her shoulder and softly patted his back.

'Are you hungry Ben or do you need burping?', she

whispered.

She watched her husband as he slicked his hair with Brylcream combing it severely back from his face. He was tall, just less than six foot and she delighted that at five foot three she fitted neatly under his breastbone so that when he held her close she could hear his steady heart beat. He had a broad face, a straight nose and a strong jutting chin. To her his blue eyes blazed a surety but to others the steeliness of his gaze was often translated as arrogance. He scooped up the loose change and car keys from the bedside table and put them in his pocket, his forearms sparse of down a contrast to his head of thick black hair. Even now, after nearly five years together, whenever he spoke his Australian accent excited her.

'What's for breakfast Katie?', he asked.

'Bacon from the smell of it. Lucky, lucky us!', she said following him down the stairs.

The kitchen was spacious with more cabinets than they could fill with crockery, cream laminated surfaces and a white tiled splash back. A large picture window overlooked the back garden. In the centre of the room an orange melamine table and matching chairs gave a splash of welcome colour to the clinical brightness of the room.

Ally was hammering her plastic cup on the highchair table, her face crumpled into a gooey smile when she saw her parents. Greg captured one of her flailing hands as she lunged forward to throw her cup to the floor. He kissed her sticky soft knuckles before picking up the cup and replacing it.

'Hello cheeky face hope you've been a good girl for your grandmother?'

He shook his head as Ally threw it to the floor and giggled at the game. This time he left it where it lay.

'Morning Lucy, Frank gone already?', he asked.

Kate's mother Lucy nodded as she placed two plates of bacon and fried eggs on the table. The yokes had started to congeal from their stay in the warmer drawer of the oven.

'How were the night feeds?' Lucy asked as Kate put the sleeping baby into the carrycot.

Kate shook her head. 'Roll on three months. Who says four hourly feeds are best for baby, but which baby, not either of mine.' Kate smiled at thirteen-month old Ally wriggling in her high chair. 'Yes you too, puddin' chops.'

Kate's mother Lucy Taylor was in her mid fifties but her smooth skin and trim body denied her age. She topped the teapot with boiling water and poured herself a cup.

'Daddy and I are thinking of going home this weekend. You seem to be coping well now,' she said.

'Don't know about coping well but we can manage can't we Greg? We are so grateful Mummy, I couldn't have done it without you.'

Greg nodded, placing the knife and fork together neatly on his empty plate,

'Yes, Lucy, we really appreciate the help. It meant I was let off the hook,' he gave a theatrical wink and blew a kiss to his amused mother-in-law.

'You're a bugger Greg Sinclair,' Kate whispered twisting a strand of her hair.

The hall was dark, lined with timber panelling. Kate wanted to paint the panels white and lay black and white tiles down on the timber floor for a more contemporary sixties look but Greg preferred the traditional look of natural timber.

The diamond paned windows in the front door spilled patterns of light on the hall carpet runner. When Greg and Kate first moved into the house, Kate thought they were stains in the early morning light and had attempted to scrub the offending marks. The previous owners had left them the runner as well as the big uncomfortable gold brocade settee in the lounge; two tapestry wing back armchairs and the dressing table. They were appreciative, as they had no furniture apart from nursery furniture, two double beds and a television.

Greg slipped his arm under her dressing gown and circled her waist. He kissed her cheek. 'I'm going to the aero club after surgery.'

Kate pulled away from his embrace 'Oh Greg do you have to, yesterday it was a game of squash, today you're flying. What about home time, and helping out with the children?' Kate's eyes narrowed.

'Come on Katie, it's just circuits and bumps, I've got to get my hours up if I'm to keep my licence.' He put his arm around her again and pulled her closer. She could feel the buttons on his shirt grazing her breasts and she tried to push away but he held fast.

'Katie come on now stop making a fuss, your parents are here helping you out and you can manage. I'll be home before you know it. Come on give me a kiss.'

'Is your sister coming this weekend?' Kate's voice was a hiss, a blur of words.

Greg raised his eyebrows and his hold on her relaxed. 'I don't know Katie, she may or she may not.'

'I don't want her here Greg, she causes trouble between us,' Kate said watching his face intently.

'She's my sister, Katie.'

'And I'm your wife Greg,'

Kate shook her head. But she did not move.

He sighed as he stared into her eyes. 'What am I going to do with you Katie?', he asked. His lips were soft as he kissed her mouth.

'Don't be late tonight, please?'

'Whatever you say Katie,' his eyes sparkled.

He opened the front door and stepped away from her. She watched as he threw his blazer into the back of the car and slipped into the driving seat. The motor coughed and steadied, before he reversed his old Citroen down the driveway. At the road the Citroen stopped while he put it into first gear. She saw him wave and shout something into the breeze and he was gone, the old car leaving a trail of exhaust.

A frieze of blue and pink bunnies etched the top of the pale lemon walls of the nursery. Kate had painted the nursery when they moved into the house ten months ago. She made the curtains from a fabric with a similar theme of long eared yellow rabbits.

Ally fidgeted as Kate changed her, she dropped the sodden terry-towelling nappy into the plastic bucket. With one hand holding Ally's legs high Kate liberally sprinkled the damp pink cheeks with talcum powder. Ben cocooned in his muslin wrap slept deeply in his carry-cot beside Ally's big white cot.

'Amazing,' Kate said 'During the day he hibernates but at night it's one big party.' Ally scrunched her eyes. 'It's okay Ally just your mother sounding off. Nap time I think for you Miss Sinclair.'

It was a funny muggy sort of day when the nappies hung wet and limp on the line. In the afternoon Kate wheeled the children in the black and cream carriage pram to the park. Ally sat facing the path ahead and at her toes lay Ben. Comforted by the movement of the pram, the infant's dark blue eyes stared at the tree line above, Some trees, affected by the harsh winter were bare of leaves but the horse chestnuts were green interleaved with white Christmas tree shaped blooms. The sweet sound of a birdsong caught Ally's attention and she twisted her head searching for the source.

'Probably sitting on her nest sweetheart somewhere high overhead, we might not see her but we can listen to her song,' Kate said turning the pram around for the homeward journey.

Lucy, fresh from an afternoon rest, was peeling potatoes. The *Good Housekeeping Compendium* lay open on the kitchen table.

'Some lovely recipes in there Kate and look at this novel centre piece for the table,' she flicked the pages stopping at a picture of a fat yellow grapefruit studied with squares of cheese and tiny red and green pickled onions on cocktail sticks.

Kate lifted Ally into her highchair and opened a jar of apple puree. She read the recipe as she fed Ally.

'That's so easy, good for a cocktail party. Oh by the way I forgot to tell you Greg is going to the aero club after surgery I don't think he'll be back in time for dinner,' Kate said.

'And your father is going to the golf club for a meeting so it's just you and I. That's nice, how about we have ours on a tray watching the telly. We can put theirs onto steam when they get home,' said Lucy.

It was mid evening. The *Z Cars* credits scrolled down the small television screen and the familiar theme music competed with Ben's hungry cries when the telephone rang.

'I'll get it,' Lucy called from the kitchen.

Kate lifted Ben from his cot and undid her blouse.

'I think you'd better take the call love,' her mother said walking back into the lounge. 'It's someone from Greg's club, I told them you were about to feed Ben but they won't give me the message. I think you had better speak to them.'

Kate took the call cradling Ben to her chest to comfort him.

'Kate, my name is William Ryan, I'm President of the Laurelford Aero Club.' His voice had a singular flat tone like he was reading from a script. 'There's been an accident. Greg has been injured and is being taken to hospital.'

'Accident, hospital?', her voice trembled. She clutched Ben tighter.

'We believe it's minor so try not to worry. We're not sure which hospital yet. My wife and I will come over and drive you there.'

She shivered as she put the phone back into its cradle.

'What's happened?' Lucy's tone was sharp.

'Greg's been in an accident.'

Lucy's face paled. 'Accident?'

'The fellow said it's not serious. He's being taken to hospital. They don't know which hospital yet but he will take me there.' Kate tried to button her shirt but her fingers wouldn't work 'I'd better get ready, but Ben…'

Lucy took the baby nestling him in the crook of her arm.'You need to get changed Ben's spew is down the front of that shirt,' Ben squirmed and started to cry. 'There there young man Nana will make it better. Greg will be fine you'll see. Don't worry about Ben I'll give him a bottle,' she said.

Kate shook as she put on a clean shirt and skirt. Brushing her hair back from her face to secure into a ponytail she remembered that Greg had said he was going to do routine circuits and bumps to get his hours up to maintain his private pilot license. She imagined his Auster taking off, going around the airfield in a set pattern before coming into land, putting the wheels down neatly on the runway. As the wheels touched the ground he would immediately gun his small plane down the runway to take off and land again, and again, and again. She had seen him do the manoeuvre safely a hundred times. She looked at the pale image in the mirror. Her eyes looked huge, her green eyes eclipsed by the dark pupils. She patted a little blusher over her cheeks. She placed her hand softly on her cheek. 'He'll be okay. You know he has more lives than a cat.'

At the front door William Ryan stood tall, his grey-flecked hair slicked back and curled around his ears. Kate recognised the Laurelford Aero Club tie.

'Be a good girl for Nana' she said giving Ally a cuddle.

Cradling Ben in one arm her mother hitched Ally awkwardly onto her other hip. 'Give me a call from the hospital and try not to worry. You know Greg always comes up smiling from a scrape.'

'Yes he'll be fine.' Kate dug into the bottom of her bag to find her purse. She fumbled as she opened it. 'Yes I've got money for a call. He'll be alright Mummy.'

Her limbs felt watery as she walked down the path. She turned and blew kisses to the small tableau at the front door as William held open the car door.

Judy Ryan, a short woman with a thick mask of beige foundation that rimmed at her chin, introduced herself as Kate settled into the back seat.

'No more news yet I'm afraid,' her fuchsia lips pursing.

'We don't know which hospital he's in but best we just head out and find out the details when we get to the police station,' William said.

'Where did the accident happen?' Kate asked.

William briefly looked at her in the rear mirror before focusing again on the traffic. 'In southwest London, we're not sure of the exact location, the police did not tell us much.'

'What was he doing in southwest London?', she asked.

'I'm not sure Kate,' William answered. There was edginess in his voice.

She clasped her hand over her lips and rocked silently on the leather seat.

Through the car window Kate gazed at the dense cotton wool clouds with hardly a lift of blue sky between them. She was unaware of the traffic and the throng of pedestrians enjoying the long summer evening.'How did you fare this January? Judy asked not waiting for a reply from Kate. 'We were snowed in for days and what with all those power cuts, it was dreadful. They say it was the worst winter for a hundred years.' She clicked open her handbag and rustled through the contents to find a packet of peppermints.

'Peppermint Kate? I always get a dry mouth in the car, don't know why but a peppermint does the trick,' she said. Kate shook her head, her stomach felt queasy and she wished the woman would stop talking. She looked at her watch it was over an hour since they had left home.

The sun was low in the sky and starting to patch the clouds with pink when the car turned into the small parking lot of a red brick police station. William switched off the engine, took off his driving gloves and opened his door 'I think this is it. Judy you wait with Kate in the car I'll find out where we have to go.'Judy turned to Kate. 'Once William has got the address of the hospital, we'll go straight away.' She reached across and put her moist hand over Kate's. A diamond ring cut into the fleshy fold of her finger and her dark pink fingernails looked as if she had come straight from the beauty salon. 'Try not to worry dear.' Judy said. Kate shook her head and snatched her hand away.

William's face was pale when he returned. 'Still no news I'm afraid. They suggest we wait here till they have the details of the hospital.'

'Why is it taking so long, surely by now they would know where they have taken him?' Kate asked.

William held the car open for her. He swallowed. 'I don't know why Kate,' he said lowering his gaze.

The waiting room smelt of sweat and stale cigarette smoke. Metal chairs with brown vinyl seats were grouped around the dark green walls. Kate's chest felt tight and every now then she audibly gulped for air. She picked at imaginary lint on her skirt, frequently getting up to circumnavigate the small room. The only sound was Judy's child like voice frequently reassuring her that everything would be all right. William loosened his tie and sat silently with his hands clasped between his thighs watching Kate. The sun had set when the policeman entered the room. 'Kate Sinclair, Mrs Greg Sinclair?'

She noticed that his sandy hair was starting to grey at the temples and evening stubble was budding on his chin. The seam of his left breast pocket of his shirt had a blue stain where a biro had leaked.

She nodded.

Without preamble he said 'I am sorry.' Kate stared down at her hands, watching her fingers twist her wedding band. She was underwater where everything was distant, the policeman's words echoing, bouncing slowly off walls drifting towards her in the deep.

Judy's gasp punctuated the silence. Kate again saw the policeman's mouth shaping the words I'm sorry. All eyes watched her waiting for her reaction. William got up from his chair. Kate lifted her eyes and stared blankly ahead. Her whole body was rigid, warding off the inevitable destruction that these words would inflict.

William took her arm 'Kate my dear, Greg is dead, I am truly sorry.' For what seemed an age she did not move. Judy stood up and her bag clattered to the tiled floor. Kate sprung to her feet and with a sense of urgency announced that she needed to pee. In the light of the white tiled bathroom she realised that she had already done so. As she stared down at the spreading bloodied stain on her skirt and the breast milk seepage on her shirt she started to laugh uncontrollably, her hysterics rattling her body. Spent and silent she bent over the sink to splash cold water on her face before returning to the waiting room.

Chapter 2

· · · · · · · · · · ·

Dark Times

Kate was still asleep as Lucy put Ally in her highchair and ran water in the kitchen sink for Ben's bath. Lucy's eyes were red rimmed as she tested the water with the back of her wrist.

'Okay bath time for you young fellow,' she said softly.

She lifted the naked baby from the change mat and carefully lowered him into the warm water. A spray of water splashed her face as Ben's legs kicked playfully. Briefly her eyes lit before a frown settled again into despair. Lucy had heard of Greg's death on the nine o'clock news.

'A single engine plane crashed into a block of flats in Handsworth, earlier this evening. The young pilot from Essex died at the scene. No one else was hurt in the crash. A bystander reported that he had seen the plane spiralling out of control to crash into the roof of the building.'

She knew straight away that it was her son-in-law. The televised footage showed the stretcher with the blanketed body being carried by the emergency rescue team. She sank to her knees still cradling the sleeping Ben in her arms. Frank found her when he came in, on the floor doubled over but holding Ben tightly. Lucy's friend and neighbour Molly arrived. She carried with her a cloth bag; in it was a wrap around apron, a pair of comfortable shoes, rubber gloves, smelling salts and her favourite potato peeler. Her reading glasses hung on a gold chain around her neck and bounced off her grandmotherly bosom as she moved. She made them both a pot of tea as Lucy fed Ben. As his mouth clamped tightly round the teat of the bottle Lucy took his small dimpled hand in hers and kissed it gently. His face was flushed with the effort of sucking and his eyelids flickered. She burped him and wiped the dribble of milk from his chin. Her knees buckled as she put him into the pram. Molly took her arm.

'No arguing Lucy you need to get some rest, you're exhausted from the shock as well as looking after these two little ones. I will take over.'

Lucy put her arms round her friend and kissed her cheek.

'Thank God you're here Molly. I'm desperate for sleep, what with the shock,' her face puckered and Molly held her closer. 'And getting up through the night to feed Ben, was ghastly.'

The sun shone in a blue cloudless sky when Kate's father, Frank Taylor walked into the City of London Mortuary. Frank had a hint of movie star Clark Gable about his appearance, the same fluidity of smile accompanied with a raised eyebrow and a thin moustache that stretched across his upper lip. He had shaved it off once during his army career but Lucy hated it and insisted he grow it back.

He asked a man at reception for directions to the viewing room. The man looked up briefly from his paperwork and pointed to the corridor to the left of the desk.

Frank thrust his shoulders back, lifted his chin and marched down the long corridor his shoes beating out a metallic rhythm on the tiled floor. The coroner's assistant stood with him as the dark blue curtain revealed the body of his son-in-law killed when his light plane crashed into a block of flats in south west London. Frank verified that the deceased was his son-in-law, Gregory Robert Sinclair. The assistant slipped out of the room allowing Frank to be alone.

Frank stood with his right arm flexed on the glass his breath smudged the window between himself and Greg. He had a dull pain in his chest that would not shift. He stared at Greg's chalk white body half hidden below a sheet. His face disfigured with purple contusions and a cut that ran up through his cheek tearing his nose and mouth with such ferocity that Frank flinched. Frank was thankful that Kate would not see him this way. He arced his hand down the window 'til it was in line with the body and closed his eyes in a silent farewell.

He imagined the years stretching ahead knowing that he and Lucy would have to carry the profound emotional responsibility of a grieving daughter and her two infant children. The assistant returned and stood silently beside Frank. He coughed and said in a reverential tone, 'We need you to sign some papers sir.'

Frank nodded and moved away from the window. The man closed the curtains and opened the door to the corridor.

'Did he die on impact?' Frank's voice was strained and gruff. He cleared his throat and signed the papers confirming the body was that of his son-in-law.

'He was pronounced dead at the crash site sir so I would not think he suffered. But the exact cause of death will be determined when the autopsy is completed,' the assistant said.

'Look I know it's not your area but I wonder if you can shed some light on why it took over three and half hours after his death before his wife was told and why they made her, a nursing mother of a two week old son, travel half way round London to be told in a police station?'

The man's eyes were sympathetic as he leant towards Frank.

'I know they had to cut his body from the plane, there would be a risk of fire with a plane crash and they would have cordoned off the area. All that takes time. I would think that they probably thought your daughter could identify the body and they would able to get the necessary paperwork underway. But sir that is simply my opinion, don't hold me to it.'

One of the mortuary doors flew open and a ward man pushed an empty gurney past the desk.

'I'm most grateful, for your help, makes sense. When do you think you will be able to release his body?' Frank asked.

'Providing the autopsy, which we anticipate will happen today, is straight forward the coroner will authorise for his body to be released at that time.'

Frank thanked him and headed back to the car park. He sat in the car in the multi-storey council car park, with its high-street landscape of red brick buildings and its steady stream of shoppers weaving their way across the thoroughfares. Bile rose in his throat and he put his handkerchief to his mouth until the nausea passed. He wound down the window. The cool air refreshed him. He was startled by the echo of a car door opening and watched as a woman packed a basket of groceries in the boot before reversing her car out into the line of cars waiting to exit. He was clearer now on the possible cause of time delay in giving Kate the news but he still wanted to understand what Greg was doing over southwest London. He decided to visit Laurelford Aerodrome.

He had a good run through the city traffic and soon the built up areas of the city thinned and a patchwork of fields and groves of trees heralded the Essex countryside. Green hedgerows and the whispery tall grasses framed Beechwood Road and he knew he was in the right place when he saw the plumped orange windsock catching the breeze. The entrance to Laurelford Aero Club was sign posted and Frank dropped into second gear as he entered the car park. There parked in a spot close to the road was Greg's Citroen. He had forgotten that it would be here. He pulled into the bay next to it. The windows of the Citroen were splattered with bird droppings and sap from the overhanging trees. He wiped the window with his handkerchief and peered inside. Ally's car seat was still hooked over the rear seat and Greg's briefcase was on the front passenger seat. He tried the handle of the door but it was locked.

The small wooden clubhouse was next to the car park and on the other side of this were three aeroplane hangars. A couple of Austers and a yellow Tiger Moth stood in front of the hangar doors. Beyond lay the grassed runways that had recently been mown.

The clubhouse doors were locked so he walked over to one of the hangars where a couple of mechanics in their grey overalls were working on an engine.

'Sorry to bother you boys but I am looking for William Ryan and the clubhouse is shut,' Frank said. One of the men stood up, wiping his hands on an oil-stained rag.

'Yes, no one has been in today and we haven't seen Bill. They got a bit a shake up last night. One of their members was killed.'

'Oh?' He coughed, it sounded false. 'What happened? Was something wrong with the plane?', asked Frank.

The man looked down at his black greasy hands and stuffed the rag in his pocket.

'Not making much difference with this,' he said 'No nothing wrong with the plane at all, couldn't be, it just received a certificate of airworthiness a couple of days back. No the poor bugger took off before a weather warning came in about dense cloud cover. So no sooner was he up when the cloud came down, he would have been hard pushed to know where he was. Nasty business, Young fellah too with a young family I hear.'

He took a spanner out of his pocket and bent over the engine once again. 'I'll tell Bill you were looking for him, shall I?'

'No don't bother I'll give him a ring at home. Thanks for your help,' Frank called as he walked back to the car park.

The tyres crunched across the gravelled surface before he turned left onto Beechwood Road. He chewed over the mechanics comments as he drove to Kate's home. It explains why Greg was so far from Laurelford, in all probability he had got disorientated in the low cloud cover. Of course it is only hearsay, he thought, but still I will call William Ryan to get confirmation.

Kate's sister and her husband arrived just after Molly had got the children down for their late morning sleep. The two sisters were different. Jane had inherited her parents' dark hair and brown eyes. Kate was fair to blonde with green eyes. Facially there were resemblances wide set eyes with long lashes, sculptured noses and good skin but very few would pick them as sisters. Occasionally with the odd lift of an eyebrow, a flared nostril when angry or a smile that played with the corner of their mouths, people could see that they were related.

'I just can't take it in Molly, it doesn't seem real.' Jane's brown eyes were puffy and she snatched at her nose with a tissue.

Molly patted her back with a cupped hand, like she would do a small child. She had always found Jane easier, more artless than Kate. With Kate she was never quite sure what was going on behind her veiled reserve.

'Terribly sad day Molly,' Ian said bending to kiss her cheek. Ian was the type of man that people warmed too instantly but later found they couldn't recall his name, more often he was referred to as the nice man who married Jane. He was solid both in build and temperament and the fact that others thought of him, as an appendage to Jane did not worry him.

'Yes. Just too dreadful, unbelievable God knows how she will cope with those two little ones on her own,' she said. Ian nodded.

Molly squeezed Jane's hand. 'Your mother is all in, what with the shock of it and doing the night feeds, all too much for her. She's asleep and the little ones. Kate hasn't stirred, thank goodness. Lucy said that she was given some strong sleeping pills to knock her out. They didn't bring her home from the police station until nearly midnight. Why they had to drag her halfway round London to tell her was criminal.'

Ian remembered the bag of pink iced finger buns he was carrying and placed them on the table. 'We thought there'd be people calling in,' he said clearing his throat. 'And we'd probably need something to go with a cup of tea.'

Molly nodded and set about putting them on a plate.

The doorbell rang, as it would do off and on throughout the morning with people delivering floral arrangements, telegrams and bringing dishes of food. By late morning the house resembled a florist shop and the kitchen table was covered in a selection of casseroles, cakes and cookies.

Kate stirred early afternoon. The curtains were drawn and chinks of light filtered through the room. Her body ached. She closed her eyes tight and turned on her side. She stretched her arm across the bed. She felt the cool smoothness of the sheets and the unruffled pillow and she remembered. It took all her will to sit-up; her limbs were stiff and heavy. She pulled herself to the edge of the bed and looked around the room. Her clothes from the previous evening lay in a jumble on the floor by the bed. On the dressing table in front of the mirror sat a brown shoebox with a crimson Bata logo. In this were Greg's watch, minus the watchstrap, his keys and small change. The blood spattered watch face was smashed, the minute hand twisted upwards and the hour hand bent and fused to seven o'clock. Both the cardboard box and its contents smelt sickly strong of petrol. She could smell it even from the distance of the bed, its pungent chemicals burning her nostrils.

The bedside digital clock read two ten. Greg's tee shirt was by his pillow. She pressed the softness to her face. She could smell him. She saw him walking down the path with his blazer over his shoulder, climbing into the car. She traced her lips with the cloth, his kiss still alive in her mind.

Faint noises reached her from downstairs. Clutching Greg's tee shirt she opened the curtains and light flooded the room, revealing one of Ben's unwashed bottles on the side table. The soft cotton shirt fell from her hand.

She ran across the landing to the nursery. Ally and Ben were both asleep, Ally with her soft blanket coiled around her little fist, and Ben snugly cocooned on his side. In the guest room her mother, fully dressed, lay on top of the bed asleep. She tiptoed to the bathroom. A tremor caught her off balance she sat on the edge of the white enamel bath and waited for it to pass. Greg's towel, neatly folded, hung on the rail. She bent to turn on the bath taps. His toothbrush, placed upright, alongside hers, in the glass. Yesterday he put a line of toothpaste over the bristles and wound it around his mouth, spitting the paste and his spittle into the sink.

She took his toothbrush and applied a worm of paste. Her mouth was dry and tasted foul. At first she brushed slowly, the peppermint taste refreshing her mouth. Gripping the brush tighter she scrubbed her teeth with a fierce determination until her gums bled. She put his brush back in the glass and rinsed with cool water until it ran clear. Taking his towel she wiped her mouth and muzzled her face into the soft soapy faintness of the cloth.

Taking off her nightdress she caught sight of her body in the mirror over the sink. Her breasts, normally gorged with milk, had shrunk visibly, sitting emptily on her chest. Her dark brown nipples were chafed and raw. Her once girlish size twenty-inch waist was replaced by her bulging stomach with folds of white flesh rolling over her lower abdomen. She removed her soiled sanitary pad, wrapped it in toilet tissue and put it in the small white pedal bin. The tail end of her episiotomy scar throbbed. The cut had been cobbled together and she was left with a nub of skin that rubbed sorely on her sanitary pad. She stepped into the bath.

She tilted her head back into the warm water, until her forehead, chin and cheeks were submerged. The bathroom was no different to yesterday morning, still filled with his presence, licks of shaving cream cleaving to the bristles of his shaving brush, the cap of his deodorant lying on the bathroom shelf. How can it be, she thought, that one second of an ordinary day you were here? Then you are gone, and no more?

Bathed and dressed, Kate went down to the kitchen. She hesitated at the door staring out through the window above the stainless steel sinks, to see Charles Barker, their accountant and friend mowing the grass and his wife Susan cutting back overgrown bushes. Flowerbeds lined either side of the lawn and midway down the garden was a terrace with stone steps that led into the vegetable garden. She watched the couple work. The mower was carefully aligned before Charles cut a neat pathway down the length of the lawn. Susan sat back on her hunches, flicked her dark hair from her face and with her hand shielded her eyes as she surveyed her work.

The sound of her sister's voice broke her trance and

Kate stole into the kitchen. The afternoon sun shafted through the window making the room bright and surreal. On the kitchen table sat a variety casserole dishes and cakes that had been left for Lucy to prioritise and allocate. Deep in conversation with Molly and Ian, Jane did not see Kate until she was beside them. Jane swept her into her arms and rocked her like a child.

'Darling are you alright?'

Ian wrapped his arms tightly round them. Jane gripped Kate's hand as they disentangled and quizzed her younger sister intently. 'Okay?'

Kate squeezed her hand in response.

Molly stood back waiting for the moment to speak to Kate. She clung to her as she kissed her cheek. 'Don't worry about a thing, Kate. I'm here as long as you and Lucy need me.'

Molly's voice was husky. She turned away to discreetly wipe her eyes on the edge of her apron.

Lucy refreshed from her sleep heard Ally playing in her cot. Ben was still asleep. She carried her grand daughter downstairs into the kitchen. Lucy's eyes were swollen and she had to keep biting her lip to stop herself crying. Kate kissed her cheek.

Ally put her arms up for her mother to take her and she snuggled into Kate's chest. Charles and Susan came in from the garden. Seeing Kate, Charles was hesitant, unsure of how he should act. Kate took his hand and kissed his cheek and folded her arms around Susan.

'Thank you for doing the garden for us, Greg would have been so grateful.'

'Kate, I'm so sorry,' Charles paused, clearing his throat noisily 'But seeing you now so composed I know you will be an inspiration to us all,' he concluded.

Kate gave a thin smile and patted his arm.

'Time for a cup of tea,' cried Molly her voice unnaturally high. 'Who's for tea and we have iced finger buns, Jane will you butter them and I will make the tea.'

Ally was intent on pulling herself up on a kitchen chair where Lucy sat. With a huge effort she made it and stood for a second, a smile lighting up her face before losing her balance and sitting down heavily. But she started again, holding first onto the leg of the chair and pulling on Lucy's knees to right herself and try once more to take her first tentative step. Molly sipped her tea, 'That child is not going to be beaten, look at her determination.'

Frank's sister arrived straight from work still wearing her navy suit with a gold metal badge identifying her as Joyce Lewis, Case Worker, Church of England Adoption Society.

Joyce put her cup awkwardly onto the saucer, it looked precarious and Lucy collected it and took it into the kitchen. Kate sat in the other wing back armchair waiting. She knew that Joyce would want to counsel her. Joyce brushed the crumbs off her skirt and pushed a strand of white hair behind her ear. Her entire head of hair had turned white almost overnight when her husband died in a motor accident after her fortieth birthday celebrations leaving her penniless to raise their two rebellious sons.

Picking up her life in those early years after his death was hard but her determined character served her well. During the day she worked in a typist pool and at night she studied for her degree in welfare counselling.

Joyce leant forward in her seat her face flushed. At first her voice was soft.

'Darling, I'm so sorry. To lose Greg in this way when you had your lives ahead of you, leaving you with two babies, is an unbelievable tragedy. '

Joyce took her hand and leaned closer, her voice firmer.

'Darling I'm not going to sugar coat it, that won't serve you. It's bloody hard but it will get harder as the weeks progress and you really start to come to grips with the grief, of being on your own and the thought of life without Greg.'

Kate pulled her hand away.

'Christ Aunty surely it can't get harder,' she said sharply.

Joyce took her hand again. 'I'm sorry love but you need to get to grips with this. You have two choices here Kate; you can either be a victim or a hero. In other words you can let this ruin your life and become bitter with self pity or you can use the experience to grow.'

Kate turned her head and stared through the French windows to the garden.

Joyce released Kate's hand. 'Do you understand Kate?'

'Yes…' Kate's voice was flat. 'I just can't take it in. I keep thinking I'll wake up and …'

'But my dear it is not a dream and the quicker you start to deal with it the better it will be for you and the children.'

'Thank you,' Kate whispered and stood up, she was

trembling and felt sick.

Joyce put her arms around her. 'Remember Kate you need to be strong to get through this.' She kissed Kate's cheek and smoothed her hair. 'Be strong Kate, be strong,' she whispered.

Jane had fed and bathed Ally while Kate was talking to Joyce. Kate carried her daughter up to the nursery, grateful for the excuse to get away from Joyce. Her head throbbed as she looked down at her daughter winding her blanket around her hand and snuggling into the pillow. She stroked Ally's forehead, soon the child's eyes flickered her body relaxed and the blanket fell from her hand.

Jane closed the front door and ran up the stairs, two at a time. She met Kate on the landing as she was coming out of the nursery.

'Kate I just asked Aunty Joyce if it was possible to get live-in help for you and the babies and she said yes she thought she could probably get a young unmarried mum-to-be, obviously one who was used to babies, growing up in a family with younger brothers and sisters. I mean it would get you over this first few months and then if it worked well you maybe could think of doing it again. What do you think?'

'I don't know, I can't think. Do you think it would work Jane? If you think it could work...' Her eyes were on the nursery door. 'Jane, how do I tell her that her Daddy's dead?'

Ian made coffee and took it into the lounge. Frank poured a stiff brandy for them all. He wanted to talk about the funeral arrangements. With her arms wrapped round her chest, Kate wandered the lounge stopping at the bay window to gaze out to the road. She watched as a car drove into a neighbour's driveway.

'Come and sit down,' Lucy said and patted the cushions of the settee alongside her.

'What happened to Greg's car?' Kate asked.

'It's at the aero club, Ian and Jane will pick it up tomorrow,' Frank said draining his coffee cup.

It was ten past seven when a sharp pain cut into Kate's chest just below her breastbone. With each breath the pain seared deep into her breast. She shivered and took shallow small breaths hoping it would ease, but it would not go away. Her face paled as she tried to concentrate on Frank's words.

'The coroner's people told me that following the autopsy, which I understand took place today, sorry love, but we do need to discuss this,' Frank said looking at Kate. 'They think they should be able to release Greg's body for the funeral.'

Kate nodded.

Frank continued 'I'll make an appointment with the undertaker tomorrow so that we can get on with the arrangements.' He put his forefinger over his lips as if to stop the question he needed to ask. 'Kate do you know if Greg would have wanted to be cremated or buried?'

Tears washed down Lucy and Jane's faces but Kate was dry-eyed. The pain pummelled sharper and deeper into her chest.

'I think his preference would be cremation,' she said.

'Does she have to decide this now Daddy, God he has only been dead for twenty four hours, let her get her head around it before we start thinking about a funeral.' Jane said sniffing into her handkerchief.

'Yes Jane she does, it has be discussed now before Erica arrives tomorrow. You know that Erica will want to take control and I don't want Kate's wishes to be over shadowed by her.'

'Sorry, I didn't mean...' Jane's voice faded as she heard Ben's tentative cry from the pram. She jumped up. 'Kate I'm doing the feeds tonight I think you need to go to bed, you look very pale love.'

Lucy took Kate's arm, 'Come on darling I will take you up, you look all in,' at the bedroom door she held her tight and whispered 'I love you sweetheart. Try to get some sleep.'

Kate felt across the bed for his tee shirt, nuzzling it to her face her tears soaking the soft cotton. She lay listening to the voices downstairs gradually the pain in her chest, like the voices, faded to a muffled hum.

The following morning Erica telephoned and spoke to Kate.

'I'm not coming today I have too much to organise. I phoned my parents yesterday and they have decided not to come to the funeral. The journey would be too much. They told me they would be sending a telegram to you, have you received it?' Erica said.

'Yes I have it. It would be a very hard journey for them to make. Greg would have understood, perhaps they can have a memorial service over there at the same time. I'll will speak to them once I know the funeral arrangements.'

'That will be up to my parents.'

'Yes, just a thought.' Kate said the irritation in her voice barely disguised.

'Now, the funeral, no papist burial I trust?'

Kate grasped the telephone receiver tighter.

'No it's a cremation.'

'I will organise the service and minister Kate.'

Kate eye's narrowed as she stared at the mesh face of the mouthpiece.

'Erica I have not had time to think of this yet, can we discuss it after Daddy gets back from the undertakers and I've had time to consider things.'

'Of course you have not thought about this,' Erica's words leapt down the line like a slap. 'But I have Kate and I will take this off your hands and make sure the service reflects the stature of my brother and my family.'

A tremor came and Kate held the edge of the telephone table.

'I've no fight in me today Erica. Do as you wish. I'll ask Daddy to ring you with the time and place of the funeral.'

Erica's manner had been hostile towards Kate and her family since the day she arrived from Australia. They all found her unpleasant even at the best of times.

'And this is not the best of times,' said Frank to Lucy after visiting the undertakers 'but if organising the order of service keeps her away from Kate, this is best.'

From the first day Kate found her future sister-in-law difficult. There was an uncomfortable sharpness to her, a nose that looked as though it could cut butter, black wing eyeglasses accentuating her small eyes and a smile that never progressed further than her lips. It was obvious to Kate that she believed she was right and the rest of world, save her family, was wrong.

At the lunch given by Frank and Lucy to welcome Erica into the Taylor family Kate was alarmed by Erica's witting, or unwitting either way it made no difference, tactless comments. She told Lucy that it was a shame the vegetables were undercooked and recommended that Lucy use a pressure cooker, which would take the risk out of giving her guests half cooked vegetables. As Lucy swallowed her al dente vegetables and annoyance, Erica promptly followed up by contradicting the knowledgeable and passionate cricket lover Frank, not once but repeatedly, about English batsman Tom Graveney's test match scores. Jane and Ian were next in line with a couple of insensitive observations about their child rearing before finally asking Kate if she dyed her hair. When Kate replied just very fine streaks she exclaimed 'I knew it, you need to get rid of them before you meet my parents as they disapprove of dyed hair.'

Erica found work as a clerk with a London stockbroker and accommodation with three other Australian girls in Wimbledon. When Kate and Greg returned home from honeymoon she drove across town in her small three-wheel car to stay with them most weekends. When her brother was not present she took every opportunity to badger Kate.

'My brother works very hard and Kate you need to understand it is not appropriate to ask him to mow the lawn, wash dishes, or set the table.'

She stared unblinking at Kate.

One weekend, Kate pushed to the limit with Erica's criticism, retorted angrily, 'I'm not your Eliza Doolittle to bully and browbeat and I resent your implication that I nor my family are good enough for your brother.'

'How dare you speak to me like that,' Erica said and flounced out of the room.

Any pretence of regard for each other was gone from that day onwards.

The day before the funeral it was warm and the cloying tobacco scent of lilies from condolence bouquets pervaded the house making Kate edgy.

'Don't you find it oppressive?' Kate said to Lucy as they put all of the floral arrangements into the dining room 'Why do they always send lilies for funerals I hate the smell.' She kicked the dining room door; it shut with a loud crash. The noise woke Ben who started to cry. 'That child never stops, he's always hungry, always crying,' she said and turned her back on the pram in the hall.

Lucy put her arms around her but Kate pushed her away. 'Don't Mummy, don't try and make this better and tell me I'm lucky to have him and that everything will work out in time. Because it won't.' She raced into the garden and threw herself down on one of the deckchairs under the shade of the tree. Lucy pushed the pram out onto the patio and within moments the rhythm of the motion sent Ben back to sleep. She took the other deckchair beside Kate and they stretched out silently, each lost in their own thoughts.

The hall was cool and quiet as Frank dialled William Ryan's number and almost immediately it was answered. After introducing himself Frank got to the purpose of his call.

'I visited the airfield the day after the crash with the hope of catching up with you. Unfortunately you were not there. But a mechanic who was on duty indicated that Greg got lost in dense cloud cover.'

'Yes we think that is what happened. A weather warning came in after Greg was in the air. I take it that you know these small planes are not equipped with radio? So there was no way of notifying him that the cloud cover was forecast to get denser.'

'How much time was there between Greg taking off and the weather forecast coming in?' Frank asked.

'Greg was in the air when it came in. Look it's all logged on the records Frank. We have nothing to hide. One must presume sadly that he got lost almost immediately.' William's conciliatory tone changed, his voice sounded defensive.

'I was told the plane was mechanically sound, is that right.'

'Yes it had received the airworthiness certificate only a couple of days before the crash.'

Frank was silent.

'How is Kate?' Ryan asked.

'Trying to cope, it's a hard time for her. Just a dreadful tragedy for the young family.'

'Unimaginable. Please give her Judy and my regards.'

'Of course. Look William I'm grateful for your help, just trying to piece it all together in my mind. I suppose we might know more at the inquest. From what I understand that won't take place for some months.'

'I think you'll find Frank that it will come down to lack of experience flying in those conditions. I just hope that is some comfort to you and the family.'

Lucy's voice startled him as he put the receiver back on its cradle.

'I'm just about to make us all a cup of tea, do you want one?'

He went out to the kitchen and through the window he could see Kate in the garden. He needed to talk it through. Lucy nodded in agreement as he told her of his visit to the aero club and subsequent telephone conversation with William Ryan.

'Well it all makes sense doesn't it? I wondered why he was so far away from Laurelford. I think you need to talk to Kate, but not today, she's really struggling this morning.'

'Yes, after the funeral would be best, too much for her at the moment,' he sighed putting his arm around Lucy's shoulder. 'Such a waste.'

The dry leaves of the sycamore tree fluttered in the breeze, some floating gently to the ground, Kate remembered the touch of Greg's soft-skinned hands that made her feel safe. When she kissed his fingertips her nostrils were filled with the smell of the antiseptic hand wash— clean, clinical hands, twice the size of hers. With these hands, the night before he died, he had stroked her arms tenderly and sensing her reservation he had taken her hand and guided it down past his taught stomach. Instantly she felt him moist and erect and she snatched her hand away.

'Come on Katie,' he started to massage her outer thighs, kissing her neck and ears, moving in steady circular movements to her inner thighs.

She pushed him away. 'Just stop it Greg, please. Just stop it.'

'Katie, come on give me a hand here,' he took her hand again.'It's been weeks since we've had fun and I am getting a little impatient.' He turned her face to him and said quietly 'Or would you prefer that I go elsewhere for sex.'

She pulled her hand away. 'Give me a break Greg it's too bloody soon, I have a scar a yard long that isn't healed and you still want sex,' she said, and turned her back to him. He didn't answer. Kate stared into the darkness.

The bed started to creak rhythmically. She heard the slap of skin on skin as he steadily stroked, his whole body thrusting with each stroke. Soon she felt him reach to his bedside table for tissues. He was done with a loud sigh. Within minutes he was asleep and Kate lay wide-eyed and disgusted.

She turned her head away from the sycamore tree. It had been some time since she wanted or even enjoyed sex. He had called her frigid when time after time following Ally's birth she had refused his advances. The word froze in her brain in Gothic bold capitals, he thought I was like ice, cold and uncaring.

⁓

Jane went with her to buy the outfit for the funeral. The shops were full of black dresses but these were mainly cocktail dresses. In Best's Department Store in the High Street, the dressing room was overflowing with black dresses on hangers and a growing pile of discarded dresses that Jane was hard pressed to replace on their hangers.

Kate struggled to zip up a dress. Her problem was that the weight sat roundly on her waist and with each larger size that she tried the top was too big and the fabric of the shoulders and neck hung like a windless sail while the waist was still snug. The reflection in the mirror was that of a pale faced overweight matron.

She had started to stack on the extra pounds at the beginning of her third trimester. In her twenty-seventh week while standing in the supermarket line-up with a pile of groceries and Ally in the trolley, she suddenly felt something warm running down her legs. She was still bleeding when she saw her gynaecologist four hours later, who diagnosed placenta previa and hospitalised her for two months of enforced bed-rest before Ben rushed head first into the world just two weeks before his father rushed head first to his death in Handsworth.

'What about this Kate?' Jane handed her a plain crepe dress with cap sleeves. 'It doesn't shout cocktail party.'

'No but it will shout gross body fat,' Kate's nostrils pinched. 'Jane its crepe it would show every roll and spare tyre. Christ there must be something that I could look half decent in,' she said putting on the clothes she came in.

The shop assistant popped her head around the door and unaware of the purpose of the outfit suggested maybe there was more choice if madam went for a bright colour. Kate snapped. 'Yes but not for a funeral.' The assistant, either not hearing her properly or choosing to ignore the warning flag, replied 'Yes but think of the wear you can get from a brighter colour.'

'Listen to me. I will say this just one more time, I need black, not colour—I am going to a funeral.' She paused and added stingingly. 'My husband's funeral.'

The assistant's hand flew to her mouth and her cheeks flushed crimson. Jane thought for a moment the woman was going to be sick as she could only make a gagging sound. Kate marched out of the store, with a sorry band following her. Jane apologising to the assistant who was desperate to catch up to Kate to make amends.

'Kate calm down, you really upset that poor woman,' Jane said as she strode behind her sister.

Kate stopped and turned on her sister.

'I have one more date with my husband,' She brandished her finger at Jane. 'His funeral, his sodding funeral, I want to look my best for him, is that too hard for you or anyone to understand,' her voice screamed. 'One more, just one more,' she sobbed and Jane held her.

They motored home to the local shops where they found a dark navy sleeveless dress and lace coat, which they teamed with a straw pillbox hat.

The sky was blue on the morning of the funeral. The sun warmed Ian's shoulders as he brushed the front path and driveway. Frank carried cartons of wine and spirits from the car to place behind the makeshift bar in the lounge. In the kitchen Molly and two friends from Lucy's canasta group chatted as they prepared neat triangles of chicken sandwiches. Susan was laying out sausage rolls and mini quiches on oven trays. In the lounge Lucy was putting the finishing touches to the serving table dressed with a white cloth that draped to the floor. Either side of the centrepiece of white roses and trails of ivy stood empty cake stands waiting to be filled with pastries and cakes. One side of the table was a stack of side plates, cups and saucers and a fan of paper napkins.

Ally and Ben were not going to the funeral. Kate agreed with her father that it would be too harrowing. Molly would care for them while waiting for the mourners to return to the house for a light lunch.

In the bedroom Jane speared the navy straw pillbox to the back of Kate's hair with a pearl tipped hat-pin. With a loving hand she applied Kate's make up. When she finally brushed mascara onto Kate's lashes she said. 'Now remember you can't cry otherwise your mascara will run.' She stood back and surveyed her work. 'You look lovely

Kate, Greg would be proud of you.'

The funeral cortège arrived. Kate ran into the lounge and stared in disbelief through the windows at the shiny black hearse carrying his coffin. The oak coffin was longer than she imagined it would be. Its brass handles gleamed in the morning sun. The morning-suited driver of the limousine stepped from the driver's seat, put on his white gloves, opened the front gate and walked up the path. A passerby, a man in a suit, stopped by the hearse, removed his trilby and stood for a while with his head bowed before moving on. Kate watched him as his stride picked up and he disappeared from her sight. For a moment behind the safety of the windowpane she felt her eyes filling. The thought of mascara trickling blackly down her cheeks curbed her tears.

Her father came into the lounge and offered his arm.

'Are you ready?', he asked.

'I don't think I will ever be ready,' she said as she took his arm and they walked out to the car.

──────

The chapel was full when they arrived the music of Elgar's Nimrod was playing as the undertaker escorted the Taylor family to the front pew. Erica and a friend sat in the front pew to the left. The minister, a gangly young man with a pronounced Adam's apple, went to the lectern. The last bars of the music punctuated with the odd cough and murmur as the congregation settled.

'Today we are gathered to farewell Gregory Robert Sinclair, a son, a brother, a husband and a father taken

from us in his prime. Gregory grew up in Sydney. He was
a bright student. His involvement in the boy scouts and
an alter boy with Church of England earned him the respect of both his teachers and fellow students. He was
house captain and then school captain in his final two
years of schooling. He studied dentistry at Sydney University, gaining honours…

Frank looked at his daughter who was staring ahead
to the coffin. He squeezed her hand but received no response; Kate was unaware of the minister's words or her
father's touch. She was far away remembering how she
and Greg had met.

She was eighteen and had been filling in as a waitress at
her mother's café for a few months in between secretar-
ial jobs. It had been a busy day all the tables were taken,
save a table of four. She had just given the cook an order of two cottage pies, when two of their regulars and
a third man came into the café and took the table by the
window. He sat tall in the chair. His hair thick and dark
was slicked back off his face, where he had run the comb
through the parting it gleamed wetly like a snail trail.

He looked up from the menu and smiled. She was
amazed, his eyes were so blue, like the bluest of oceans
ready to sail her into new and exciting shores. She watched
him as he examined the menu. He had a strong face and
a mouth that compelled you to watch as it creased into a
smile, whenever he looked up his eyes teased as he held
her gaze.

'I think I'll go for the steak and kidney pie. You know Katie, may I call you Katie?'

She nodded, delighting in his old fashioned courtesy.

'Meat pie is Australia's national dish but we never do it with kidneys, so you have a lot to live up to,' his voice was low pitched.

Vistas of beaches, surfers and lifeguards with little cloth hats tied under the chin danced in her head.

'You can't make a decent steak pie without kidney. What are you colonials thinking about?'

With a cheesy wink and a warm face she went to the kitchen. Every day Greg came into the cafe Kate's heart beat faster. His accent excited her, the broadness of the vowels and the Australian habit of adding 'ie' to nouns and adjectives alike suggested a roguish disregard for everything establishment. She stood close to him as she took his order.

'Katie what would you suggest today?', his eyes searched her face.

'It's all good Mr Sinclair. What do you fancy today?', her voice was breathy like a little girl.

His arm brushed hers and the thrill was so intense that she had difficulty holding her pad and pencil.

When Greg asked if she would like to go to the opening night of *My Fair Lady* starring Julie Andrews, Rex Harrison and Stanley Holloway, she did a jig in the kitchen.

After the theatre they walked down the Strand. Greg took her hand in his and guided her through the crowd. They stopped in a shop doorway and he serenaded her with Professor Higgins' song *I've grown accustomed to her face.* In the midst of the nightlife of the west end they were alone. With a hand cupped on her waist he pulled her closer, her hand was on his breast and like a graceful pas de deux they moved into an embrace. *Her smiles, her frowns, Her ups, her downs.*

The congregation was restless the coughs and rustles of the printed order of service had become more frequent. Rivulets of perspiration ran down the Minister's face.

'Greg's passing is a tragedy and we may not yet understand why a this young man with his life ahead of him is taken from us; but comfort can be taken from the bible - First Corinthians Chapter 13 verse 12. Now we see as a poor reflection in a mirror then we shall see face to face. Now I know in part; then I shall know fully. '

Kate was safe in Greg's embrace, *Are second nature to me now; Like breathing out and breathing in.*

'Kate, Kate.' The minister's whisper was insistent.

She flinched when he took her arm and invited her to say her farewell to Greg before the curtains closed around the coffin for the final time. He led her to the catafalque where she looked past the dusty velvet curtains through the window to the Memorial Rose Garden the breeze was catching the rose blossoms and tossing them gently in the air.

He whispered 'Are you alright?' Kate nodded.

He switched on the tape recording of Jesu Joy of Man's

Desiring and asked the congregation to bow their heads. 'Giving you a moment to say farewell to Gregory in your own way.'

She stood by the coffin willing her memories of their music to override Bach's, I was serenely independent and content before we met; Surely I could always be that way again—*And yet I've grown accustomed to her look; Accustomed to her voice; Accustomed to her face.*

She focussed on the floral arrangement with the sculptured white and cream roses. Their shiny stems were devoid of thorns. She ran her finger down the denatured surface feeling the scant nub of scars where the thorns had been removed. Will that be me one day, she thought, just the nub of scar where once I was whole?

She stroked the card she had written at the florists. *To my darling husband and our dearest Daddy. We will miss you forever. Kate, Ally and Ben xxx.* Tears pricked her eyes; she pinched her nose tightly with a lace edged hanky that had been balled in her clenched hand throughout the ceremony.

Frank took her arm and escorted her back to the seat where she watched the dark purple velvet curtains edged with silver brocade close around the coffin to the final lines of Bach's hymn. The music covered the ugly whirr of machinery as the coffin made its jerky passage forward.

Kate stood between her father and Erica as people arrived at the house. As people lined up to offer their condolences she remembered greeting the same people, at her wedding almost two years before. With each embrace the repetition of her sentiments that Greg was the finest fellow and she and the children were immensely grateful to have had him in our lives sounded more and more hollow.

Clusters of mourners spread through the lounge, some making their way into the garden and the sunshine. At first people murmured softly, their faces adopting a mask of sadness. But as the wake progressed and their glasses were refilled the sombreness of the day gave way to memories, the chatter grew louder and their faces creased into smiles and laughter.

Kate slipped away and went into the garage, opened the door of her Mini Minor and perched on the driving seat nursing her glass of whiskey and soda. She wished she could drive away. Somewhere, wherever the open road would take her where the pain could not reach her.

After the last guest left Frank took Kate back to the crematorium to look at the flowers. The car radio played Bobby Vinton's rendition of *Roses are Red My Love* as they drove up the driveway. They walked to the site beside the chapel where the flowers had been piled up directly under the black-framed notice that stated simply Gregory Robert Sinclair and stood reading the cards attached to bouquets and wreathes. The Laurelford Aero Club had sent a large wreath. Kate read the card that was written in a bold hand with heartfelt condolences William and Judy Ryan and fellow members.

'What do you think he was doing Daddy so far away from the Laurelford? I asked William Ryan the night he died but he said he didn't know.'

'I had the same question Kate. But from conversations with Ryan and a mechanic at the airfield I gather that Greg was in the air when a forecast of worsening conditions came in. They think he got lost in dense cloud cover. He also said that there was absolutely nothing wrong with the plane mechanically, it had received its certificate of air-worthiness just a couple of days before the accident.'

'He got lost,' her voice was soft. 'Nothing can bring him back.'

'Yes love nothing will bring him back,' Frank echoed. He kicked the gravel under foot and spray of flinty stones flew up.

Many of the flowers had begun to wilt. Kate used Greg's camera to take a shot of the carpet of floral tributes and a close up of the wreath from his parents.

'It was a tough day, love,' Frank said as he put his arm around her shoulder.

'The worst,' she said. She picked a couple of the better roses from her and the children's bouquet before she took his arm as they started walking back.

As they strolled through the memorial garden that led to the car park, a dramatic gust of black smoke came from the crematorium chimney and stained the blue sky ahead. Kate shivered as she watched in disbelief as the dark smoke slowly spiralled upward. They stood like sentinels mesmerized, monitoring the trail of smoke as it thinned. The last wisp disappeared through the clouds.

'There's some poor bugger going up in smoke.' Kate said shattering the tension.

Her irreverence caught them both by surprise and their nervous giggles built rapidly into hysterical laughter. People walking past looked at them, their faces grim with disapproval. Trying to look suitably sombre just made Kate and Frank laugh more until the bittersweet relief of tears washed down their faces.

Ben woke at four in the morning Kate stumbled out of bed and put a bottle onto warm.

'Shush, shush,' her voice was thick with sleep. She took him out of his carrycot and laid him on the bed. Ben's cries grew louder. 'Shut up, shut up, shut up,' she whispered, twirling the bottle in the warmer. She tested the milk on the inside of her wrist it was warm enough. She sat on the edge of the bed cradling Ben. She sighed when he took the teat with a determined tug. The doctor had given her pills to dry up her milk and recommended that life would be easier for her and Ben if she bottle fed him. The chest pains that visited every evening at seven, he said were psychosomatic and not uncommon amongst the recently bereaved.

She cupped her hand under Ben's small chin and lifted his soft body upright. The darkness of the room, lit only by a distant streetlight pressed in around her. She reached for Greg's tee shirt under her pillow and pressed it close to her. She patted Ben's back until at last he burped, his lips bubbling with milk that ran down Kate's hand onto the sheet. She wiped his chin, changed and wrapped him tightly and put him back into his cot. He slept but she could not.

She switched on the bedside lamp and went to Greg's wardrobe and opened it, his clothes were hanging in a neat row. Below his shoes were untidy, like he had been in a hurry and flung them in the cupboard without care. She picked up a tennis pump from the far corner of the wardrobe. His hand had been the last to undo the lace and pull off the shoe. She put it to her cheek. She searched through the clutter of the shoes to find it's matching mate. It lay face down, its orange rubber sole a beacon in the assortment of leather. She pushed the jumble of shoes to one side. Her tears splashed onto the canvas shoes as she straightened them, the tongue tucked neatly under the eyelets before tying the laces in a bow. She placed them on the wardrobe floor rubber sole touching sole. She climbed back into bed, curved her body around Greg's bundled tee-shirt and waited for sleep to claim her.

⁓

The call from Eva and Angus Sinclair came through promptly at eight o'clock the morning after the funeral. At first the connection was scratchy. 'Sun spots,' said Angus his voice echoing down the line. He listened when she told him what she knew of the accident. But it was Eva who spoke mainly, asking about the children. Saying how she wished she could meet them adding that she wondered if Kate would bring them to Australia for a holiday.

As Eva spoke Kate's chin lifted, her eyes fixed on the mahogany panel in the hall, the whorls of the dark timber veneer was transformed into the curve and spread of the beach at Bondi. With sailing boats dancing on the Sydney Harbour the voice in her head was insistent and persuasive—you would be honouring Greg's memory by giving his parents the opportunity to meet the children, it would give you something to plan. The children would see kangaroos and koalas. An escape from the pain, the winter...

'May be a holiday early next year when the children are easier to manage. Let me think about it. Take care of yourselves.' She put the telephone back on its cradle.

The day was hot and the sycamore tree provided welcome shade as the Frank and Lucy sat in the garden having their morning coffee. Frank was executor of Greg's estate. His will was straight forward leaving everything he had to Kate, or in the event of her death to his issue. His worldly goods included the dental practice and the house both were mortgaged to the limit. His life insurance policy provided an amount of financial security but not enough to maintain this large house. Frank gazed back at the cream rendered house it was impressive of scale and size and should be easy to sell. Five bedrooms, large family bathroom and a half bathroom downstairs, two large reception rooms, a glass conservatory, double garage and an expansive back garden.

Ally squirmed in Kate's arms as she carried her out into the garden. Kate sat down on the grass and let her daughter free as she side straddled across the lawn.

'Is this a good time to go through the will with you Kate?' Frank said

Kate nodded her eyes watching Ally.

'Really you would know the contents of his will. Everything goes to you and he has left you reasonably secure.'

'How secure or poor will I be after all the debts are paid? I presume selling the house and the practice will help.' She got up and retrieved Ally from a flower-bed and bought her back to where the family was sitting.

'Will I have sufficient to live comfortably? And, I haven't told you this yet, as I will need to see how feasible it is, but I would like to take the children out to Australia early next year to meet their grandparents.'

Lucy raised her eyebrows, 'Australia, next year, have you any idea Kate how difficult it would be to travel with two little ones on your own?'

Kate shrugged her shoulders. 'Will I be able to afford that Daddy?'

'You and the children will be able to live a relatively comfortable life, you will be able to take a regular annual holidays and of course, if you feel you must, a trip to Australia next year. But it's not a bottomless pit and you'll have no income save the interest from Greg's life insurance money but I'm pretty sure you're eligible for a widow's pension to augment this.'

'But I do think you need to sell this house. Not only

is it costly to run but it is too big for you to look after without help and that is a cost you could ill afford.' Kate turned her head towards him.'I want to sell this house. I hate it here without him. It was our dream home and now it just feels a mausoleum. I want to live closer to you both and Jane.'

'Yes and it would make it easier to give you the support you need.' Lucy said sipping her coffee.

Kate turned her head to see Ally heading for the edge of the terrace. She raced down the garden just in time to stop the toddler from falling over the terrace into the vegetable garden below.

Chapter 3.

· · · · · · · · · · · ·

New Beginnings

She walked her parents and sister to the front gate of her new house. The house was in a leafy suburb in Redford, Essex not far from the A12 main road to Chelmsford. A few blocks away was the small shopping area. The wide street was domicile to a branch of Barclays bank, a number of small essential shops, a good delicatessen and the café where she had met Greg and which Lucy had sold a year before their marriage.

Kate and the children had moved in that day to the three-bedroom semi-detached house which was just five minutes walk from her parents and sister's homes. She looked across to the park where a man and two children were walking a dog. She waved as her family tattoo-tooted their farewells as they pulled away. The garden path was fringed with flowerbeds stocked with standard rose bushes. She pinched off a few of the dead rose heads. Her car was parked on the small flagged driveway and an untidy privet hedge hid the small square of lawn from the street.

She closed the front door and wandered through the rooms making a mental list of things still to do or buy. The only visible sign that the lounge had once been two rooms was the freshly plastered doorway and support beam that framed the division. At the far end of the long room was the reproduction Queen Anne walnut table with eight matching chairs and sideboard that she had purchased from the previous owners of the house. The furniture contrasted with the white matt painted walls with high gloss window trims, skirting boards and shelves. The wing back armchairs flagged the fireplace. She noted that she needed a settee and lamps, and thought maybe something a bit more contemporary, orange is trendy.

Kate loved the breakfast nook in the kitchen with its built-in lime green vinyl seats and Formica table. Sitting proudly in the old chimney-breast was a cream and black cast iron Aga stove belching out warmth. It provided the hot water for the house and featured two ovens, one for baking and the other for slow cooking. Off the kitchen was a glass sunroom that ran the width of the house, which Kate had designated as the children's playroom. In the utility room was her new washing machine, its white enamel gleaming and the instruction book lying on the lid. It was plumbed in ready for its first wash. Tomorrow no more hand washing the nappies, she thought, fingers crossed it's a fine drying day so I can christen it.

The children were asleep when she started unpacking one of the large cardboard boxes. This one was full of slides taken on their honeymoon. She held a few up to the light; one had been shot by the water's edge with the Sydney Harbour Bridge in the background. In it she was looking up at Greg. He had his arm around her shoulders and returned her gaze, his smile and eyes alive with laughter. She remembered they had asked a passer by to take the picture. They had laughed at the clichéd pose but the picture had captured the radiance of the moment.

The familiar pain came again. She tossed the slides back into the box, taped it shut and dumped it in the hall cupboard. The pain grabbed tighter like a cramp around her chest and she panicked, her breath short, sharp and painful. She needed fresh air. She dashed through the house and unfastened the back door. The evening air was rich with the smell of jasmine. She inhaled deeply, and slowly breathed out. Gradually her breathing calmed and the pain lessened. She found the muffled noises coming from neighbours' homes peculiarly comforting. A dog barked and she heard her neighbour call out to quieten him. She smiled it felt good to have neighbours so close to her.

The following week Isabella Cunningham, sixteen years old and nearly five months pregnant arrived accompanied by Joyce. Thick dark curly hair framed an almond shaped face and her long limbed body showed no sign of a baby bump. She was the eldest of three children and had helped her mother with her younger brother and sister. She knew how to feed a baby, change them and bath them. Kate had been told that Isabella was anxious when she was first told that her parents had given their permission for her to leave the unmarried mother's home and live with a widow and two babies for the remainder of her confinement. Although Isabella hated the church run home, she was nervous about leaving the friends she had made.

Kate visited Isabella at the home, a grey brick manse that had been built in the late 1800s. Its gardens had long fallen into disarray, as had the interior of the large, draughty house. In the common room she saw evidence of the church's view of illegitimacy, above the fireplace hung a framed biblical text. James l: *15 When lust hath conceived it bringeth forth sin.* On meeting Isabella, Kate held out her hand and the young mother to be shyly shook Kate's hand. 'How silly of me,' Kate said. She put her arms around Isabella and kissed her cheek. 'After all we are going to live together for four months at least and we should be friends.' Isabella nodded looking up at Kate through her long dark lashes. 'What I need most is help with the children. I hope we will work as a team and if between us we get round to the cleaning and dusting it will be a bonus. Your friends are welcome to visit but always the babies must be our first priority. Are you happy with that?' Isabella nodded and her smile lit up her eyes.

⁕

Kate showed Isabella to her room and left her to unpack and settle in while she and her Aunt made lunch.

'Will she keep her baby?' Kate took out the makings

for a sandwich from the refrigerator.

Joyce sat in the breakfast nook, clasped hands resting on the table. She shook her head.

'No, Isabella's parents have already decided it is in the best interests of Isabella and the family to put the child up for adoption.'

'What about the father of her child?' Kate set the containers on the table and reached for a breadboard in the cupboard.

'It seems he was sixteen and denied it all. His parents said if Isabella or her family contacted them further they would make sure the world knew about her loose morals.'

'Loose morals?' Kate stopped the words ricocheting in her head, the breadboard slipped out of her hand and crashed onto the table.

'Well I think the term they used was slut.'

'They called her a slut, are you serious?' Kate hissed. She glared at her Aunt.

'Yes they called her a slut,' Joyce waved her hands like an orchestra conductor. 'The Cunningham's were mortified and felt they needed to get her away from Nottingham and when their GP recommended the church-run Home for Unmarried Mothers...'

Kate banged the bread knife down on the board.

'The boy is only sixteen; you can understand to a point. But his parents? I'm speechless.'

'Well, love, sorry to disillusion you but this story is not uncommon. Denial is an easy way out and of course there is no proof so it comes down to her word against his.' Joyce said picking at a slice of ham from one of the containers laid out on the table.

'Tell me does Isabella have a say in this?'

'She is under eighteen so the final decision will rest with the parents. But the reality is that most young un-married mothers are encouraged to give their children the right start in life and that right-start means with-out the stigma of illegitimacy. If I'm honest, and this is just between you and me, they really do not have much choice in the matter.'

Joyce's hands rose again to punch and emphasise her words. Her words so urgent that she took breath in quick gulps.

'Society and the state has created a culture where women who don't give up their babies for adoption are seen as morally weak and self serving while those who do are lauded as brave and selfless. So imagine Kate, if you are a young woman, without parental and financial sup-port, what would you do? You accept the way it is' Joyce nodded. 'Six years ago the Mental Health Act was abol-ished, which allowed unmarried mothers who wanted to keep their babies and who did not have family support or financial means to be detained in mental institutions.'

'My God aunty that is unbelievable, how were they able to do that?' Kate whispered.

'On the pretext that these women or young girls were morally deficient.' Joyce's fists and voice raised in crescendo. 'Their babies were forcibly taken from them at birth and adopted out but the mothers were retained long, sometimes years after the birth in these mental in-stitutions.'

Kate stopped buttering a slice of bread. 'Why are you involved in this? It's pretty obvious you're disgusted with the system.'

Joyce paused trying to find the right words. 'Well, first I can't change the system, second this is what I have been trained to do and last but certainly not least there are some agencies that do not scrupulously investigate would be adopters. I can't do anything about that but I can make sure that all the babies that I place go to the right parents. Not only parents capable of love and understanding of a child's needs but those that have genuine and abiding respect for the birth mothers gift to them.'

Isabella poked her head round the kitchen door. 'Alright if I come in?', she asked.

'Definitely, and just in time for lunch.' Kate said.

After lunch Kate lifted Ally down from the highchair and let her loose in the kitchen. With a side stepping crawl she reached a kitchen cupboard and tried to pull it open. Dodging Kate she pulled herself up with the aid of the kitchen bench.

All three women watched closely as she stepped away from the bench. 'Clever girl,' they shouted as one.

Ally's eyes focused on her mother's outstretched hands and she took two more steps before dropping onto all fours and crawling until the fabric of her dress caught her foot and she rolled onto her back with an infectious chuckle, deep and sweet.

Isabella was content. The small butterfly kick of her own child did not register, as she was delighting in the sleeping Ben who was curled so warmly in her arms.

Kate ruled that she would never quiz Isabella on the how
and why of her situation. But one night while they were
watching television, an episode of Dixon of Dock Green,
Isabella volunteered the answers to Kate's unasked questions. The plot line playing out in black and white on the
screen was about a young mother's difficult pregnancy
and her husband who did not want the child. Dixon was
unsuccessful in trying to stop the man before he boarded
a cargo ship for Canada, leaving the heroine of the story
to raise the child on her own.

'Why didn't she just have an abortion? Abortion was
my parents first thought when I told them I was pregnant
but then they said we couldn't, as it would be breaking
the law. I would have done it,' she spat the words out, her
eyes fixed on the programme credits scrolling down the
television screen. She ran the flat of her hand over her
bulging tummy.

'I will be so glad when this is all over and done with so
I can get back to a normal life.'

Kate patted her hand as she picked up the cups and
saucers and took them out to the kitchen.

'Don't be too sure sweetheart it's not that easy,' she
whispered as she ran them under the tap to rinse them.

She lay awake, she could not sleep. She looked at the illuminated clock face another two hours before Ben would
wake. She could not get Isabella's comments out of her
mind. Round and round she wove her own slippery dip

of remorse like a sickening fairground ride. She got up stealthily putting on her dressing gown, easing the nursery and Isabella's door shut before flooding the landing with light. In the kitchen she put on a saucepan of milk to heat. She sat at the kitchen table sipping the warm milk hoping that it would allow sleep to come.

But there was no relief in the warm milk, still her mind spun shameful webs of the babies that she had aborted. Embryo's Greg had called them, as though the clinical name justified the act. Greg was so open-minded in so many ways but when it came down to the stigma of illegitimacy he was just one of the crowd. He had been an enigma.

It was a month after the engagement that she became pregnant. They were in a country pub drinking gin and tonic when he told her that he had managed to contact a doctor. She was twelve weeks pregnant. She ran her finger over and over the milky rings that stained the mahogany table as she listened.

'He'll do the abortion next week at my flat. Katie I'll leave you the money, you'll be fine it is just a routine procedure,' he said quietly.

'What do you mean you'll leave the money, won't you be there?' Her voice was shrill and loud. The other drinkers in the bar turned to look at them.

'Shush,' he said patting her hand. I'm sorry Katie you know I'm going to the Rome Olympics. My tickets are booked and paid. It's a once in a lifetime opportunity. After all you are a big girl now and I'm assured that it is a simple and safe procedure.'

'Christ Greg I can't believe you are leaving me to do this on my own,' she pulled her hand away sharply almost knocking over her drink.

'Come on Katie, you'll be fine, I'm only away for ten days.' He put his arm around her and pulled her close.

The backyard abortionist was exactly as she had stereotyped him in her mind, a greasy haired fellow in a shiny suit. He was foreign and spoke little English. When he arrived he asked her to boil the kettle and supply him with a bowl. She left him in the kitchen preparing and went to lie on her bed. She took off her pants. She drew her knees up as he directed. 'Open,' he commanded and impatiently pushed her legs apart. She closed her eyes as his fingers examined her. She felt some sort of tubing being pushed up hard and high into her. She remembered little else, her mind held fast in thinking of their wedding day and it was not until he announced it was done that she came back to reality.

'You will lose the foetus tomorrow maybe or day after,' he said pushing a sanitary pad firmly between her legs. 'Remember you don't speak of this to anyone and you don't know me, you understand?'

She nodded.

She gave him the money that Greg had left her and felt a little dizzy as she showed him to the door. The empty flat with its faded red curtains echoed with her cries of pain the following day. But the day after the memories seemed surreal, the only reminder being her copious bleeding. It's done don't look back, she repeated over and over to herself.

'Rome was amazing Katie, bloody Russians were on fire they topped the medal tally well and truly beating the States but Australia got eight gold. Not bad I suppose for a young country,' Greg smiled broadly and with his golden tan he looked even more handsome to her.

Pinpricks of dust danced in the stream of sunlight spilling through the lead lighted windows near their table. A cacophony of Australian voices almost drowned out Greg's words. A man balancing three pints of lager bumped against them spilling beer over Kate's skirt. Greg took a gulp of his beer.

'I've been thinking while I was away we need to do something about birth control, Katie. We don't want this happening again. I think sex would be better for us both without a condom so I think we need to get you a diaphragm, a Dutch cap.'

She nodded, thinking anything would be better than a flawed rubber.

She disliked the Harley Street gynaecologist, a middle-aged paunchy man wearing a red spotted bow tie. His manner from the very outset of the consultation patently showed that he took pleasure in intimidating women. She lay flat on her back with her legs in stirrups while he examined her pelvis to determine the size of the diaphragm. Without making eye contact he explained that the diaphragm, correctly used, offered a high degree of protection from unwanted pregnancies. He put the latex cap in her hand, pulled up a foot stool for her to place one foot on and directed her to squeeze the sides of the diaphragm and insert it by opening the lips of the vagina, pushing it gently towards the backbone, keeping the index finger on the outer rim to guide it and making sure the front edge of the diaphragm was placed just behind the pubic bone. At her first try the latex cap with its springy rim sprung out of her hand onto the floor.

'You need to take this seriously Miss Taylor,' he said. Emphasizing 'Miss' with a hissing sound as he looked over the rim of his reading glasses.

'Sorry, it just jumped out of my hand,' she said, her cheeks patched crimson.

After a few more tries, to her amazement and his satisfaction, she got it in.

'Make sure that you insert the cap sometime before, but no more than two hours prior to sexual intercourse, putting one teaspoon of spermicide into the dome of the diaphragm beforehand or with this applicator if you already have the diaphragm in place.'

She was shown how to look for possible holes in the latex before putting the round cap into its metal case.

'You will find that you and your fiancé will get complete satisfaction using this,' he said with a smile that never reached his eyes before ushering her out of the door.

She hated it from the outset and confided in Jane. 'I'm supposed to second-guess the moment to put it in. If Greg finds stopping to put on a condom slows his libido, any desires I have completely disappear when I try to get the wretched thing, with its messy spermicide into the right spot. And I am totally repulsed having to keep it in place for six to eight hours after sex.'

'Sounds ghastly to me, so glad it was only French letters in my day. What about this new pill, Kate? Why don't you get that?' Jane asked

'Because the medical world, do not allow unmarried women to go on the pill,' her voice squawked with indignation.

Four months later, pregnant again, she tearfully pleaded with Greg to move the wedding forward.

'Greg it's only two months away, why don't we elope or just marry in a registry office. Think of it, I would only be four months pregnant and hardly showing even if we kept to our plans.'

'Katie, come on now you're not thinking straight. You know it would be impractical for us to change our plans at this stage. We have people coming from Australia for the wedding, it's all organised. Anyway Katie, I'm not going to debate this as we both know it would not be right for you to be pregnant on our wedding day. We don't want to start married life with that cloud hanging over our head, or the child's for that matter. We have no choice here, I'll work something out.'

———

Her scream echoed around Greg's flat when he told her that he intended inserting a long needle into the middle of her back.

'It is called an epidural, Katie, and I promise you will not feel anything from your waist down. I've researched this thoroughly and am confident this is the best way. I'll give you a pill to relax you before we start.'

She shook her head.

'I know what I'm doing. You trust me don't you Katie?'

She took the pill with a glass of water while he made the rest of the preparations. He laid out a collection of equipment on a stainless steel tray; a selection of probes, different mouth retractors, local anaesthetic spray, dental syringes and needles. Finally he plugged a sterilising unit into the wall socket. She was completely relaxed by the time he was ready to start. After scrubbing and putting on surgical gear and mask he helped her slip off her dressing gown and got her to lie on the clean sheet that covered the dining table. Feeling down her curved back with his fingers he found the site between the vertebrae where he would inject the Novocain. First he swabbed the area with antiseptic and sprayed it with a local anaesthetic.

'Now Katie you are to be absolutely still, do you understand?'

'Yes,' her voice was muffled.

As the needle went into her spine she winced.

Greg reassured her, 'Doing well Katie, you are doing well.'

She held her breath as the shaft of the needle pushed hard into her.

'Just discomfort, Katie, remember to breathe,' Greg said, his professional manner building her confidence.

She felt the pressure spreading across her lower back until all was numb.

'You did very well Katie. Now just relax, close your eyes and think of Mother England,' he said with a laugh as he turned her on her back and opened her legs.

She closed her eyes. The mouth retractors made a squelching noise as they opened up the passage to her uterus and the sharp metal instruments chattered as they hit the metal tray. All she remembered was seeing the vibrancy of her blood dripping onto the faded blue carpet with yellow roses before Greg put a pad into place and carried her to the bed to rest.

She told no one of the abortions, not even Jane. She never allowed herself to think of her shame or think of the foetus as a small form of a baby. Instead she focused her anger on Greg and when Greg started his overtures towards her, a couple of weeks after the abortion, she turned away from him. He understood and left her alone. But he did not understand as the days went on and Kate still did not want sex.

One evening as she turned away his advances, he said 'Enough Katie, time to put this behind you, we have a life ahead as man and wife, you need to let go of what happened.'

Her dressing gown was damp from her tears. She would never ever know whether she was enough for him. A notepad sat on the kitchen bench. She picked up a pen and turned to a fresh page and started to write.

Has God punished me or have you? Night after night I dream of seeing you in the distance and I shout and cry but I can never get you to turn around. I hate you for leaving us, tearing apart our family. Was I...

The pen slipped from her fingers as Ben's cries reached her. She ripped the page out, shoved it into her dressing gown pocket and went upstairs.

It was late September when Kate had her first social outing after Greg's death. Susan and Charles Barker laid on a barbecue for his clients; several of these clients were also dental friends of Kate and Greg. Kate sat on the patio with Charles and Susan either side of her, talking to two of Greg's grooms men at the wedding. Tom was tall and well groomed; conversely Bruce was the type of man that looked enduringly untidy. His shirts collars always lay at odds and today his jacket sat rumpled and uneasily on his broad shoulders.

'Do you remember Katie when Greg did that naked saucepan samba at the party when you and he were first an item?' Bruce asked. 'And the old colander he used had a fucking big hole in it,' he said roaring with laughter.

Kate smiled, a small fleeting smile. 'Yes it was something like our second date and suddenly these three naked blokes came into the room with a saucepan held over their heads and another over their nether regions.'

Tom interjected, his brown eyes teasing. 'What do you mean by nether regions, Katie?'

'She means their cock-a-doodles,' Bruce chuckled.

Kate relaxed it felt good to be with lively Australians calling her Katie. 'Ignore him, as I was saying, well Greg either was the last in the saucepan cupboard or maybe he was the first, you know what he was like.'

They all nodded laughing in agreement. But seeing the quizzical looks on the very British Charles and Susan's faces Kate continued her explanation.'So the thing is, they sing saucepan samba, saucepan samba and instantly, when some one douses the lights for a second, they switch the saucepans,' Kate mimed the act being careful not to spill her drink. 'Unfortunately when Greg removed the colander from his head to his cock-a-doodle all was revealed, in all its glory or otherwise, depending on your point of view,' she said a smile lighting her face.

The group broke up, Charles went off to barbecue the lamb chops, Susan to lay out the salads.

'Another drink Katie, I know your Dad's picking you up so come on lets get sloshed,' Bruce said, taking her glass.

She nodded and smiled. It was first time, she realised since Greg died that she felt a flicker of life pulsing within her.

Tom agreed, 'It would be good for you to kick up your heels once in awhile,' he said.

Tom Appleton was in his mid twenties, he was tall, ironed shirt, knife-creased pants. She remembered he had the job of giving out the order of service for the groom's side and he escorted Erica down the aisle after the service. Kate had only met him on a couple of occasions before the wedding.

'How you're doing Katie?,' he asked when Bruce left.

She flushed, her stomach tensed, she felt unsure how to answer. 'Oh you know, good days and bad days,' she said.

He took a business card out of his pocket and put it on the table in front of her. 'Katie If there is anything I can do for you,' he put his hand on her arm, his voice now an earnest whisper, 'just give me a bell.'

Kate was dusting the lounge when the window cleaner climbed the ladder to polish the bedroom windows. He wore red socks pulled high over his calves and she noticed how shapely they were, round and smooth like legs on Queen Anne furniture. He must be cold she thought as she watched the edge of his leather shorts disappear from view. When he cleaned the lounge windows she could see that his muscles flex in his arms as he polished. As he lifted the chamois to reach the top of the windows his windcheater pulled from his pants and her throat caught as she saw the bare flesh of his taught stomach with a fine line of hairs running down from his navel. Immediately she felt a longing to run her hands down his body. Her duster slipped from her hand as she stared at him. He saw her through the windowpane and tipped his cap. Her face flushed and her eyes were downcast as she paid him.

'See you next month love,' he said as he swung his ladder and bucket effortlessly over his shoulder. There was something about his jaunty manner as he sauntered down the path and she knew that he knew.

The following morning Kate woke unwillingly from a dream. She had dreamt that a man dressed in white without a face was making love to her. She lay cradled in his arms naked as he kissed her beasts, his kisses becoming more and more persistent. It was at this moment she felt the familiar hot moistness trickling down her inner thighs onto the sheets. She leapt out of bed, her nightdress and her sheets stained with blood, pulled the sheets off the bed, took them into the bathroom and stashed them in the linen basket. She turned the taps on the bath and removed her nightdress. She saw her reflection in the bathroom mirror the smoothness of her skin, the shape of her waist and the roundness of her small breasts. She felt the pressure of arousal deep in her body and she brushed a hand over her nipples. She dropped the nightdress to the floor and cupped her breasts gently massaging them. The water was deep enough and warm enough now. She locked the bathroom door and slipped into the water. Sitting, she bent forward, her nipples brushing her knees and pressed open her legs against the side of the bath. She fingered herself her slowly at first exploring tentatively until her body demanded gratification and then rapidly her fingers moved like a piston until she sighed a low appreciative moan. She laid in the pink waters her body warm and relaxed.

The weather on that November morning was dry but bitterly cold and from the window they could see the people going about their business, their breath steaming the icy air. The gas fire in the living room was turned to its maximum warming the room. Ben slowly rolled on his tummy a big dribble of saliva running down his chin and dripping onto the yellow plastic toy grasped in his hand. Ally sat on the arm of Kate's chair her arms folded around her mother's neck. Isabella had gone to the local doctor for her prenatal check.

The television was broadcasting live coverage of John F. Kennedy's funeral. Kate was addicted to the coverage of the American President's assassination and the aftermath of events leading to the funeral. She had watched as Jackie, wearing her blood spattered suit, stood numbly beside Lyndon Johnson being sworn in as the new President. She stared at the screen as the sad figure of Jackie strode determinedly behind the caisson with the Kennedy brothers. The commentators acclaimed her courage and composure. Kate knew that she and Jackie shared a secret bond, a sisterhood. She wanted to tell her that she understood the pain, the physical searing pain that came each day as an echo of the timing of their passing. She watched a tissue balled in her fist ready to wipe the tears, as Jackie stood with her children watching Kennedy's coffin being carried down the cathedral steps. Three year old John Junior was given a whispered prompt by his mother and smartly raised his little outstretched hand to his eyebrow to salute and symbolically farewell his father's coffin before it began the last journey from St. Matthew's Cathedral to Arlington National Cemetery.

Ally was kicking the back of her chair and Ben was crying as he crawled over to her. It was lunchtime; she blew her nose, wiped her eyes and picked up Ben, his hands moist and sticky with fluff from the carpet. After lunch, while the children took a nap, she sat at her desk trying to reply to one of the many condolence letters that people had sent. She reread the handwritten letter on the lilac paper. It talked of her journeying through death's dark valley and that in time she would smell the roses again. But the writer also said how lucky she was that she had the children to comfort her and that Greg would live on through them. Kate screwed it up and threw it across the room.

She started to write, her hand pressing down hard on the nib.

> *How dare you say how lucky I am? Why do you think that having two infant children to raise single-handedly is fortunate? My children are not inanimate objects to be clung to, to ward off depression. They deserve the wholeness of two loving parents and not to be raised by an emotionally absent mother. I hate Greg for leaving me to do this on my own.*

Her tears spilled down onto the paper. She snatched the sheet off the pad and ripped the page into pieces. She imagined Jackie Kennedy feeling the same anger and despair and she was comforted that she was not alone in this maelstrom of grief. She picked up the crumpled violet paper and smoothed it out. She wrote once more.

> *Thank you for your kind words at this difficult time.*

They have given me comfort. I look forward to smell-ing the roses again one day. Love Kate and the children.

Her sexual needs had incubated slowly like a sick-ness. With each passing day her longing for a man to hold her grew more insistent. She spent longer time in the bathroom her fingers no longer giving her satisfac-tion. One day after the window cleaner had been and she got Isabella to pay him the seven and six pence, she knew she could no longer ignore the drive within her. But how she wondered as she fed Ally her lunch. The answer came easily: Tom Appleton. Her eyes were moon like, bright shining out of a dark space. I will ask him if he wants sex without obligation.

That afternoon on the pretext of doing some shop-ping while the children and Isabella had a rest she drove to a call box several streets away. With her heart beating a staccato in her ears, she dropped the pennies into the machine and dialled his number. As the number rang she felt sick but steadied her mind. His voice answered and she pressed the button to speak.

She had rehearsed her question over and over before ringing him and decided upon the umpteenth version there was no polite way to ask except boldly.

'Tom, I am very much in need of sex, that is sex with-out obligation, would you be interested?'

'Of course Kate, when and where?'

If he was surprised by the directness of her approach he didn't register it. She thought his response was courteous but detached much as though she had asked if he could give her a dental check up. But when he asked if she was free Tuesday evening next week and that they could go for a drink first she knew he had understood.

She told Isabella she was going out for a drink with an old friend of the family and not to wait up for her. The children were in bed when Tom arrived. He held the car door open as she climbed into his sports car; he closed the door and got into the driver's seat. As the car slowly navigated its way to the main road she felt the throaty thrust of the engine waiting to be unleashed. When they reached the arterial road Tom put his foot hard on the accelerator pedal and they roared past the cars on the inside lane. They drove through suburbia turning onto a narrow country road before they reached a small country pub. The dark blue and gold painted sign of the Bull and Bush swayed in the wind and the gold lettering glittered in the light from the pub windows. The bar was warm. They picked a small table by the log fire and Tom went to the bar to get a couple of whiskies and to order two rare roast beef sandwiches with horseradish sauce. Kate looked around the snug, only a handful of drinkers were present. Two couples were perched on barstools talking to the barmaid and a couple of men in a corner table, poring over a racing form guide. Around the red brick fireplace hung wide leather straps that displayed a collection of horse brass. At one end of the bar a woman in a white apron carved the roast beef and assembled the sandwiches.

Tom came back carrying the whiskies.

'Thank you.' She took the glass and lowered her eyes. 'Sorry, Tom, I'm not sure how to be. I'm embarrassed,' she said her face flushed from the warmth of the fire and her discomfort.

'Why don't we forget about the purpose of the evening and just get to know each other, have a bit of fun.'

At that moment their beef sandwiches arrived. Kate asked him where he had met Greg.

'At University, but while we were in the same year, we were at the opposite ends of the alphabet and consequently in different study groups but as you know, a few of us decided to come to Britain to make our mark. So I got to know Greg more during the time we were at sea on the five week trip to Southampton on the Fairsky.'

Kate had heard about that trip from Greg where four of them shared a quad cabin in the lower decks. 'I believe it was one long party,' she said.

'Yes, that's for sure. You know we left Sydney just a couple days after graduation. It was just great to be done with studying and to be able to get on with our lives.' He smiled at her. 'You okay? How about another drink?'

'Yes that would be nice, thank you,' she said. My God, she thought, I sound like a vicar's wife at a tea party when really all I am after is his body.

She watched him as he went to the bar. She imagined that he had been raised in a middle class family on the north shore of Sydney, like Greg and had wanted for little. He was tall and well built; his fair hair was cut short tapering into his neck. He wore sharp creased beige slacks, a pale blue shirt open at the throat and a dark grey jacket.

Her eyes stung, so powerful was her desire to touch him. She shifted in her chair and took her jacket off. She draped her jacket around the back of the chair; her creamy silk shirt was unbuttoned at the neckline. She crossed her legs and turned towards him, in a single gesture she pushed her skirt higher so it set mid thigh, her lacy stocking tops teasingly visible. She used her hands as she talked, elegant open palmed gestures.

'Did you like being a hostie?,' he asked. She saw the desire in his eyes.

'I absolutely loved it, my one regret was that my flying days were so short, the employment policy was single women only so it all came to a halt when I married Greg.'

'Did you ever get to Australia?,' he asked. She saw him bite his lip gently,

She ran her hands down her thighs again, watching him. He coughed.

'Not as a hostie but of course we visited on our honeymoon.'

The publican's voice rang out. 'Time gentlemen, please.'

She took his arm as they walked out to the car, their shoes crunching across the gravel forecourt. In the car the engine spluttered to life and Tom put on the heater as they drove home. Neither of them spoke. When they arrived at her home, he turned the engine off and turned to look at her.

'Do you still want to go ahead, Tom?,' she said, her

voice sounded deeper.

'Most definitely,' he said as he swung his legs out of the car in one easy move.

She hesitated for a moment at the front door, she turned round to look at him, and was about to say lets not rush into this, when he took her key from her hand and opened the door. The lounge was warm and the curtains drawn. She offered him coffee. He shook his head. He helped her slip out of her coat and jacket and laid them across a chair back. She locked the lounge room door and moved into his arms and placed her head under his chin. They swayed, a gentle motion until he lifted her head and bent to kiss her. His hands smelt evocatively of a dental surgery, filling her senses, reminding her of Greg.

She watched as he removed his suit jacket and trousers and laid them neatly over a chair. He stood tall, his shirt and tie hanging over his dark underpants. He kissed her neck and ears and his hands were on her body caressing her breasts and pulling off her shirt. From the moment she had moved into his arms her longing, a fierce and determined desire, fuelled her. She wanted nothing more than to feel him hard inside her, being as one as they moved. She unzipped her skirt, and slipped it to the floor. She was in his arms again as he fumbled with her bra strap. She yanked her pants down. Hungrily she slipped her hand into his underpants pushing them down to his knees. She waited impatiently as he pushed a condom over his penis and rolled it down into the darkness of his pubic hair. He had pulled the cushions off the settee and threw them down on the floor and she fell on them and dragged him down to her. She cried out as he entered her. Moving slowly at first. She wrapped her legs around him and lifted her body to strain with him. She whimpered with delight before he climaxed. Her hair was mussed and damp. She felt him move again and with renewed energy they fucked once more. After they lay quietly before he rolled over and said 'hope it was as good for you as it was for me.'

She sounded polite when she thanked him, all traces of the lustful libertine now spent. She echoed his words: it was good. He stood up asked for the bathroom. She gave him directions to the downstairs bathroom and asked him to be very quiet so as not to wake Isabella or the children. She put the cushions back on the settee and gathered her clothes buttoning her topcoat over her naked body. When he came back he was dressed and ready to leave. At the front door he kissed her on the cheek.

'It was great, Katie, how about Tuesday fortnight, is that okay?,' he asked.

Kate nodded. A gust of cold wind blew her coat open. He waved as he got into the car. She closed the door. She stood by the lounge windows listening to the sound of the engine as the car purred down the road. She saw the headlights catch the black shadowy shapes of the trees until he turned the corner of the street and was gone. Up in her bedroom she hung up her clothes and went into the bathroom to wash. She caught site of herself in the mirror, her skin was flushed and her eyes glittered brightly. I can't believe I did that, she thought.

She went into the nursery to check the children. Ally

lay flat on her back, her hand holding fast to her blanket and Ben curved almost into a ball, his covers kicked off. She covered Ben up and picked up Ally's blanket and tucked it in beside her. She slept deeply that night hardly moving and when the alarm rang she woke refreshed.

Kate sat with a coffee in her hand by the kitchen door as she watched the children, warmly rugged playing in the sunroom. The morning was cold and their breath made misty imprints in the cold air. Ally was busy taking Dolly in the pram out for a shopping spree and as she walked the length and breadth of the glassed-in sunroom she stopped at imaginary shops to make purchases. Ben was occupied with his Tonka dumpster and bulldozer as he corralled other small toys into a central pile.

Kate wrapped her hands around the hot coffee mug to warm them, her mind analysing why it was that sex normally made her feel ashamed and uncomfortable but the sex she had with Tom left her feeling free. Maybe, she thought it was because I did not have to worry whether he still loved me in the morning. After all my only expectation was getting shagged.

Isabella came into the kitchen and told her that they needed some more milk for Ben. She prayed that Isabella had heard nothing last night. She collected her car keys and purse and went to the local shops.

Chapter 4

• • • • • • • • • • •

Isabella

On the first Wednesday in December Isabella was in the kitchen making a cup of tea when her waters broke.

'Kate! Kate!,' she screamed.

Kate raced from the utility room where she had been loading the washing machine. She saw the very large pool of water on the linoleum floor and Isabella's grim face as she bent double over the kitchen table.

'It's okay, Isabella, your waters have broken. Do you have any pain?'

'No, not yet,' Isabella muttered, her teeth gritted.

'That's good but I think we need to get you to hospital as soon as we can.'

'I would like to be with her,' Kate said as Isabella nervously signed her name on the admission papers at the hospital. The admission sister's eyebrows arched and she turned to Kate, her eyes signalling that she did not like to be questioned. 'We will not allow that,' the sister said.

'She is under my care and only sixteen, surely I can stay with her during the early stages,' Kate appealed.

'These are the hospital rules so I suggest you make yourself at home in the waiting room. This young woman will be in capable hands.' The sister steered her patient away in a wheel chair.

The woman was inflexible, Kate thought, starched from the tip of her crisp white cap to the hem of her blue uniform. Kate ran after her and blocked the wheelchair's passage, placing both hands on the armrests.

'Isabella, I'll be here and won't budge. Don't be frightened sweetheart you'll be fine.'

The sister's sucked her breath in sharply as she thrust the wheelchair forward out of Kate's grasp.

'If she is not in labour at visiting time you will be allowed to see her,' she called out as the wheel chair rolled on squeaking across the cork floored corridor.

Kate found a call box and phoned her mother who was looking after the children. Lucy assured her that the children were fine and not to worry about time as she had everything necessary for them to stay the night.

In the waiting room three men were seated eyeing the clock nervously. A round-faced man with a heavy build paced the floor smoking a cigarette; another read a magazine and a third man in overalls was busy trying to scrape the blackness from under his nails with a metal nail file. All three looked up when she came in and took a seat. Through the smoke haze she watched each of the men, her fingers nervously twisting her wedding ring. Her loss separated her from their joy. Her eyes glazed with tears. She stood, blew her nose and went to the centre table where piles of magazines were untidily displayed. She chose a glossy travel publication.

She flicked through the pages. The full-page photograph of Waikiki Beach made her pause. The scene showed surfers riding their long boards as the rolling sea-green waves of the Pacific carried them onto the pale fine sand. Palm trees edged the beach alive with tanned bikini clad girls and young men in thigh length shorts. The article's headline read Christmas in Hawaii. She flipped the page and looked at a couple of pictures of the Royal Hawaiian Hotel, dubbed Honolulu's Pink Palace. The interior shot was of the foyer of the hotel with a huge icing-pink feathery Christmas tree decorated with baubles, every hue of pink and a model train running around it's faux snow base. She sighed. She looked up as the chubby faced man, struck a match to light another cigarette. There was one window in the room that looked out over a grey and cheerless streetscape below. Another sigh escaped her lips. The man cleaning his nails looked up and nodded sympathetically. She turned the page, skiing in Austria did not interest her. But over the next page was an article that captured her. A white cruise ship crested the dark blue waves. The headline read *Cruise to Australia in Style*. Two smaller pictures showed an angle shot of cabin with a square window and it's own bathroom and the other showed a good looking couple, on deck, their faces alive with excitement as they gazed at Cape Town's Table Top Mountain. The images mesmerized her. She read and reread the article:

The one-class ocean liner S.S. Antares provides an around-the-world service to Australia and New Zealand and returning to Southampton via Panama. The graceful liner with minimalist decor carries fourteen hundred passengers in air-conditioned comfort. The large open sports and sun deck with an outdoor pool provide ample space for passengers at play. The liner has two restaurants fore and aft, an expansive forward lounge, library, writing room, smoking room and an impressive two-deck cinema lounge. The favourite watering hole on the ship is the Ocean Bar with live music each night at sea.

The ship was built to take advantage of the many migrants leaving our shores for new lives down under but many other travellers revel in its quality accommodations. The next trip to Australasia leaves Southampton on 4th February 1964 with two ports of call, Las Palmas, Canary Islands and Cape Town, South Africa before making landfall in Australia.

Her eyes were bright as the kaleidoscope of sunshine, palm trees and beaches that filled her mind. She tore the page from the magazine and slipped it into her bag. This trip is obviously meant to be she thought. Tomorrow I'll see if a cabin with a bathroom is available and if it is, I will book it.

Two hours later, family visitors filed through the doors of the maternity hospital for the afternoon visiting hour. Kate joined the throng as they moved up through the corridors to the wards. She decided not to ask at the desk for directions to Isabella's ward but simply worked her way through the corridors checking names outside the wards. Isabella was in a two-bed ward but only her bed was occupied. Kate could hear her frightened cries from outside in the corridor. Isabella was sitting on the edge of the bed, wearing a blue hospital gown. Her pains were coming steadily and as Kate came into the room she was having a strong contraction. Isabella bent double with the pain and moaned as Kate took her hand.

'How long between them Isabella?,' she asked. The pain subsided and Isabella breathed deeply.

'Oh Kate, this is so awful, they shaved me, how embarrassing and gave me a thing called an enema, it was awful. The pain won't get worse will it? I don't know how long between but they…' She grabbed Kate's hand as the pain started again like a deep wave steadily and determinedly moving through her lower body. Sweat trickled down the side of her nose onto her lips and chin.

As the pain ebbed Kate asked 'When did you last see a nurse?'

'I don't know, they gave me buzzer to use if it got bad, but it doesn't work as I have pressed and pressed it and no one comes.'

The pain came again, only this time stronger and longer, which left Isabella whimpering and spent.

Kate bent over her.

'Listen to me Isabella, I am going for a nurse, if they won't let me back in, know that I am in the waiting room. You'll be alright Isabella, I know you're frightened but promise you will try to relax, like we practiced, it will help you get relief from the pain.'

At the ward desk she found a young nurse in a lavender and white striped uniform.

'I am responsible for Isabella Cunningham; she is sixteen years old and terrified. She is in Room 2D and she is having regular and strong contractions. With less than two to three minutes in between. She has been using the buzzer as directed to summon a nurse but has not seen one for some time. I would like you to either go to her or get someone competent in there to assess her and reassure her.'

The nurse saw the determination and concern in Kate's eyes. It had been a busy afternoon and probably no one had answered the buzzer.

'I will get someone to her immediately but you must go to the waiting room,' the nurse said firmly.

'Thank you. I'll go into the waiting room directly I see someone has gone into see Isabella.'

Kate stood guard by the desk watching the corridor ahead. Within a couple of minutes one of the ward sisters entered Isabella's room.

Kate got a coffee from the canteen before it closed for the afternoon and went into the waiting room. The chain smoker that had paced the floor had gone. But the man with the magazine and the man in overalls were still waiting.

'No news?,' she asked.

'No news,' they both spoke in unison.

'These babies take their time,' she said.

Half an hour later a nurse came through the door and told one of the men that he was the father of a baby boy. He let out a whoop of joy and left the waiting room with the nurse to meet his new son. Others joined them in the waiting room. The man who tried to focus on reading a magazine was looking very tired and stressed. At six o'clock a nurse came to tell her that Isabella had given birth to a girl, both mother and child were fine and Kate could now visit them.

When Kate arrived in the four-bed ward, three of the beds had visitors clustered around and she saw the man who paced the floor and continually smoked. His arm encircled his wife, her blonde hair a damp mess of Shirley Temple curls. They gazed in amazement at the baby cradled in her arms. Kate stood silently watching the family scene. The pain in her chest had returned and she absently rubbed her breastbone with her fist. The curtains were drawn around the fourth bed. She peeped through a chink in the curtain and stepped inside where she saw Isabella being coached by a nurse to encourage her baby to breast-feed.

Isabella smiled at Kate. 'I have a daughter,' she said. 'A beautiful daughter.'

'Best looking baby in the ward, Isabella well done.'

The nurse pulled open the curtains.

'I have named her Laura. Would you like to hold her Kate?'

Kate took the tiny infant in her arms and inspected the wrinkled face. The baby yawned and opened her dark blue eyes for a moment, staring up at Kate almost in recognition.

'How was it Isabella?'

'Bloody awful and I have six stitches,' she smiled proudly.

Kate gave Isabella her baby and took a chair beside her. Isabella opened the baby's blanket and laid the newborn across her lap. The baby's limbs suddenly unrestricted by the blanket did odd little jerks.

'It's okay sweetheart,' her mother said reaching out to steady her.

'Look at her hands, Kate, have you ever seen anything so tiny but so perfect?' Not waiting for an answer she continued to investigate the baby's feet and count her toes.

'Yes of course,' Kate said biting her lip to check her tears. 'She is simply perfect, Isabella.'

The visiting bell rang Kate got up to leave.

'Give Ben and Ally a cuddle from me.'

'Of course,' Kate bent to kiss Isabella's cheek and her infant's pudgy fist. 'I'll see you tomorrow, Isabella.'

The temperature outside was freezing and the walk from the hospital to the car park left Kate chilled. She put the heater on in the car. As she drove out of the hospital driveway onto the orange-lit main road she turned on the car radio. The car filled with the distinctive yodel of Frank Ifield singing I remember you. The traffic slowed as they came to traffic lights. As the lights turned green the radio disc jockey announced 'Now let's have one from the top of the charts this year, the Ronettes with *Be My*

Baby.

The night we met I knew I needed you so, and if I had
a chance I'd never let you go

Soon the orange lights of the main roads turned into the odd white street light as she ducked around the back streets to her house. She drove into her driveway, turned the headlights off as the last bars of the chorus sang out. *Be my, Be my baby, My one and only baby, Whoa oh oh oh.* The house was warm. Lucy had washed dishes and mopped the linoleum floor in the kitchen. She rang her mother.

'She had a girl at 5.12pm. She weighed in at 6lb 5 oz. She's called her Laura. You should see her Mummy, she's gorgeous. Isabella was very proud of the fact that she had six stitches.' Kate's voice sounded thin.

'That's wonderful news Kate, a little girl and six stitches. God bless her.'

Kate smiled and cradled the phone closer to her cheek.

'Are you okay? Must have been a stressful day for you. Get some rest and pick the children up tomorrow, not tonight. They're fast asleep and look like little angels. We'll have breakfast together and we can work out a roster for visiting Isabella.'

Kate checked the Aga furnace before putting in another shovelful of coke. She went into the lounge and pulled a bottle of Remy Martin brandy from the sideboard. Pouring herself a large slug in a brandy balloon she took it back into the kitchen. She could not be bothered to eat. The first few sips of the brandy burned her throat but with each sip she felt the warmth spread through her body. She took out the folded glossy pages from the magazine and examined it again. The cabin looked good like a hotel room and had its own bathroom. If I left in February I would be in Sydney for Easter, beautiful time of year Greg always said.

The only sound was the hum of the Aga. It was strange without Isabella. She thought about ringing up Isabella's parents to demand that they see first-hand the love between their daughter and granddaughter. If only they could see this they would never separate them.

In the bedroom she slipped her coat onto the hanger in the wardrobe next to Greg's navy cashmere sports jacket. Taking his jacket off the wooden hanger she slipped her arms down inside the silk lined sleeves traced with Monsieur de Givenchy cologne that she had given him one birthday and folded the large jacket around her body, lifting the soft collar so that it sat round her chin and neck. Wrapped in the softness of the cashmere she rubbed her cheek into the collar. Her eyes filled and spilled gently. She thought of the round-faced man in the hospital so happy as he gazed at his child and an image of Greg holding Ally and then Ben so proudly in his arms at their births. She shook her head and her tears flew across the room. She remembered each tiny detail of his delight, his eyes shining as together they had checked every finger and toe and found them perfect.

Tears and mucous streamed down her face. She looked out of the window, the moon a silver slice in the night sky and like a werewolf she howled damming God for the loss of Greg and damming society for the injustice shown to young unmarried mothers. She raged for Isabella's child who would be taken from her and for Isabella who would have to live with the terrible secret all her days. Her head pounded as she crawled onto her bed.

She fell asleep, still in Greg's jacket with the soggy spent tissues lying on the floor, her body giving little shudders. As the heating in the house went off and the temperature dropped she pulled the eiderdown around her. She slept through till the clock radio switched on at seven playing a Bob Dylan track *Blowin in the Wind.*

Breakfast was eventful. Kate was ready to defend her decision to book the trip to Australia with less than two months to organise it. She showed her mother the magazine cutting. But Lucy was enthusiastic, the ship looked impressive and how wonderful, she said to have a cabin with its own bathroom, two restaurants and a swimming pool, indeed the best way to travel. Kate rang the travel agent and found there was still a cabin with bathroom available on Promenade Deck for the February voyage and there was a cabin available for a return voyage if she chose leaving Sydney in the middle of June. By lunchtime she had sent a telegram to the Sinclairs telling them the proposed dates of their stay and asking them to confirm.

Kate was buoyant when she went to the hospital for the afternoon visiting hour. She took some fruit and a cold sausage sandwich with a daub of HP sauce, Isabella's favourite snack and a pink potted hyacinth. Isabella was sitting in bed with her pillows bunched behind her, the white rough hospital sheet folded over the loose weaved fabric blanket, which had been pulled tautly across the middle of the bed.

'Hi sweetheart, how're doing today?' Kate quizzed.

Isabella eye's moistened. 'They won't let me have her except for feeds,' she said.

Kate looked at her expectantly waiting to hear that perhaps the baby had colic and was confined to the nursery. 'What do you mean is she sick?'

'She is fine, perfectly well but Miss Higgins, the Moral Welfare Officer, came round first thing and left instructions that she was only to be given to me at feed times.'

Kate's nostrils pinched. How dare they deny her child and simply use her as a milking machine, she thought. Her anger built steadily. Shaking she tried to quieten her mind. She sat on the edge of the bed and held Isabella's hand. 'How often are you feeding her?,' she asked.

'They say I have to do it every four hours. She seems very hungry and is always crying when they bring her in.'

Kate stood and smoothed her skirt. She handed Isabella the paper bag that held the greaseproof paper wrapped sausage sandwich. 'You need your strength my girl, eat your sandwich. I'm just going to have a word with the sister.'

Kate strode down the hall past the viewing window to the nursery. At the desk she demanded to see the Ward Sister. Her heart was hammering and her thoughts scattering as she tried to piece together a sound argument to get a more humane outcome for Isabella. The Ward Sister wore glasses and her hair was pulled back into a bun, so tightly from her face the frown lines on her forehead were smoothed. Her voice had an edge of impatience as she asked what Kate wanted.

'My name is Kate Sinclair, Mrs Sinclair and I have been responsible for the welfare of Isabella Cunningham for the past four months. Yesterday afternoon she delivered a baby girl. Today I believe she has only had limited access to her daughter, at four hourly feed times and I would like to know why she cannot feed her on demand and have her child with her like all of the other mothers in that ward.' Kate hoped that the sister did not hear the tremble in her voice.

The Sister's eyes narrowed. 'If you have been responsible for the young woman this length of time, I have no need to tell you that she is an unmarried mother and as such her baby will be put up for adoption at the end of six weeks. To make this transition easier it has been decided to limit the time she spends with the child. It is in her best interests so that she does not get too fond of the baby.'

Kate looked at her reddened hands and noted no ring. 'Sister, I'm sorry I didn't catch your name?' Her voice was strong.

'My title is Ward Sister Baker,' the nurse replied pointing to her badge pinned to her dark blue uniform. 'Ward Sister Baker, my charge is sixteen years old and as a minor the question of whether her baby will be adopted will finally be decided by her parents. But I believe you do not have a right to limit access to her daughter. There is no way in the world that anyone can make this transition, as you like to call it, easier but denying her rights will only increase her grief and I would imagine her milk supply.'

'I will take what you say on board Mrs Sinclair but not promise anything,' the Sister said.

'No Ward Sister Baker you will organise to bring Isabella's daughter to her now. If not I will take this matter to the hospital administrators.'

Kate did not speak loudly; her threat was clear and concise. She held her chin high and stared unflinchingly at the ward sister. Her righteous fury gave her a feeling of exhilaration.

It was obvious that the sister did not like Kate's manner but she did not argue. Instead, as she walked back in her office, she bit her lip to control a smile. Maybe, Kate thought, Ward Sister Baker was equally pleased to have an excuse to defy Miss Higgins's directive.

Kate needed air. As she went through the vestibule to the front door she saw the round-faced father light up a cigarette, the acrid smell of tobacco smoke filling her nostrils. It felt good. It was a good couple of years since she had her last cigarette. She asked if she could have one of his cigarettes. 'With pleasure love,' he said with a flourish.

She took the cork tipped Rothman cigarette and bent her head as he offered her a light. The smoke curled up through her nostrils and flowed through her like tiny bubbles released into her bloodstream. She felt light-headed like she had drunk a glass of champagne. Feeling much calmer she walked back into the hospital and up to the ward. Isabella had eaten her sandwich and was looking at a magazine one of the other mothers had given her. She looked up when Kate came into the ward.

'What did she say?' she asked.

Before Kate could answer the door opened to a young nurse pushing a mobile cot.

'Cunningham?' she queried. Isabella jumped off the bed and took the cot with a smile that could light up a power grid.

'Thank you, thank you,' she threw her arms around Kate's neck and hugged her.

Joyce phoned that evening. 'I hear you have been putting them all in their place at the hospital. Miss Higgins is very down in the mouth, well done.'

Kate beamed. 'I couldn't stand by and see her used as a wet nurse for her own child.'

'Yes love you are right, but I want you to think beyond this moment. The bottom line is this: Isabella will endorse her parent's decision to give her child up for adoption. She is a loving caring girl who will want the best for her child. And in the eyes of her parents, the welfare system and society, adoption will give her child the opportunities that she could never give her. After six weeks she will go back home and all this time that she has had with you will have to be forgotten, never talked about, if she is to rebuild her life.'

'Yes, I hear you and know I have to let things run their course. But I still say this is wrong, Isabella should have the right to decide, as should any young woman in the same situation without being badgered or vilified by society. In the best interests of the child is moral blackmail or propaganda or whatever you like to label it. I'm sorry but it stinks, you know it does.'

'Look Kate I don't think any of us know whether adoption is the best way, but at this point in time this is the way it is. Illegitimacy is a hard pill to swallow. Remember Kate, the term bastard is part of our every day language and is still used as a shameful slur. I promise you that I will find the best parents for this baby, ones that will raise her in a loving environment and who will be able to financially give her the best quality of life.'

———

Isabella asked Kate to do the hand-over of her daughter to the adopting parents. Kate sat in an armchair in the common room as Isabella wrapped her baby girl in the soft wool shawl that Lucy had knitted. As they waited for the new parents to arrive, Isabella sang, her voice sweet as she cradled her baby in her arms, willing the lullaby to be imprinted into her child's memories so that she would know how much her mother loved her.

Go to sleep my baby. Close those pretty eyes. Angels are above you. Watching over from the skies, Big blue moon is shining. Stars begin to peep. Time for you my baby. Time for you to sleep.

Isabella's eyes never left her child's face absorbing the soft down of her cheeks, her long eyelashes, wispy eyebrows, pouting mouth and a tiny chin that disappeared into the folds of her sweet smelling pinkness.

Isabella's parents arrived to take her home. When Kate

took the baby from her arms, Isabella grasped her arms around her chest and swayed, Kate thought she might faint and put out a hand to steady her. The pupils of her eyes were dilated making her eyes look black and her face was contorted with scream that made no sound. She turned, her shoulders rounded as she walked from the room closing the door softly behind her.

The new parents were shiny faced, well-groomed and alive with excitement as Kate handed the baby to them.

'Her name is Laura. Please let her know that her mother is a beautiful soul who loved her dearly. She only wanted the best for her.'

Kate eyes were red rimmed but the couple did not notice they only had eyes for the sleeping baby. 'She is due for a feed shortly,' Kate called as she walked from the room.

She was shaking as she drove home. Sighting a red telephone box she pulled over. The phone box smelt of stale tobacco. She dialled Tom's surgery number, his nurse answered. She drummed her fingers on the graffiti covered telephone book until she heard his voice.

'I've had a wretched day any chance of you coming round for a drink tonight?', she asked.

'I'm playing squash but will come later,' he said. She sighed as she replaced the phone on its cradle.

He arrived at nine and there were no preliminary drinks and chats. She took his jacket at the front door and was unzipping his fly as they backed into the lounge. With one hand on her shoulder he held her at arms length as he undid his pants, she slipped her skirt and pants down and her hands reaching out wanting to touch and be touched.

Best's Department Store that day was crowded. The store was festive with holly wreaths and garlands of silver balls strung high across the counters and walkways. Lucy and Kate foot sore from the last of Christmas shopping sipped their hot milk and dash of coffee only too grateful to have secured seats and two highchairs in the busy store café. Oily crumbs coated Ally and Ben's fingers and faces as they made short work of toasted cheese fingers.

'I keep thinking about Isabella and the baby,' Kate said

'Yes but she's home now with her family, she'll pick up,' Lucy said.

'The new parents seemed nice I wonder if they will tell her that she is adopted? If she grows up knowing that, do you think that'll be enough for her, or will she question why her birth mother gave her away?' Kate said.

'I don't think about it love.'

Kate heard the exasperation in Lucy's voice. Her mother's toes were sore where her new shoes had rubbed. Ben was tipping his feeding cup upside down watching the milk trickle down on to the carpet. Lucy took it from him.

'As I've said before you think far too much, just accept that is the way it is, live your life not others'

'You weren't there to see it, Mummy. It was awful.' Lucy shook her head. 'You're always saying I think too much, what is wrong with thinking?' Kate stared at her mother.

'Nothing Kate if it's productive but questioning things you can't change is pointless. That baby is a very lucky child she will have everything. I know Joyce said she has gone to a well-to-do couple who love her dearly. She will have a good life. ' She put her coffee cup down and leant across to caress Kate's cheek. 'They'll both be fine Kate, stop worrying.'

Chapter 5

. . . .

The Voyage

Ally threw Dolly into a suitcase half full of neatly layered clothes. Kate put her pile of folded clothes down on the bed and pushed the doll back into Ally's arms.

'No Ally, not in the suitcase please,' she said. The bedroom was chaotic with piles of clothes and shoes waiting to be packed. Kate had underestimated the amount of luggage she would have to take with her on the five-month trip to Australia. She sighed as she folded her navy jacket with tissue paper, she could not get it to sit evenly.

Ben gave a howl of rage and she dropped the jacket and raced onto the landing. His face red with indignation as Ally held tightly onto his favourite truck.

'Enough you two, enough. Give him back his truck, Ally.'

Reluctantly Ally let go and picked up Dolly and disappeared into the nursery. Kate checked the gate at the top of the stairs and picked Ben up and his truck and carried him into the bedroom. 'Play here, where I can see you,' she said putting him down close to the bed.

She tugged and pulled at the crepe material but still it was too bulky for the suitcase. Once more she tried but still the finished result was cumbersome. In exasperation she flung the jacket to the floor.

Ben commando crawled the bedroom, a line of concentrated dribble hanging off his chin. She picked up the jacket. Slowly and carefully she started the folds again. This time the jacket packed reasonably flat and she placed it in the case.

As Kate sat on top of the final case to shut it, the thought came that this time tomorrow she would be on the high seas getting herself dressed to go to the dining room to have dinner with adults, no cooking, no washing up. Clipping the lock on the suitcase she scooped up Ben under one arm, grabbed Ally from the nursery and bounced down the stairs to start dinner.

⁓

Frank and Lucy drove the family to Southampton docks. As they arrived at the terminal they could see the white hull of S.S. Antares towering above them, its single orange smoke stack at the aft barely visible. Porters rushed to help as Frank unloaded the cases. Frank checked each piece of luggage carefully to make sure that they had the correct labels as they were piled high on a trolley.

The family with the children, safely strapped in the double pushchair, joined the line waiting for passport inspection. Having finished all the formalities they were ready to board. The covered gangway was set at about a thirty-degree angle, steep enough to make two children in a cumbersome stroller a difficult task. Lucy took Ben and Kate carried Ally while Frank manoeuvred the stroller up the gangplank. Crew members in their winter navy uniforms greeted them in the boarding area. One of the pursers directed them to Kate's cabin telling them to take the elevator to promenade deck. The lift with its laminate faux marble walls was close to her cabin. A man, his steward's uniform hanging loosely on his thin frame, ran to greet them. He took the pram from Frank and set it outside her cabin.

'Number thirty-three Signora—this is yours. My name is Roberto, I am your cabin steward.'

Leading Kate into the cabin he darted into the bathroom to allow the rest of the party to enter. He stood at the bathroom door.

'Little squeezy with Momma and Poppa here but the three of you will be good. When you unpack, I take the cases so you have plenty room and I store the pram down in my utility room, you can get when you need it,' he said.

A smile lit his face. 'In Napoli I have four children, two little ones like these.' He knelt down to talk to the children. 'Bella, bella,' he gently chucked Ally under her chin. 'What's their names?' he asked.

'Ally and Ben.' Lucy beamed

Frank followed Roberto out of the cabin. He told him Kate was travelling alone with the children and would need all the help he could give her. He pressed £30 into his hand promising that Kate would give him another £45 at the end of the voyage if she was satisfied with his service.

Roberto nodded in agreement. 'I'll look after her and the babies, you know need to worry sir,' he assured Frank as they solemnly shook hands.

The cream painted cabin was cramped as all of her cases had been delivered and these were taking up valuable floor space. A cot separated the two single beds on either side of the room. A dark green patterned curtain looped on one side of the window that looked out on the promenade deck, a smallish wardrobe and a small writing desk/dressing table. Most importantly it had its own bathroom.

'At least I have a bath for the children, rather than a shower stall,' Kate enthused to Lucy. 'It's small but it will be fine,' she said.

All too soon the loudspeakers crackled with an announcement for all visitors to go ashore. Kate clung to both her parents as they said their farewells.

'Kate try to have a bit of a rest and fun. Roberto says he'll take care of you and remember to give him the £45 I promised him at the end of the trip.' Frank said as he stepped onto the gangway.

As the ship slipped her berth, people threw paper streamers from the decks to those waiting hands below. The coloured ribbons stretching until either the wind whipped them from the farewelling hands or the ship's slow progression broke the tie. Below on the dock the band played *Now is the Hour*, Kate held the babies tighter, her eyes firmly fixed on her parents. The music faded, tears trickled down her face and the wind chilled them instantly, she stayed until she could no longer see their faces.

Roberto was in the corridor when she returned. 'Such beautiful babies,' he said as he opened the cabin door for her. 'We work together your voyage will be good.'

She lifted Ally off her hip and let her run into the cabin. 'I could do with the help.' She tightened her hold on Ben. 'Is there a babysitting service, can you arrange that?'

'Yes signora, I can but I am here on duty most times, I can listen for them and if you speak with me before you go to dinner I will listen out for them and any trouble I will get someone to get you,' he rubbed Ben's back. 'We'll be fine won't we Ben?'

'Grazie, Roberto,' she said, her voice sounded more cheerful. 'Did I say that right?' Roberto nodded. 'I'll let you know when I'm going down to dinner.'

Roberto had cleaned and tidied the cabin while she had taken the children down to the dining room for their evening meal. The suitcases were in a neat pile next to the dressing table. Surprisingly the children snuggled down into their respective bed and cot and watched her as she went to and fro. She didn't bathe or change, there wasn't time but she wiped her face clean and put on fresh make-up. The children were asleep when she came out of the bathroom. She gazed at them, hesitant about leaving, the dining room seemed so far away. Roberto had heard the dinner gong and was waiting as she left the cabin. He patted her arm and told her to have a nice dinner and that he would watch over them.

She made her way through the dining room, conscious of her crumpled slacks and twin-set. Other passengers that she passed looked as though they had gone to some effort. She tugged at her slacks trying to smooth the creases.

She was the last to arrive at her assigned table and her fellow diners had already started to eat. Her face was flushed as she stumbled through an apology for her late arrival explaining she needed to get the children settled first.

The waiter stood close to her elbow, tapping his pen on his pad as she studied the menu.

'I'll have the asparagus soup and the roast duckling with orange sauce,' she said.

The waiter tapped his pad again. 'Just soup and duckling? No fish, no entrée?' he said.

Kate replied, 'No fish, no entrée, just soup and duck, thank you.'

She placed her napkin over her creased pants. The woman beside her sat tall in her chair. Her dark hair framed her broad brow and deep-set light grey eyes. Twenty four year old Prue Ponting came from a world of wealth and social position. Her clothes, her self-assurance and voice flagged all the clues.

Her voice, loud and accentuated with its BBC plummy articulation, demanded attention.

She turned to Kate. 'Are you going to Oar-stralia?'

'Yes, Aus-tralia,' Kate replied. She turned away and broke open her bread roll.

'Oh are you a £10 POM? What fun,' Prue said.

Kate shook her head.

A husband and wife opposite said quietly that they too were going to Australia and how nice it was that we were all travelling together. Kate smiled and was about to speak when Prue cut across the conversation.

'Your husband, is he in Oarstralia?'

Kate did not reply.

In Oar-stralia? Prue was nothing less than persistent

Kate swung round her shoulders squared, her face pinched with irritation—her bread knife clattered heavily on the plate

'No, he's dead,' each word slowly articulated knowing how shocking it would be to the women beside her.

'What?' Prue's lip trembled.

Kate saw the pallor on her neighbour's face. Her voice softened, 'My husband is dead.' She felt her chest tighten and she took small shallow breaths.

Other diners at the table looked away in embarrassment. Prue's hand flew to her mouth,

'I am so sorry,' she said taking Kate's hands in hers. 'Please, please, I never thought.'

Kate lowered her head in disgust she felt disloyal to Greg's memory using his death like a weapon but worse still that these strangers saw her anger. 'No, I'm the one who should apologise. I'm sorry it has been a long and emotional day.'

Prue did not speak as the meal progressed. Kate glanced at her she no longer seemed to sit so tall and straight in her chair. Other diner's excused themselves from the table as they finished their meals. Kate's dessert was the last to arrive, Prue had pushed hers to one side and when Kate's arrived she picked up her spoon and started eating. Soon they were the last at the table.

'I'm truly sorry. Talk about putting your foot in your mouth—and I have very big feet,' Prue said, her spoon poised as she looked at Kate.

Kate smiled 'Look it wasn't your fault, I've been angry ever since Greg died, it does not take much to set me off.'

'So can we start again? Do you want to go for a drink in the Ocean Bar.'

Kate nodded. 'I think that sounds perfect.'

She checked the sleeping children and told Roberto she would be in the Ocean Bar for an hour. Prue was already seated in the lounge when she arrived and had got a small table to one side. Kate took out her purse to pay, but Prue insisted on buying the first round.

'What do you drink?', she asked.

'A whiskey with ice and a splash of soda water.'

Prue's voice boomed, 'Oh my God, that is my favourite tipple. We are going to be great pals, gal.'

Kate giggled. She watched as the tall angular girl with an easy gait made her way to the bar. Even from the distance she heard her order the drinks. She grinned when Prue's voice boomed across the room. 'Keep the change, barman.'

When Kate found that Prue had been raised in Wales she told her how during the war she had spent time in a town called Llandrindod Wells, that in fact she thought she even went to school there for a day.

Prue leant forward, her face alive with excitement. 'I don't believe this, my family lives near there. I started at the village school and was there for a couple of terms, before boarding at Boxham, do you know it?'

'Boxham? D'you mean the supposedly best boarding school in Britain for girls? Only by reputation. What was it like?'

'Fabulous. The school was quite broad in their thinking, yes we did the academic stuff but the school's philosophy was to develop each of our individual talents and focus on those. So perfect for me as my passion was interior design. What about you? Where did you go to school?'

'I went to a local all girls Grammar School and have to say it was dull by comparison. Closest thing to anything creative was home science where the highlight was learning to make a good cup of cocoa, which of course every girl needs to know.' The women laughed. As they continued chatting they discovered that they both loved cooking and. As they talked, Prue's accent and fortissimo voice no longer bothered Kate. Prue asked about Greg.

Unexpectedly Kate found herself confiding, 'I miss him dreadfully and it is so bloody hard on my own with the two babies.'

Prue swallowed hard; she imagined that Kate would hate her pity. 'Well my dear we will just have to get pissed together each night.'

With that she told her that she had just broken up with her man after five years and this trip was to have a bloody good time and put it all behind her.

'Pissed it is,' said Kate, 'but not tonight. I'm all in, but tomorrow night sounds good.'

As she made her way back through the labyrinth of public rooms, corridors and stairs, the ship weaved a gentle heaving motion that intensified noticeably by the time she got to her cabin. The bow of ship eased down into the waves of the North Atlantic and shuddered as she rose. The children were sleeping soundly, Ben looked as though he was glued to the mattress of his cot, as it gently rose and fell with the motion of the ship. She managed to change into her nightdress by clinging onto the bathroom door. Topside, things that weren't battened down rumbled across the deck. Gusty rain tattooed on the cabin window. In the darkness of the cabin she reached her bed by holding onto the dressing table and Ben's cot. She pulled the covers over her, gripping the sides of the mattress, as she lay rigid staring at the shadowy ceiling. As her body adjusted to the ship's movement she relaxed and focused on its rhythm, first her head dipped then it rose, head dip and rise, dip and rise.

She was woken by Ben's tentative cries as daylight was filtering through curtains. Ally stirred. Ben stopped crying, rolled over and sat up. Wide-eyed, Ally and Ben looked at each other in the small space. The ship's passage was smooth with no trace of the previous night's squally seas. Ally bounced onto Kate's bed.

'Blimey, Ally ,I thought it was calm sailing this morning,' Kate said, reaching out and grabbing her daughter. 'Breakfast for you two I think, now get off me you pesky monkey and let me get up.'

Children's nursery was on the sun deck, one deck up from the cabin. She registered both of them into the nursery programme that was structured for small children up to the age of five years. Kate hovered to one side of the nursery watching to see how they would fare. Ally made friends instantly and squeezed herself into the middle of a small group of other toddlers who were busy removing furniture from the large painted dolls house. As she watched one of the nursery assistants took Ben out of the playpen to sit on her lap.

'They'll be fine. Most of the children on board this trip are older so we have plenty of time to indulge these little ones. Just relax and make the most of your time off,' she said.

Roberto had already cleaned the cabin and all was neat and tidy. She unpacked the suitcases and set up the Milton Steriliser and washed Ben's bottles in the sink and popped them into the steriliser. She ran a bath and lay soaking in the warm water. She did not move until her fingers became soggy and wrinkled and the water was almost cold.

Both Ally and Ben were ready for their nap after lunch and it didn't take long before their restlessness turned into sleep. Kate's bed was by the window, which offered her natural daylight to read by. She plumped the pillows to support her head as she lay, her paperback in hand. She read a few lines of her novel but could not get into it. Kate looked at the children as they slept, watching their small chests, like small soft bellows filling and emptying.

She stared beyond them to the steel bulkheads. I wish

you could see them Greg she thought. They sleep well on the ship; it must be the gentle rocking.

Four days after leaving Southampton the ship sailed into Puerto de Las Palmas the first port of call on the voyage. The two friends, with the children in the pushchair, disembarked as soon as the gangplank was in place.

Even this early in the morning the sun was hot, a light breeze was welcome as they strolled. Open-air restaurants and cafés speckled the promenade that framed the three mile golden stretch of Playa de las Canteras beach. They stopped at a small café, its table and chairs facing the ocean. A natural reef protected the bay and the waves rolled softly into shore. They ordered coffee, warm milk for the Ally and a plate of churros.

'According to this,' Prue said, reading the shipboard daily news, 'Las Palmas de Gran Canaria, is said to have the best climate in the world.'

Kate nodded her mouth full of the delicious sugar dusted Spanish donut.

On the beach they hired a couple of deckchairs. Prue hitched her skirt, her white legs a shock in an abundance of golden-limbed sunbathers arranged on sun-beds.

'God Kate, we could go crazy here with all these spunky men.'

Kate laughed and kicked off her sandals feeling the warm sand trickle through her toes.

'Yes, like kids in a sweet shop,' she called as Ben straddled her hip and Ally held her hand as she took the children to the water's edge.

Prue settled back into her canvas chaise longue and lifted her face to the sun.

Kate took Ben off her hip, tucked her skirt into her panties and squatted down holding him firmly by his hands as she put his feet in the water. The water was warm and he stomped his small feet soundly up and down. Suddenly the water sprayed up into his face. At first he turned to his mother with a look of amazement and excitedly he stomped again, this time synchronising his action with a bigger wave. The water covered him and he was soaked. He looked up at his mother and his face crumpled and let out a howl. Kate laughed, tickling him under his chin until a smile plumped his face. She put him back on her hip where he happily watched Ally run and splash until Kate tugged her reluctant daughter back up the beach to change.

'Time for a walk again before lunch?' Prue rallied pulling her skirt down over her now rose pink legs. Kate nodded intent on buckling up Ally's sandals.

They walked for nearly an hour. The promenade a heady landscape of palm trees, the air fragrant from coconut oil from the sun worshippers on the beach with elegantly dressed people strolling slowly to stop every now and then to greet friends or to read menus outside of the many open-air restaurants and cafés.

They found a small restaurant just off the main thoroughfare for lunch and ordered thin steaks and salad bathed in olive oil.

'I think I'll come back to the ship with you. I've had

enough sun for today and I don't want to go looking at cathedrals or museums, I have seen more than enough of those in my time.' Prue said, as the children finished their ice cream.

Ben was almost asleep when their taxi arrived at the ship.

'I'll settle them and meet you for a coffee in the forward lounge,' Kate said.

With most of the passengers still sightseeing the lounge was quiet and they got a table in front of the huge forward window where they could see the town and the port below.

'Don't look now but I think we may have company,' said Prue, staring over Kate's shoulder at a couple of ship's officers walking towards them.

Leo Grasso, the ship's Chief Engineer and Fred Ashton the ship's doctor, impressive in their summer whites introduced themselves and after a few courteous enquiries about their welfare, whether their cabins and food were satisfactory, they asked if they could join them. Leo clicked his fingers to a steward to get another round of coffee and launched into an impressive monologue about the tonnage of different foods that would be eaten by passengers and crew on the voyage. Fred joked that most passengers he saw would be unable to keep food down as sea sickness was the most probable cause of a trip to the ship's doctor.

Prue curled her hair around her fingers as she chatted with the brown-eyed Italian. Leo leaned towards her, his eyes settling on her breasts when he felt her eyes were elsewhere. He licked his lips and said grandé and bella frequently whenever Prue spoke.

Kate figured that Fred was in his early forties and liked the way his eyes never left hers as they spoke. He was tall, a little on the heavy side but had a great smile and blue eyes. He was not wearing a wedding ring.

Without a doubt, she thought, these fellows with their gold epaulettes could have their pick of the female talent on board and obviously are well practiced at it from their pick-up lines but I wonder if Fred would want me knowing…

As they talked her pulse quickened and a familiar desire gnawed in the pit of her stomach. She quickly looked away in case he saw the hunger within her. But it was too late.

Fred said quietly 'Kate you have the most come to bed eyes I've ever seen in a woman.'

Her cheeks flamed. For God's sake she thought I'm giving out signals like a bitch on heat. What the hell am I doing? She turned her head, staring at the curved lines of the bow of the ship through the forward window.

'Kate I am sorry about your husband and I know you have two young children,' he said quietly.

She turned and held his gaze. 'Thank you, but what's your point?'

'The point, as you like to put it, is simple. I enjoy your company and would like to get to know you better. I suggest that we meet for a drink in the bar after dinner. So what do you think?

She was quiet momentarily, her fingers twisting her

wedding band. She looked up and smiled, any conflict she my have had now pushed firmly away, 'I think I'd like that,' she said.

They left Prue and Leo in the lounge. Fred walked Kate back to her cabin. At that moment Roberto came up to tell her that the children slept well and enquired if she was feeling sea sick seeing the doctor with her. 'Thank you Roberto,' her shining eyes looked past him at Fred. As his broad shoulders disappeared down the corridor she returned her gaze to Roberto. 'I'm fine thank you Roberto. But I will need a babysitter tonight as I will probably be later than usual.'

Dr Fred Ashton's opening play was seamless. After a drink in the lounge with Leo and Prue he suggested a walk on the deck. On the deck it was cold and windy.

'Not the best night for a walk,' he said as he took her arm and brought her back inside, 'and the public rooms are too busy for us to get to know each other and I would really like to know you,' he smiled. 'My cabin is quiet and we can talk, I have a good bottle of malt whiskey.'

'Well,' said Kate 'what can a girl say to an offer like that?'

He took her on a tour of the empty hospital. It had two wards one with four beds and the other with two, a dispensary and consultation room. His cabin was located at the bow end of the hospital. She saw the cabin was twice the size of hers with a couch and coffee table along the inner wall, a double bed, a desk and a large bathroom with a shower and bath. He poured her a drink, put on a record, took her arm and led her to the glass doors that went out onto the deck.

'Too windy now to take you out there, but it leads onto a portion of the deck for patients' use, but rarely do we have anyone in the hospital long enough for them to use it. It's very private and away from the main passenger areas, and a perfect place to party when the hospital is empty.'

'Do you have many parties?' Kate asked quietly.

'Not many I am quite selective.' He smiled at her and raised his glass. 'Good health,' and clinked his glass with hers.'Tell me about Kate,' he said as they sat on the settee.

'Well you seem to know the latest facts about me. What more is there to tell?', she replied.

'There is a wealth to tell I am sure, Kate,' he said his eyes never leaving hers.

'You first, tell me about you.'

'Let me give you the short version and you can decide whether you want to stay. I'm divorced. My ex-wife has the family home and custody of our children. This ship has been my home for the past two years. I love women but hate complications, so my rule is to have one relationship per voyage that ends when she disembarks. Am I too direct?

'No, I like your honesty. That suits me perfectly.'

'Then let's take our time to get to know each other.'

Tony Bennett singing *The Good Life* was playing on the record player. 'Don't you love this number?', he said, taking her glass from her.

In one easy movement he took her hand in his and gently pulled her up beside him. He placed his other hand in the small of her back and swung her round in his arms, slow dancing to the melody, his thigh warm and insistent against her legs. *Please be honest with yourself don't try to fake romance,* crooned the velvet voice of Tony Bennett. Fred was an impeccable lover. However lustful and needy she was to urgently complete the act of intimacy, he redefined sex for her. His pleasure was in pleasing her. To him making love was an art form and with each gentle progressive move to penetration he was in control. Kate was at first embarrassed when the good doctor and his soft warm mouth and impassioned tongue continued their heady and exciting journey south of her navel. But her hunger for satisfaction soon overcame any self-consciousness that she felt. Satisfaction when it came was all the clichés that any filmmaker could use exploding gloriously deep within her and rippling through her body until she was played out.

She woke early next morning with Ally climbing over her. 'Oh no get off Ally, let me sleep.' She pushed Ally off her but Ally would have none of it and grizzled as she tried to climb onto the bed again. Ben joined in the chorus of anguished cries for attention. Reluctantly Kate eased her heavy limbs from the warmth and comfort of the bed.

'Stop now...that is enough,' both children looked at her, their eyes amazingly dry but both mouths open ready to howl. 'Enough I am up.'

Taking a deep breath she set about the morning routine of changing, breakfasting and by the time she left the
children in the playroom her energy had returned.

When she got back to the cabin Roberto had cleaned
and tidied. The beds were smooth and taut, the bathroom
smelt clean and fresh and where there had been slight
sprays of toothpaste speckling the mirror it now shone
without a blemish. She made the daily laundry visit with
her pile of washing and back to the cabin to sterilise Ben's
bottles before dashing back to the laundry in time to put
the clothes in the big spin dryer. Within an hour it was all
done and she had time for herself.

Kate took a jacket and went outside to sit on one of the
padded deck chairs that lined the side of the promenade
deck. She opened her book but the wind from the ocean
blew and scattered the pages as she tried to read. She
closed the book and stared out to sea. Lost in a reverie
of detailing every moment of the previous evening. Re-
calling the sweetness of the touch of this man she hardly
knew and with it came the uneasy knowing that intimacy with Fred surpassed any lovemaking she had experienced with Greg.

Maybe in time sex would have been better, but Greg,
we had no bloody time to find out.

She remembered vividly that first time they had
sex. They motored in Greg's open MGA to the local forest on a hot summer evening, both knowing this was the
night. Greg laid a plaid travel rug on the grass and they
sat for a while waiting for the sun to wane. Their conver-

sation was stilted; she remembered she was jubilant that at last she was going to do it, not just petting but the real thing.

She had mused you could call it a right of passage and had giggled. Her chortle had stilled the air and Greg, startled by the randomness of the giggle, responded as though it were the starting gun. Rapidly he moved across the blanket and clasped her in his arms. He kissed her neck and her lips, his fervent kisses building until his tongue urgent, warm and fleshly drove itself deep into her mouth. He pushed her blouse up but his large hands were not nimble enough to undo the bra strap. Instead he forced her bra roughly upwards till it sat under her chin. Cupping her breasts, his thumb and forefingers pinched her nipples. His hands moved lower down her body, murmuring her name as he thrust his hand between her legs. She knew all this from before with previous boyfriends but now the moment was here, the moment that she had fantasized ever since the *My Fair Lady* evening.

She kicked off her pants and he cupped the small of her back in his hand and lifted her bottom off the ground, his sheathed penis urgently trying to gain entry, bashing at her genitalia like a bird at a window pane. He was in and she felt nothing. No stars, no rolling ocean crashing onto the beach, simply discomfort because he was large and pushing higher and higher into her body with every thrust. She lay looking at the outline of the tree above, shadowy in the twilight. With each determined thrust she responded as she thought she should. Like a puppet master she directed her actions, you should touch, you should hold, you should moan. When it was all done, he discarded the condom onto the grass beside them. They adjusted their clothing and lay together quietly.

She gazed at the spent rubber with its milky filling. Why, she thought, don't I feel satisfied and blissed beyond my wildest dreams like the magazines and my friends tell me? Why, oh why do I feel ashamed like I did something dirty?

'I love you,' she had said to Greg each time they had sex. She always hoped that he would say I love you my dearest, loveliest girl in the whole world who makes my heart sing, but he never did.

A dull ache spread across her chest. With the flat of her hand she rubbed her breast bone to relieve the pain while rebuking herself for her disloyalty to the man she loved, whom she had married for better or worse until death do us part.

But Greg the deal wasn't for you to die so young it should have been when you were old and feeble. Would we have lasted the distance Greg, would we have grown old together if it had been different, or would you have grown tired of me? God I'm so tired of feeling like a victim. She stared through the rails of the ship watching the white-flecked waves of the ocean. Her mind shifted and she was back in the escape world of Fred, slow dancing and measured lovemaking. She started going through her wardrobe in her mind deciding on what to wear for the date tonight in his cabin. She wanted to look desirable, ravishing, a knock-out.

Prue plumped down on the deckchair beside her.

'I have been looking for you all over the ship, how are you?' She leant forward to kiss Kate's cheek.

'I am fabulous, did you have a good time?' Kate queried.

'Rather! Never had an Italian lover before.' Prue's voice boomed out, easily heard by the passing passenger traffic out for a walk.

Kate nudged her and with a nod of her head and raised eyebrow she indicated the passengers clipping past on their rounds of the deck.

Prue put her hand to her mouth 'Why hush my mouth,' and giggled. 'What about you and the good doctor?'

'The sex was amazing,' she whispered as a man in shorts jogged past them. 'And I have another a date tonight, directly after dinner,' Kate said.

'Same here, isn't life grand,' Prue responded.

⁓

A smudge of pale light sliced through the window curtains when Kate woke the children. She was determined to see the magnificence of Table Top Mountain as the ship arrived into Cape Town. Both children grizzled as she changed and dressed them and took them up in the morning sun on the top deck. Already the deck was alive with camera waving passengers waiting to catch the first glimpse of the spectacular landmark. Prue had claimed a good position on the port deck rail. 'She took Ben from Kate and turned to show him the first glimpse of the mountain. Passengers clicked shutters of their cameras as the mountain came clearly into focus. Its flat top kissed with the barest whisper of mist.

'Its amazing, it just looks as though the top has been sheared through horizontally its so flat and straight,' Kate yelled into the morning air.

Ally was intent on wriggling off Kate's hip, to get down and dirty on the deck. 'Ally stop, you are not getting down' she said sharply as she rejigged her on her hip. 'You know there is a cable car that takes people to the top of the mountain and you can walk around up there.' Kate said.

'Yes but with only six hours in port we won't have time to do that, they say the wait to get on a cable car is horrendous,' Prue answered.

Both the children were hungry and becoming increasingly crotchety. Reluctantly Kate took her last look at the ruler flat expanse of Table Top with its craggy outlines of Lion's Head and Devil's Peak that sat either end of the plateau.

The large black saloon taxi waited for them on the dockside. It gleamed with an abundance of chrome fittings and white walled tyres, looking straight out of a fifties American gangster movie. A middle aged, solid man wearing mirrored sunglasses, a white short sleeve shirt, grey razor-creased slacks and brown shoes with toecaps that shone in the morning sun stood by the gangplank holding up a handwritten notice that read Sinclair & Ponting. Prue smiled at him and pointed to herself as she lowered the pushchair's front wheels on to the dock.

'Good morning mevrou welcome to Cape Town, my name is Nick,' he said in a strong Afrikaans accent as he led them to the car. Both Leo and Fred had too much to do in the short time in Cape Town to come ashore and had organised the taxi to take the women and children on a short sight seeing tour of the city.

'Okay ladies, Officer Leo said to give you a tour of the city and afterwards take you to the Mount Nelsen Hotel for lunch, is there anything you want to do beforehand?', Nick asked as he turned to face them.

'Yes, we want to buy gold signet rings, but don't want to pay tourist prices. Do you know somewhere?', Prue asked.

Over a whiskey one evening, before they met their officers, the friends had decided they wanted a memento of their trip and preferably gold seeing as South African gold prices were so attractive. Both liked the idea of signet rings.

Nick started the engine. As the large car pulled away from the dock he looked at Prue through the rear mirror. 'Ya mevrou, I know the best.'

The town was not as large or as cosmopolitan as they had imagined it to be. The roads they travelled were frequently unpaved and the dust rose in clouds behind them. Soon they were in the small city centre with its unremarkable collection of shops and offices. The car crawled to a walking pace as Nick looked for a parking spot. They passed a bus stop its wooden bench stencilled with large white letters EUROPEANS ONLY/ BLANKES. The streets were busy, the throng dominated by white people. The few black people they saw looked strangely out of place. At last a space became free and Nick reversed the vehicle neatly into the curbside. They put the children into the pushchair and Nick led the way over the wooden walkway to the end of the block. On a corner of the block was a jeweller; the windows covered with strong wide mesh bars and in the corner a dusty sign that read Best Prices for Gold Shop Here. On either side of the drab emporium were neon lit display cases full of gold jewellery that spun pools of pale golden light onto the dusty wooden floorboards. The women were fascinated by the yards and yards of gold chain in all weights and styles that filled one display case. In the other were necklaces, pendants, bracelets, charms and rings.

Nick spoke softly in Afrikaans to a man in a beige suit. They presumed he was the manager. He gave a small bow and smiled showing gold inlays on his upper lateral teeth. Nick found stools for the women to sit on and turned his attention to amusing the children. The manager laid a worn leather flat cushion on the counter before sliding out a tray of gold signet rings from the cabinet. Both women examined each ring before placing it on their little fingers stretching their fingers across the cushion to see if the shape and style suited. With each ring the gold-toothed man murmured obsequious comments about how well it suited their hand. Both settled on heavy 9ct rings, a Fleur De Lis emblem for Kate and a very fancy engraved P for Prue.

'They're nine carat.' His vampire like gold teeth sparkled in the light as he smiled. 'Just right for a ring as a higher carat gold would be too soft.' The manager bowed before taking out his calculator to agree on the price.

Elated with her purchase, Kate was not concentrating as they came out of the jewellers and nearly wheeled the pushchair into the path of a native African dressed in mud-encrusted overalls

'I'm so sorry I was not looking where I was going,' she said.

She met his eyes for an instant before he lowered his gaze, dark brown eyes that were sullen and fearful. He stepped backwards out of her way into the path of Nick. 'Move man, move,' Nick growled.

The man jumped off the sidewalk into the dusty road his posture cowed and his eyes downcast, as they filed past.

'Please it was, my fault,' Kate said 'don't blame him.'

Prue took her elbow and quickly steered her and the children away from the scene. ' Shush Kate you'll just make it worse for him,' she whispered.

Both women were quiet as the taxi drove away from the city. As they looked out of the windows they became increasingly aware of the segregation of black Africans. They drove past sprawling collections of small lean-tos some simply made from cardboard boxes and the more established built of recycled timber and corrugated iron.

'Ya shanty towns like these are a blight, an eyesore but as quick as the authorities try to clean them up, they start up again. But I show you the good sights of Cape Town now.' Nick said. Shortly the vista changed with neighbourhoods that were well kept with manicured lawns and flowering shrubs. 'These are the suburbs where we white South Africans live, many homes as you see are fortified with high fences or walls. We have to do this with our problems, you can imagine,' Nick said.

As they stopped at one cross street waiting to turn right into the flow of traffic again, Kate nudged Prue and pointed to the sign on a building *DANGER—natives, Indians and coloureds—if you enter these premises at night you will be listed as missing. Armed guards shoot on sight and savage dogs devour the corpse. You have been warned.*

Kate interrupted Nick's description of white South African lifestyle. 'I think Mount Nelson Hotel now please Nick, the children need a milkshake.'

'And we need something stronger,' Prue whispered.

Both Kate and Prue were relieved to be back on board the ship. Kate stayed defiantly in the cabin as the ship cruised out of Cape Town and into the Indian Ocean. Her spirit was mollified by the sense of order and cleanliness in the cabin. She tackled the routine of changing, bathing and dressing the children in their nightclothes with an enthusiastic energy. At tea-time both children glowed from their mother's attention and merrily slurped up worms of spaghetti, splattering their shiny clean faces with tomato sauce and when Kate jiggled and shimmied the plate of red jelly Ben rocked with laughter and only took breath when she fed him a spoonful of the slippery deliciousness. Ally copied the fun and wobbled the jelly precariously on her spoon. They were still smiling happily, warm faced from another lick of the flannel, as Kate tucked them into bed.

Dinner that night offered a choice of flank steak or fresh fish. Sautéed Cape Salmon with a Beurre Blanc the menu read. It was a pleasing contrast from the frozen fish normally served at sea. Their table was in an ebullient mood. A fellow diner rolled his eyes as he lifted a forkful of glistening buttery flakes of fish to his mouth.

'At last I can taste fish, I haven't been able to distinguish between pork, beef, chicken or fish for the past ten days.'

Amidst the ensuing laughter their steward arrived with a bottle of South African Chenin Blanc for Prue and Kate. 'With the officers' compliments ladies,' he said with a small bow.

'Don't be jealous folks we can share, providing Kate and I have the lion's share, which means you lot may only get a thimbleful,' Prue said and once again the table erupted with merriment.

'Of course and it would have to be white being South African,' some wit at the end of the table piped up.

That night when Fred started his gentle overture of foreplay she could not wait. She unzipped his fly and found him hard and erect. 'No Fred, no foreplay, I just want you in me.' Her carried her to the bed and undressed her, slowly, his fingers teasing her, until she cried out for satisfaction 'I want you,' she grasped his penis, 'dam it not your fingers I want you.'

As the days counted down to docking in Sydney she wanted to keep cruising the oceans forever with her doctor, children's playroom and all meals provided. The remainder of the voyage passed in a daze. When the children got a chest cold three days before the ship arrived in Fremantle, Fred brought the whole family down to the empty hospital ward next to his cabin for a couple of days. Knowing the children were safe and close by, she felt completely free, making the sex she enjoyed with this man even sweeter. Fred told Kate that this was the first time he had had an affair with a woman who was widowed and was trying to deal with her loss. Normally he chose married or attached women so that disentanglement at their port of disembarkation was cleaner. He said he liked feminine women and he particularly delighted in making love to her, as she was always responsive and appreciative of his lovemaking.

'Well that's because you're bloody good at it,' she said as they lay together in his bed.

But she knew that she was his nemesis as her loss reminded him that cruising the oceans with a new affair each trip masked his abandonment of his family. She noticed how quiet he was when she expressed her guilt about her lack of wholeness for her children and she saw him flinch when she told him that she felt ashamed because she was more than glad when the children spent their mornings in the ship's playroom and she had time to herself. Once when he tried to tell her one night, as the children lay asleep in the ward close by that she was a good mother, her answer made him turn away from her.

'I don't think good is enough, do you? Most of the time I am emotionally absent, just going through the motions,' her voice that was normally pleasing to the ear sounded harsh. 'And tell me how I can be both mother and father to them? How will Ben learn to grow up to be a man? How will your son's learn, Fred?'

He got up and pulled on his dressing gown. 'Sorry Kate I have work to do, go to sleep, I'll see you later.'

'You know we are similar you and I,' Fred said as she lay in his arms the night before they reached Sydney.

'Apart from liking sex?' Kate said hungrily planting kisses on his shoulder.

'Be still woman, the truth is we are both running away.'

Kate stopped.

'Me from my responsibilities and you from the fear of responsibility,' Fred said.

'Is that what you think, I thought I was running from the pain of losing Greg.'

'Yes I understand you're escaping the grief but you know the reality is that you are afraid you will not be good enough to cope with the responsibility of parenting,'

Fred kissed her hand and pulled her closer.

'But at some stage Kate we will have to stop and face it, you know it and I know it.'

'The problem is Fred I just don't know how. I'm in this vortex of pain, anger and guilt. The only time I feel remotely whole is when I am with a man.'

'Yes but Kate you are very vulnerable, you need to be careful, men can be pretty ruthless especially when they see easy prey like you.'

'We can write can't we?' her voice pleaded.

He kissed her forehead and gently pulled away resolute in the finality of the relationship.

As she left his cabin that night he felt a growing sense of relief. He went to his desk, switched on the light above it and looked at the passenger list for the return voyage. He felt a surge of anticipation he would soon be back in the hunt again. The thought brought a smile to his face. He switched off the light and got back into bed. It was early morning when the ship sailed into Sydney Harbour. On the top deck Kate, Prue and the children jostled with other excited passengers to view its passage as they sailed through the Heads into the sheltered waters. Before them lay a kaleidoscope of forested land mass edging the large harbour, pale bleached beaches and houses dotting the foreshores. Ferries criss-crossed their passage across the wide harbour carrying commuters to the city. As they sailed under the Harbour Bridge a train rattled overhead on the grey iron archway that carried traffic from the north of Sydney into the city and other suburbs to the east, west and south of the metropolis. Kate asked Prue to mind the children so that she could say goodbye to Fred. With her in-laws meeting her at the dock she knew she had to do it now. Fred was waiting for her in his cabin. She started to say how much this time had meant to her when he gently put his finger to her lips.

'It was a beautiful voyage, thank you and I look forward to your return voyage.'

'Fuck you,' she said with a wink as she turned to leave the cabin. His laughter filled her ears as she walked from the cabin back to the children.

Chapter 6

· · · · · · · · · · ·

Australia

Eva Sinclair squinted up at the huge liner as it inched alongside the dock, its heavy mooring ropes thrown down to be tightened round the giant bollards. Her eyes scanning the decks looking for her daughter-in-law who she had first met when Greg bought her to Sydney on their honeymoon. Eva had found her to be a pleasant young woman and significantly she was protestant. If he had bought home a Catholic bride she would have been devastated. Eva wore a navy suit with a pale yellow straw bucket hat, her handbag swinging from her forearm and her cream pigskin gloves tightly clasped in her hand. Angus was parking the car. There was plenty of time for Angus to join her, as she knew that it would be some time before Kate would disembark. Both were determined to be there in plenty of time to greet her and their grandchildren as they docked. Eva spotted Kate on the main deck with little Ben in her arms. But where was Ally? Kate pointed to a small child held in the arms of a dark haired woman standing next to Kate. There was activity on the dock, the passenger gangway was put in place and luggage was being unloaded and taken by forklift to a holding area on the dock. They waited patiently behind the barrier watching for the family to disembark.

Prue helped Kate down the gangway with the children and pushchair. Kate could see the Sinclairs in the crowd. Customs had come on board the ship at Sydney Heads to process the passengers so there were no formalities to go through as they disembarked. Eva pushed her glasses up to dab her eyes with a small white handkerchief as the family neared the end of the gangplank. She put her arms out to hug little Ben while Ally held Prue's hand and jumped up and down shouting 'manpa, manma'.

Angus gave Kate a hug. He seemed to be thinner than she remembered and had forsaken his trademark beret for a wide brimmed Panama hat. He picked up Ally and held her out at arms length.

'My word you look like your Mum,' he said.

Kate introduced Prue to the Sinclairs. After some polite exchanges about the trip, Eva asked if they could give Prue a lift somewhere. Prue declined saying she had organised a hire car to take her to a friend's east Sydney apartment. She gave a hug to the children and squeezed Kate's hand.

Kate and Eva sorted out the luggage from the huge pile on the dock. Angus had gone to get the car and tipped one of the dock officials to allow him to bring it closer to the luggage area so they could pack the car more easily. The journey to the Sinclair home was a short drive across the

Harbour Bridge to a suburb close to the water. As the car turned into the driveway of the Sinclair home they could see the arch of the bridge in the distance. The house was an old-fashioned muddy-blue brick home with lattice paned windows, its wide eaves designed to keep the building cool in the summer months. Taut net curtains covered the double glass front doors that opened up immediately into the lounge room. The room was timber panelled and against one wall sat a large brown leather couch with two matching armchairs each with a crocheted headrest. Next door to the more worn chair sat a chrome pedestal ashtray, the stain of cigarette ash corroding its surface. Facing the seating a small-screened television was placed on a low table. The L-shaped room revealed the dining section with a dark oak table and eight heavy dining chairs. Alongside the dining table was an old piano that had come into the home when the Sinclair children were young and had piano lessons at school. The room was a study in brown and in the midday heat it felt oppressive. It took Kate all her will not to pick up the children and run outside to the blue skies to gulp in the fresh air.

Eva removed her hat and gloves and showed Kate the sleeping arrangements for the family. She had set up the children's cots in the sleep-out. In the past the sleep-out had been a narrow balcony on the side of the house where previous owners had sat to catch the morning sun. This had now been glassed in to make an additional room, normally used as Angus's study. It could only be accessed through the dining room or through Eva's bedroom. Angus had a separate bedroom on the other side of the house. Eva had borrowed a cot for Ally and used Greg's old cot for Ben. As they inspected the room the children sensed their mother's unease and clung to her. Ally now slept in a bed and Kate knew it would be a challenge to get her to sleep in the cot. The kitchen windows opened onto the sleep-out and she imagined it would be noisy, as bedtime would coincide with evening meal preparation. She had hoped that Eva would have put them all together in one room. Kate's heart sank when she heard that she was at the other end of the house and was to share a bedroom with Erica. When she had planned the trip Erica had told her she was going to be working on one of the islands on the Great Barrier Reef. Now not only was she separated from her children, she was to share a room with Erica.

'I would really prefer,' Kate stumbled over her words. 'I really think the children and I would be better together,' she said. 'If they wake in the night I have to go through your room to reach them and I don't want them to disturb you.'

'Well my dear that is not possible, this is the best solution as there is no room in the sleep-out to put up another bed. The children will be fine and I am sure you will hear the children from Erica's room.'

'Couldn't the children sleep with me in the bedroom and perhaps Erica in the sleep out, we could easily move the cots and the bed?' Kate appealed.

'No my dear definitely not, as I said the children will be fine in here.' Eva's lips formed a tight smile. She had made up her mind and that was the end of the matter. Kate and the children managed to escape the house in the afternoon when she took them in the pushchair for a walk up to the point. The point was a grassy park on the foreshore of the harbour. She put a blanket on the grass and put little Ben down on his tummy. Within no time his little body was wriggling across it to grab a handful of grass. The park was deserted and Kate had a clear line of vision and so was able to let Ally roam freely. The breeze felt good and as she gazed out at the swaying eucalyptus trees framing the harbour, now busy with sailing boats, her mood lifted. She watched Ally as she picked the bright purple heads off a rhododendron bush. Ally ran back to her with her gift, tumbling into Kate's arms.

Angus poured a jigger of whiskey into each of the heavy cut glass tumblers while Kate fed the children and Eva prepared the dinner. He added a couple ice cubes to each glass. 'You want water Kate?' he queried as he offered her a small crystal water jug. Kate nodded as she spooned a mouthful of rice pudding into Ben's open mouth.

'I have some pictures taken at the funeral, of the flowers and the mourners, which I thought you would like to see.' Kate said. She was about to take the photographs from her bag but neither Angus nor Eva replied. She hesitated as the silence stretched uneasily.

'If you want to know anything about Greg's funeral, please ask.'

Neither of them spoke until Eva weighed the topped and tailed green beans on the kitchen scales, 'This way Kate, we get the right amount of green vegetables,' she said. Eva lifted out the big heavy cast aluminium pressure cooker from a cupboard. She layered lamb forequarter chops, potatoes, carrots and finally the green vegetables into it before locking on the lid.

'All ready, to put on when Erica comes in,' she smiled brightly before crunching noisily into her ice cube.

Erica arrived home at six o'clock. She had caught the ferry from Circular Quay. Her cold lips pecked Kate's cheek before turning her attention to the children. Ally was holding Dolly by the feet and Erica stooped down to take it from her and handed it back the right way up. 'You may call me Aunt Erica. But first you must hold the poor doll the right way up otherwise you will give her a headache,' she said. Beaming at Ben she picked him out of the highchair. She waltzed him around the kitchen.

'This is where Grandma makes the food,' she said her voice fading as she wheeled through the kitchen door on a tour of the dining room and lounge,

She carried Ben back into the kitchen put him back into the highchair.

'This was your father's highchair,' she said her voice high with excitement.

Ally didn't know what to make of her aunt and sidled up to her mother. Kate lifted her on to her lap and held her tight.

Eva put the gas on under the pressure cooker.

'Dinner will be ready in twenty minutes so better get a shower Erica.'

Holding Ben's bottle and Ally's blankie and Dolly, Kate took the children into the sleep-out. Ben was tired and with a couple pulls on his bottle his eyes closed. Occasionally his body did a little jerk and he took a few more swigs of his milk. Ally didn't like the cot, she wasn't used to the bars surrounding her and she stood forlornly as her Mother tried to reassure her that she and Dolly would have a lovely sleep in this magical bed. Eventually Kate persuaded her to lie down and tucked her scrap of soft blanket close to her cheek while she massaged her head with the palm of her hand gently moving it down to cover her eyes. This ritual settled her this first evening and soon she was asleep.

She had forgotten that Eva was a poor cook but the overcooked green vegetables had turned yellow and the stewed lamb chops with a strong mutton flavour forcibly reminded her. Nervously, she ate as much of it as she could and pushed the remainder with the bone to the side of the plate.

Kate tried to make conversation, as she found the silence at the table unbearable.'Cape Town was a real eye opener, the apartheid thing is quite dreadful,' she said.

'Well they really don't have any other option Kate,' Eva answered.

Angus cleared his throat as though to speak but said nothing. As Erica stacked the plates to take out to the kitchen she saw the remaining food on Kate's plate.

'We do not leave food on our plate in this household, it is a waste,' she said.

Kate mumbled an apology more for Eva's sake rather than the viperish Erica. Eva left the table dropping her napkin on route to dish up the dessert and Angus stared through the window. Dessert was vanilla ice cream with paw-paw. Kate left nothing on her dish. Eva washed, while Kate dried the dishes and Erica sat on the stool and talked of her day's happenings. She worked in the archive section of the Sydney Morning Herald. Kate wished that Eva and Erica would speak more quietly and hoped fervently that the children could sleep through this crescendo of voices, pots and pans. She went in to check them and found them fast asleep, Ally spread-eagled on her back and Ben curled on his side his bottle lying beside him. She picked up the bottle and took it back to the kitchen to clean. Erica was pouring herself a sherry as she walked in.

'Kate you should know that my father does not appreciate empty headed small talk at the dinner table,' she said and went through the door before Kate could answer.

Kate's hands trembled. She smoothed the fabric of her skirt, lifted her chin and walked into the living room. Angus had the Scrabble box on the table and asked if she would like a game. She smiled knowing Erica would hate this but she was grateful, she knew her father-in-law had seen her play several times with Greg while on honeymoon. Angus had his medical practice in Macquarie Street. Friends of Greg had warned her that he had a temper and ruled the household with a firm hand. But she felt more comfortable with him than with the women of the house. True he was a man of few words but she appreciated this kind gesture.

Later that night, after checking the children, Kate changed in the bathroom into her nightclothes. She had hoped to avoid Erica but she was waiting for her as she came into the bedroom. 'Make sure you are up to see to the children before my mother in the morning,' she said watching Kate as she folded back the cover on her bed. Kate said nothing but got into bed and pulled the sheet up high around her neck and turned her face to the wall. When eventually the light went out her eyes searched the darkness, her heart raced until she heard Erica get into bed.

Her hopelessness came in like a low-lying fog and deadened her senses. She was unaware of the trees rustling in the night breeze and the steady and rhythmic breathing of her sister-in-law. She thought that she had wanted to share her grief with his family but it seemed that they were on a different plain to her. Eva and Angus had not said one word about Greg's death, just trite chatter from Eva and while she appreciated the kindness from Angus she was still perplexed that he did not talk of his son. She felt more removed from Greg here, in this room where he had slept as a boy and where, on their honeymoon they had made love quietly on one of the narrow single beds placed either side of the room. Now it was her worst nightmare.

<hr>

Most days in Sydney proved to be God given washing days. Ally and Ben created a constant pile of washing but the contrast in drying the clothes in Australia to Britain amazed her. At home washing required a constant eye on the weather and re-pegging and re-jigging of the garments on the line to aid the drying process. But here by the time she had pegged the last nappy out the first nappy on the rotary line was almost dry. She opted to tackle the ironing in the afternoons when the children were occupied watching television. In the early evenings she helped to prepare food, bathed and fed the children finally helping with the washing up after dinner. The time hung heavily and the only relief was her daily walk to the point or on Wednesdays and Saturdays when Eva and Angus played bowls most of the day and Erica worked.

Once she accompanied Eva and Erica to the morning service at their local Church of England church where Greg had been an altar boy. Keeping two small infants quiet and captive in the narrow pew was impossible. Eva, red faced, forcibly held Ally as her grand daughter tried to push past her to freedom of the aisles. Ben strapped in his pushchair became bored with inactivity and let out a huge wail of protest just as the minister lifted the chalice above his head. Erica glared at Kate her eyes narrowing meanly. The children's behaviour gave Kate the perfect excuse not to attend church.

While the house was empty, she was free to do the things that would upset the Sinclairs. The children ran and crawled naked in the garden basking in the sunshine. She allowed them to play the piano, their banging on the yellowing keys making raucous and joyous music. Defiantly she exceeded Eva's perceived right weight of morning tea and lunches. While they had their midday rest she wrote home or spoke on the phone to Prue.

Kate heard the postman's motorbike and the welcome flap of the mail-box lid. She raced down to the mailbox by the front gate. In the metal box was the familiar blue airmail from home. She took it to the seat in the front garden that overlooked the harbour. It was from her father telling her about the inquest into Greg's death.

According to the Ministry of Aviation Inspector, they found no mechanical problems with Greg's plane. They surmised Greg was an inexperienced pilot who was unable to maintain control of the aircraft in the difficult weather conditions encountered during the last part of the flight. Witnesses in Handsworth, some twenty miles southwest of the Laurelford airfield, who were called to give evidence, said the plane appeared below the low cloud then climbed again into the cloud under power. This manoeuvre was repeated, but at the top of the second climb the aircraft was seen to stall then dive at a steep angle into the roof of the block of flats. The coroner found that the weather played a part in Greg losing his way and that this and his inexperience as a pilot contributed to his death.

She read and reread it again, running her fingers over her father's blue inked words finding comfort from his copperplate writing. The coroner's findings rang true. She sighed. She had flown with Greg often enough before to know that he flew by correlating his map reading with the visual landmark below and she was convinced it was his lack of experience flying in those conditions that caused his death.

She sat looking out at the harbour, the grey bridge

dominated the view but she could see the ferries scudding across the water leaving white trails of foam in their wake. I should be relieved, she thought, comforted that the coroner did not find him negligent in any way, but I just see it as another bit of bureaucracy that winds up his life.

She smoothed the letter out and read her father's final paragraph again. His words made her smile.

You will be delighted to know I got a hole in one last week much to Ian's annoyance as we had a ten bob bet on the hole. Just wish I had made it a fiver! Take care of yourself and the tiddlywinks – looking forward to having you home again.

There was a nip in the air on this winter morning and Kate shivered and stood up wrapping her jacket tightly around herself as she went indoors.

When Angus came home that evening she gave him the letter to read. His face was impassive as he sat and read it. 'Has Eva seen this?' Angus said lifting his reading glasses up onto his head. 'No not yet.' Kate replied.

He took the letter into the kitchen for Eva to read. Kate stayed in the lounge with the children but there was not a sound from the kitchen, no howl of anguish, no whispered discussion, no clattering of pans, simply silence. At dinner no one spoke until Angus placed his knife and fork together on his empty plate. 'Your father had some good luck with his hole in one,' he said.

They all laughed politely. Inside her head Kate was screaming why don't you say what a fucking awful waste of my only son's life.

But instead she looked down at her half full plate of yellowish Brussels sprouts, boiled potatoes and savoury mince.'Yes he should have had a fiver on it,' she said.

⁓

Ally needs discipline Kate, children need firm handling and a strict routine,' Eva said when Ally threw herself down on the floor in a rage.

Eva, headmistress of a primary school before marriage, and Angus's views on child rearing were very different to the way Kate had been raised. It was not difficult for Eva to relate to Ben who was an undemanding baby. His gentle nature and smile made him appealing to all. Ally's giggles entranced but her frequent tantrums did not impress her grandmother.

As the days progressed the Sinclair seniors decided that they would not eat until the children were asleep. If Kate could not settle them, Angus or Eva would overrule her and disappear into the sleep-out to be firm with them until the children finally lost the battle, with sleep claiming them.

Early one morning when Kate was showering, Eva took Ally's well-loved scrap of blanket from her, marched down the hall out into the garden with Ally running behind her. Eva threw it in the garbage bin and banged the lid on tight. 'Dirty,' she said to the crying child.

As Eva continued her morning chores of examining the rain measure gauge and recording this in a small tattered notebook Ally stood beside her demanding 'Blankie. I want my blankie.' Kate could hear the cries as she dried herself and grabbed her dressing gown and ran into the garden, She found Eva standing over Ally repeating dirty, no, to each of Ally's tearful pleas.

'You need to be firm with her Kate. Not only is it unsanitary but it's time she stopped being reliant on it.' She turned to Ally, 'You're getting a big girl now Ally you don't need the blankie.'

Ally howled again and Kate's nose pinched white. 'She's had that blanket since she was a baby, it's her snuggle, her security she winds it round her fingers when she goes to sleep. Christ Eva, what are you thinking she is only three years old, she's just lost her father, can't you see what it means to her?'

'Kate, I really don't think this is necessary; the child was too young to know that...'

'Know what Eva, that her father died, is that what you meant to say?' Kate was shouting now not caring who could hear her raised voice.

'I'm not prepared to discuss this any more Kate as you are obviously hysterical.' Eva said as she turned and went back indoors.

Kate shook her head at the retreating figure of her mother-in-law. She snapped open the garbage bin inside she found the well-loved remnant of woollen blanket with its satin binding on top of pile of potato peelings. Kate, with Ally her constant shadow, took the fabric into the laundry to hand wash it.

Eva took to her bed with a migraine and did not get up until lunchtime. Kate was feeding the children when Eva joined them in the kitchen. 'The butcher cut me off a nice corner of topside yesterday,' she said as she took it from the fridge. Kate nodded. Eva pulled out the old metal scales from the cupboard and weighed the joint. 'Two pounds eight ounces, so with a bit of shrinkage that'll give us a good six ounces per serve with some left to make into mince.'

Not another word was said about the argument.

The only transport into town was the ferry with its one hundred and thirty six steps to the jetty. Occasionally she took the two children in the double stroller into town to wander around the shops or to meet up with Prue. Bumping the stroller slowly down to catch the ferry and on the way back she climbed the stairs backwards hauling the pram up one step at a time. This day Prue introduced her to a woman named Pamela who was her neighbour. Pamela had long blonde hair tied loosely at the nape of her neck and a fringe so deep it almost covered her eyes. Prue said she wanted them to meet as they had much in common as they both had been widowed at a young age. Pamela had recently remarried two and half years after her first husband died of a cerebral haemorrhage when she was pregnant with their son. Marcus was now a bright three year old with a happy disposition who ran around the coffee lounge chasing Ally as the women chatted.

'Those first eighteen months were hell I was full of anger and dark, dark spaces, day after day. I never left the house, save taking Marcus to the doctors for his injections, you know what it's like,' she said. 'But gradually I accepted my lot. I accepted my grief,' said Pamela. She paused, watching Marcus tumbling on the floor with Ally. 'I think acceptance was my turning point, not that I will ever stop missing him, especially when I look at my beautiful Marcus, but it was just easier when I accepted it. I had loved to paint as a child so I went to night school to take painting lessons once a week. That's when I met Bryan and after a few months we started to date, the rest as they say is history.'

On the ferry ride home, Kate played Pamela's words over and over in her mind. Suddenly the biblical words valley of the shadow of death made some sort of sense. The pram did not feel like hard work as she started to haul it up the steps but this afternoon it was different one of the commuters, a man in a suit helped her lift the pushchair up the steps to the road.

One Saturday she went with her father-in-law to an AFL football game and as they drove to the match they passed the half finished Opera House.

'It's a disgrace, a ridiculous design that's costing us taxpayers far too much. I'm sure part of the rising costs comes down to the time it takes to make the wog workforce understand what they have to do as none of them can speak English.'

Kate turned her head away to stare out the window of the car at the half built roof shells of the building. Nothing, she thought could be more foreign than the Sinclair family.

The football game re-energised her watching young men in short shorts. The crowd roared as the home teams full forward leapt in the air to take the mark pulling the ball hard into his chest. Her heart pounded as he lifted his leg in a long smooth kick and sent it squarely though the goalposts. She longed for one of those men in short shorts to catch her mark and score. The following weekend as the Sinclair seniors drove off in their whites to play bowls Kate and the children went by taxi to Bondi to a barbecue. Prue and her friends had rented a weathered beachside cottage in North Bondi for the week. Surfboards leant against the wall beside the front door, which was open and music of The Honeycombs' top single *Have I the right* blasted out into the garden and beyond. As Kate lifted Ben from the stroller Prue was at the front door welcoming them. She took them through to the sitting room and introduced them to the group of friends and friends of friends. 'Give her a whiskey and soda,' shouted Prue to a fellow behind the bar. Someone took Ben. Ally had already made friends with an Irish girl and was watching her face intently as she mouthed her soft lyrical words. Prue put her arm around Kate and whispered 'You've got the outer of jail card girl, it's time to have fun.'

The fellow behind the bar was from Berlin and spoke little English. His name was Max, she could imagine him on a surfboard waiting for the perfect wave, he had bronzed wide shoulders, hair tied back off his face and wearing singlet and shorts. He handed her a big tumbler full of what looked more like scotch than soda. She looked at the drink and held the glass up to the light.

He smiled and shrugged his shoulders. 'Ja,' he said, his eyes meeting hers. They were blue, like the blue in an artic glacier. His smile broadened, as he gazed at her, his eyes moving from her face to her breasts, to her waist and to her ankles. As he met her eyes again, he winked. She put her hand to her neck and ran her fingers down to the open buttons of her shirt.

'Ja, is not good enough,' she said. She put the drink on the table and her hands fluttered as though they could express a language that he could understand. 'I'll be under the table if I drink all this,' she picked up the glass. 'Do you understand?' Her question was paced and loud as though he was deaf.

He raised his hands in a questioning gesture and winked again.

Ben was getting tired, it was past his mid morning sleep and the fellow who had carried him high enamoured with the novelty of gurgling happy baby began to look for respite as Ben started to grizzle, Kate took him laid him down in the stroller with a warmed bottle to soothe.

The day was unusually warm for early winter and it was decided that a swim and surf first and the barbecue later. With the stroller beside her she and Prue sat on an old beach towel on a grassy knoll above the beach watching the others swim and surf. The Irish girl from Dublin had taken Ally in for a paddle. The sun was hot without the sting, the gentle kind of warmth that penetrated deep into the tissue and muscle, like relaxing in a hot both.

'Mind you,' she said thinking out loud. 'After that large glass of soda and whisky I don't need anything to relax me.'

Prue laughed. 'You mean whisky and soda.'

'No I got it right the first time it was a measure of soda topped up with whisky by a very heavy handed German with the bluest eyes I've ever seen and his body's not bad either,' she said staring intently out to the ocean as Max stood up on his surfboard and rode the wave.

'Ah, I see.' Prue looked beyond the breakers to where the tanned board riders straddled their boards. 'You know he hardly speaks any English don't you?'

'Yes but there are other ways of communicating.'

'I love it, you're such a naughty girl.'

Ally and Ben ate their sausages with tomato sauce at the table surrounded by adults. Some one tried to give Ally some fried onions and she turned up her nose and spat it out. The adults laughed and her face creased into smiles, infectious giggles rocking her small frame. Kate knew that she wasn't the only one that felt the freedom of the day.

The Shadows song *Apache* blasted from the record player.

Kate got up and went to the kitchen to get a glass of water. In the kitchen Max caught her by the wrist.

'Dance yes?'

She nodded. At first they shuffled separately a tidy kind of dance movement, their eyes saying words that they could not. As the beat of the music quickened they moved together his arm around her waist, her hand in his, their motion rocking more than moving. The record changed to The Animals *House of the Rising Sun* and still they rocked closer now she could feel his breath on her neck. He dug his fingers into her waist pulling her closer. Her heart raced, the bass guitar strum mimicked the gnawing in her pelvis. Their hands no longer extended in a ballroom pose but drawn close to his chest. She could feel the stubble on his face as she rested against it. Slowly they moved away down the hall. A bedroom door was ajar and he swung her inside and kicked the door closed with his foot. He pushed her against the wall and clasped one hand high over her head as he bought his mouth down on hers. His lips were firm, and she moaned. Within seconds they were naked. 'Please, please' she begged as he fitted a condom. Then he was in and he fucked her hard and fast until she cried out.

She dressed and went back to the party. Ally and Ben were still the centre of attention at the table. Prue bent her head and looked sideways down the table to where Kate stood. She wagged her finger at her friend, her face crunched up with laughter. When the taxi arrived to take them home Max appeared at the front door and gave a small bow and kissed her hand as she stepped into the taxi.

The thoughts of his flesh on her flesh, mouth on mouth and the rhythm of their bodies entwined were obsessive over the coming days. One evening while she sat waiting for Angus to shuffle his scrabble tiles into a word, she visualised Max pushing hard into her, so hard and fast that she could hardly breathe and a soft moan escaped her lips. Erica's hostile eyes immediately met hers followed by the Sinclair's startled gaze. She pretended to have a coughing jag and excused herself to get a glass of water. She opened the fridge; the cold air cooled her face. Did they recognise the naked desire in my face she wondered. If they had she was certain it would seal their disapproval.

The first anniversary of Greg's death was a day like any other day, the sky was blue and there was a nip in the early morning air. Erica dressed in her grey suit with a crimson scarf tucked into the collar stood at the door of the kitchen as Kate was feeding Ben scrambled eggs.

'I've suggested to my parents that they go to their respective clubs this morning. They need space to deal with this day in their own way and I do not want them unduly or unnecessarily upset by an outpouring of emotion.' she said.

Neither Eva nor Angus mentioned the significance of the day to Kate or that they would be spending it in their whites at their respective bowls clubs when they left the house mid morning. Kate wheeled the pushchair to her familiar spot at the point and sat with the children on the rug. A big black magpie waddled across the green park towards them, the children were fascinated and Ally ran to catch him. Wings flapping the robust bird rose rapidly in the air before settling on the branch of a eucalyptus tree focussing them with a red beady eye. Suddenly his head threw back and warbled his beautiful song. He stayed with them for some time before his last song and flew away into the spinney of trees. Kate fixed her eyes on the water as it licked the edge of the harbour leaving trails of gossamer sandy bubbles that were tossed and rolled down the foreshore by the wind. Her head and arm ached dully. The wind picked up and she shivered pulling her sweater tight around her. She looked at Ben trying to catch the leaves swirling around them, she caught his hand, it was icy cold.

'Lunchtime, I think we need to get you into the warm' she said, beckoning Ally and putting Ben in the push-chair.

She closed the door to the sleep out. Both children were asleep their faces patched with red from the wind. She took her writing pad into the back garden to sit at the weathered wrought iron table and chair, the grey paint traced with rust. The winter sun was low in the sky and bathed her spot beside the laundry that was sheltered from the wind.

My love,

It is a year today since you died. I ache for you. If some-one had dumped me in the middle of the Pacific Ocean I could never have felt more alone than I have today in this loveless house. Living here with your family is a nightmare for me. Now I understand why you never could express love.

People say the first year is the hardest and then it will

get better. That's bullshit I don't believe there is a finite time for grief. People tell me constantly that I'm lucky to have the children and that's bullshit too, they say it to comfort themselves not me. I am overwhelmed with guilt about not being good enough for the children. They say that anger is part of the grieving process and that is true. I rage at the absolute waste of your life, our lives and the children's lives.

I met a widow a few weeks back, she told me that the pain eased for her when she accepted her grief. But how to get to there Greg, I just don't know. I say it over and over like a mantra I accept my loss, I forgive Greg for leaving us, in the hope that I can absorb, digest it and move on but nothing works.

I desperately want to reach the stage where I get relief from the grief and guilt. Will I ever stop missing you?

Katie xx

Four days later The Beatles arrived in Sydney on a rainy morning and both the television and radio stations pumped out tracks from their albums. The Bakelite radio sitting on top of the fridge filled the kitchen with Love, love me do. Eva pursed her lips and snapped it off.

'Absolute rubbish,' she said loudly. But the music pulsated through Kate and she remembered life, as it should be, not as it was in this brick house that felt like a life sentence for a crime she hadn't committed.

That night as Kate walked back to the bedroom, Erica dressed in her faded floral pyjamas, stood in the doorway to the room. As Kate tried to ease past her, Erica grasped her wrist, her bony fingers holding her tight. Erica's alcohol fuelled breath was hot on her cheek. Kate turned her head away.

'What do you do to clean that make up stuff off your face?' Erica's graceless question hung heavily in the space between them.

Kate removed Erica's hand from her wrist and without turning her head answered

'With cleansing lotion.' Her sister-in-law swayed slightly catching onto the door-frame to steady her as she sucked in her breath sharply.

'You need to wash your face properly with soap and water my girl, otherwise when you get to my age you will have wrinkles.'

Erica slowly ran her fingernail down Kate's face shaving off any residues of Kate's night cream and showing her what she believed was evidence of her skincare inadequacies. 'Get away from me Erica,' Kate's voice shook.

Her hostile eyes fixed on her sister-in-law's face. She walked to her bed, her fear and loathing of Erica barely suppressed. She wanted to hit her, to take her fist and smash it into her face. She hated how this woman bought out the worst in her. Her arm now felt spent and weak where her sister-in-law had gripped it.

Kate was tired and her arm still ached the following morning. As Kate put each spoonful of porridge to Ben's lips he twisted his head away, his lips squeezed together. It was a game that tickled him but not Kate. 'Enough Ben, enough,' her voice loud and sharp. She tried once again but Ben squirmed away laughing. She took the plate to

the sink. 'That's it, go hungry then Ben. I'm not playing this game.' She wiped his face and hands and set him
down on the floor.

Eva popped her head around the door, 'It's a call for
you Kate. The shipping agents.'

Kate's spirits lifted only two more weeks she thought
and she would be back on board, back with Fred. The
voice said 'Sorry to be the bearer of bad news Mrs Sinclair but S.S. Antares had been holed up in Cape Town
for two weeks with engine trouble waiting for spare parts.
She is now sailing back to the docks in England for further work. They have had to cancel the June sailing from
Sydney to Southampton and been forced to reschedule
her sailing dates she will now sail from Sydney on 27th
August.'

Kate was silent her shoulders slumped. The voice continued. 'Of course we will give you a full refund if this is
not suitable.'

'What about alternative sailings in June?'

'Only one I'm afraid out of Sydney via Panama to
Southampton, but that is fully booked, the only thing we
can offer at the moment is the rescheduled sailing of Antares in August.'

Ally and Ben were squabbling loudly and she heard
Eva's schoolmarm voice trying to appease them. She ran
out to the front garden, she did not want Eva to see her
tears. Another seven weeks I can't bear it, even with the
thought of Fred at the end of it. She walked down to the
post box and lifted the lid she knew it would be empty, as
she had not heard the mailman's motorbike this morning

but the excuse would serve Eva if she came out looking for her. She wiped her eyes and nose with the edge of her dressing gown and went back to the house.

After her shower she walked to the point with the children. From her vantage point she saw a ferry pulling away from an urban jetty, its wake spewing and foaming the water. 'So what do you think kids, should we stay or go. I don't know about you two but the thought of another seven weeks fills me with dread. I wonder what your Dad would say, probably that I'm being a coward by wanting to run.'

The ferry tooted as it chugged towards the next ferry stop, from the distance it looked like something she would float in Ben's bath. She smiled and remembered Fred had once said to her sometimes you need distance to see things more clearly. Clearly it was not true for her to stay, not only because neither she nor the children thrived in the Sinclair household but also she knew a five-week cruise with Fred carried serious risk of emotional involvement, on her part, not his.

She told the Sinclairs before dinner that night about the delayed sailing date but she would not wait until the end of August to leave, that her intention was to fly home. Her father-in-law walked her outside to the garden. They sat on the wooden bench facing the harbour, the ice cracking in their crystal tumblers. As they sipped their whiskey, Kate was silent wondering what Angus was going to say. He cleared his throat and took a swig of his drink.

'Am I right in thinking that you and Greg planned to

live in Australia eventually?', he asked.

'We had talked about it of course but we really had such a short time together we had no plans and now...'

Her hands were cold from holding the icy glass; she put it down on the seat beside her. This was the first time that her father-in-law had spoken of his son. She rubbed her hands together trying to warm them. Angus looked out towards the harbour and the familiar shape of the illuminated coat hanger bridge. The sounds of Eva clattering pots and pans in the kitchen broke their silence.

'You have two children, surely it would be better if you left Ben here, it would be easier for you to raise one child on your own and if Ben stays here I would make sure that he had the finest education.'

Kate picked up her glass and cradled it in both hands. She squared her shoulders.

'Sorry? Leave Ben here, I'm not sure I understand?'

'Let me put this way Kate. If you leave Ben here in Sydney with us I will pay for his education, which you can be assured would be at the same school that Greg went to.' He took another nip of his whiskey. 'I would provide the finest education that money could buy.'

Her face and ears were so hot and her pulse so loud she thought any minute her head might explode like a watermelon spewing redness and flesh everywhere.

'What about Ally's education? And if I take Ben home with me?' He did not reply and turned his head to stare once more at the lights twinkling on the Harbour Bridge. Her eyes blurred with tears of anger.

She sat waiting for her emotion to calm. The evening

breeze cooled her face. A distant ferry hooted and she could hear sounds of the next-door neighbour's television.

'Angus did you really believe that I would leave Ben here with you, with Eva and Erica? Do you think so little of me as a mother that I would trade my son for the best education that money can buy? Angus was alert, his head turned towards her but again he was silent. 'The answer is no Angus, you think of education as a compensation for a lack of love, where I think love will conquer all educational inadequacies.'

'You won't change your mind Kate?'

She shook her head. She heard Eva calling that dinner was ready and she walked back inside the house.

Kate jiggled Ben on her hip as Angus packed the large case in the boot. As the car reversed down the driveway she took a last look at the emotionally sterile home where Greg had been raised. Where everything was measured from the rain in the rain gauge in the back garden, to the dinner makings weighed on the chipped metal scales and the exact jig of whiskey that went into the crystal tumblers each night. She reflected that the Sinclairs were so dominated by austere protocols that the household would not have been out of place in one of the Bronte sisters' novels. She could easily imagine Eva referring to Angus as Mr Sinclair especially as she nodded goodnight to him before they retreated into their separate bedrooms at different ends of the house.

Several of the Sinclairs' friends and neighbours had come to see her off at Mascot Airport. Fortunately Erica had decided not to come to see them off.

'Won't be able to get across town to the airport in time after work,' she said gruffly as she left that morning.

She kissed Kate and Ally on the cheek before holding little Ben close for a moment before she flew out the door running to catch her ferry. It was at the airport that Kate caught a glimpse of the Sinclair seniors' humanity. Angus and Eva held each of their grandchildren lovingly. Angus carried Ben who was trying desperately to grab his spectacles but with each lunge Angus was quicker in turning his head, their laughter and joy at the splendid game freeze framing the moment as Kate watched. Eva sat with Ally on her lap showing her the contents of her handbag, both absorbed in the finds within the deep navy leather bag. For an instant, but only an instant Kate's heart reached out to them.

With Ben on her hip and Ally stretching up to hold her mother's hand they made their way up the stairs to the cabin doorway of the Qantas Boeing 707. Kate booked the middle three bulkhead seats. She'd paid extra for a seat for Ben so that she had room for the children to stretch out during the long flight to America. She knew it was going to be a long haul but she had decided to break the journey first in San Francisco and again in New York. She had booked hotels close to San Francisco Airport and John F Kennedy Airport where she would stay overnight between each leg of the flight to London. She had sent most of her luggage home by sea a couple of weeks before she left Sydney. Apart from one large suitcase in the hold she only had her travel bag and the children to manage.

The Boeing 707 started its engines with a throaty roar and began to taxi slowly down the runway. At the end of the north south runway, the pilot revved all four engines, the plane vibrating with power before it thrust forward down the runway. Kate imagined the cockpit with the second officer checking off V1 and as the power built V2 and lift-off. The huge bird rose steadily in the air climbing high above the clouds.

The cabin staff prepared the cabin in readiness for the night flight. Window shades were lowered and extra blankets and small pillows delivered before the cabin lights were dimmed. The bassinet was fitted on the bulkhead and Kate asked the hostess to fill Ben's bottle with warm milk. Kate gave both the children a teaspoon of the pink coloured liquid guaranteed by Angus to make them sleep. She popped Ben into the bassinet with his bottle. He kicked and squirmed for a while before the magic drop worked. Ally was restless and defiant she did not want to lie still on her makeshift bed. No sooner had Kate settled her down, than she sat up. At last she crumpled mid sit up and sprawled lengthwise on the seat. Kate covered her with a blanket and lifted her head onto the small pillow. Kate half lay, half sat wide-awake in her seat she was tempted to take a large swig of the pink elixir and sleep through the next eleven hours. Instead she picked up her book and turned on the small pinpoint of light from the overhead bulkhead. The passing hostess asked her if she would like a cup of tea. Kate gratefully responded. She returned with a small round tray. Upon it was a china mug of tea and a plate bearing a chicken sandwich.

'I notice you hardly had time to eat. Where are you off to?' the hostess asked.

'San Francisco this leg, overnight in a hotel, on to New York, overnight again and home to London.'

'You have your hands full. Rather you than me,' she smiled sympathetically.

'I used to be just like you, a hostess with British Airways until I married and had to leave,' Kate replied.

'Can you believe how Victorian the airlines' policy is that they only employ unmarried women?' The hostess lowered her voice 'I'm engaged and I can't afford it to be known, I love my job and don't want to lose it.'

Kate finished her sandwich and cup of tea and placed the tray close to the bulkhead ready to be picked up. She clicked her seat back and tried to settle back to sleep. As she watched a hostess open the bulkhead compartment to get a passenger another blanket she remembered buckling into the jump seat on her first flight as a hostess at the age of twenty one and her feeling of terror as the plane took off on its leg to East Africa. Once airborne and she started to work, there never was an instance when she felt nervous again and even when the plane made the occasional bad or a heavy landing she felt no fear only gratitude to be sitting down for a short while.

Each time she put on her navy uniform and did the shiny buttons up on her jacket she got a thrill. Beaming her reassuring passenger smile as she walked down the aisle during the flight and standing at the door of the plane as the passenger's disembarked, receiving their gratitude for a smooth flight, like she alone was responsible. It wasn't work. It was fun.

An image came of Lake Victoria Hotel set close to the shores of Africa's largest freshwater lake in Entebbe, Uganda. Where turban headed punkawallahs worked the graceful swing fans in the lobby. It was their second stopover on the journey to Nairobi. The white single storey hotel squatted amidst acres of manicured grounds, where teams of gardeners kept the African wilderness out. It was a place where you could expect to see slouched hatted coffee planters sitting on the wide terrace drinking gin-and-it with wraiths of women in silk gowns with long cigarette holders.

Every time she journeyed in the rickety old crew bus from the airport to the hotel she fell in love with Africa again and again. Breathing in the tang of damp earth after a torrential downpour and everywhere the smell and sight of wisps of wood smoke tracing the sky. They wound through narrow dirt track roads passing lines of African women carrying flat baskets piled high on their heads and barefooted children joyfully chasing the van as it passed. She remembered the brightness of the shimmering sunlight as they passed fields of tall yellow sunflowers and the thin mud encrusted dogs that slept on the edge of the track.

This stopover was different to Kenya. The horror stories of the Mau Mau uprising and civil war told by young English army officers unnerved her. Especially when early one morning a young African man climbed into her bedroom on the first floor of their hotel. She woke, as he broke the windowpane and sat bolt upright in bed and screamed. The man to her amazement screamed equally loudly and threw himself back out the window. The crew and hotel staff praised her courage but she knew that it was the sight of a pale-faced white woman with a voluminous pair of lurid pink baby doll bloomers over her head that had scared him off. A smile traced her lips as she recalled she had forgotten to bring a silk scarf with her to keep her hairstyle protected as she slept and had improvised with the nylon pyjama drawers.

Soon the drum of the engines and her thoughts faded, her novel fell off her lap and slipped to the floor.

The cabin was filled with light. Blinds were being raised and people were standing pulling off their blankets and putting their seats upright in readiness for breakfast. Shortly the children woke and it was a frenzy of changing, feeding and dressing them before arrival in San Francisco. She barely had time to put everything back into her bag and buckle the children in their seats before they landed.

Chapter 7

• • • • • • • • • • •

The Opportunist

The midday weather had been iffy when she landed in London, the few dark clouds gathering as they made their way to the car park promising a storm on this summer day. But everything was pleasing to Kate, her house was warm and inviting, her well loved Aga purring with contentment and radiating out a delicious aroma of one of Lucy's casseroles.

In the lounge Kate gazed around at the built-in shelves overflowing with books and on the mantelpiece of the stone fireplace photographs of Greg and mementos of their honeymoon. Two olive green velvet winged armchairs contrasted with the bright orange settee and at either end were side tables bearing the sea-green glazed china lamps with their deep cream pleated shades. At the far end of the apple green carpeted room was the walnut sideboard, dining table and matching chairs. In the corner, her pride and joy a reproduction of a George V burr walnut secretaire desk. It was the only piece of furniture that both she and Greg had coveted in the furniture store and she purchased it shortly after the move into her new home. Besides the tangible sentiment of the piece, she loved how the desk lid, when opened, slid smoothly across the felt padded arms and presented its green leather tooled writing face. Within this upper portion of the desk there were compartments to hold papers and pens but most pleasing to Kate was the hidden drawer. Not that she kept anything in it but it was a secret and it was hers.

Ben navigated the hall slowly and headed into the kitchen. While the tea was brewing Lucy watched Ben, his legs wobbly as he pulled himself up on the edge of a bench in the kitchen and side stepped his way around clinging tightly to whatever he could until he took a tentative step on his own, rocking to and fro for several moments before sitting down on his well padded bottom.

'What a clever boy you are,' Lucy said as she held his hands and he placed one foot gingerly in front of another.

'A cup of tea please—oh Mummy it is so good to be home,' Kate waltzed into the kitchen and planted a kiss on her mother's cheek. Ally, her mother's shadow, scrambled to climb the bench seat jubilantly waving her blankie, her precious scrap of comfort, which they thought was lost forever, left on the plane. Instead Kate found it in one of the bags. She had changed into a pair of jeans and a cotton top. In comparison to the children's healthy glow Kate's face was pale and her jeans hung on her hips. 'You look as though you've lost a bit of weight Kate?'

'Yes I think I have, probably due Eva Sinclair's rations and her cooking. You've no idea Mummy, she weighs everything, the meat, the veg and then it all, yes everything goes into the pressure cooker to be cooked for the same length of time. The vegetables are yellow and mushy.' Kate giggled 'Do you remember what Erica said about your al dente vegetables.'

Lucy laughed. 'I remember only too well.'

Lucy and Frank left after the early dinner. It was still very light but Kate was grateful as she had a throbbing headache and felt jet lagged. She only had the energy to lock up and get to bed. Sleep is what I need in my own bed she thought as she pulled back the deliciously clean sheets and climbed into bed.

In early September, Cheryl, one of Kate's bridesmaids, phoned with the news that she had left her husband. She was homeless and wondered if she could use the spare bedroom for a few weeks until she got herself settled. Kate immediately pulled the vacuum cleaner out from the cupboard and trailed it excitedly up the stairs to clean the guest room.

Cheryl was a veterinary assistant at a branch of the RSPCA. She was soppy about animals, the kind of animal lover that lets an animal eat from their own plate of food and who adore slobbery mouth kisses from their pet. She always said she preferred animals to humans and certainly when it came to Ken her husband she was proved right that animals were definitely more trustworthy.

The women had met at primary school. Both shared

a similar sense of humour and a passion for movies. All through their teens they would visit the cinema once a week catching the *Movietone* newsreels before the screening of the shorter low budget B movie. Habitually they would get a vanilla ice cream as they waited for the big picture. William Holden captured their adolescent fantasies and they saw every movie in which he starred. *Picnic* was their all time favourite, William's portrayal of the charismatic drifter who stole his best friend's sweetheart left them weak at the knees and when he danced the oh so slow *Moonglow* with his co-star Kim Novak they were hard pressed to sit still in their seats.

'Time for a celebration drink,' Cheryl said holding a bottle of wine as she walked into the kitchen. She sniffed appreciatively. 'Something smells good, but we'll have to work out a roster so I do my fair share of cooking.'

'Honestly Cheryl, it's no trouble, I'm happy to cook for you. I have been slack recently, can't be bothered cooking for myself and have been making do with the children's leftovers and beans on toast. So think of it as doing me a favour. Cooking for two grown ups will motivate me. Anyway you'll have little time to cook after a full day's work.' Kate said. She found the corkscrew in a kitchen drawer and handed it to Cheryl.

'Well if you're sure,' Cheryl said as she opened the bottle, 'hopefully it won't be every night as I'm determined to get my social life on track. Anyway promise me I can cook for you on the weekends.' Cheryl said.

'What did the two-timing sod have to say when you told him you were going?' asked Kate, proffering her wine glasses to fill.

'He was sorry he had lied to me but he was hopelessly in love and it was beyond him to stop the affair. He finished by saying he hoped I understood.'

They talked as they ate. Cheryl had known little of his infidelity until friends told her. When it all came out he told her that he had started the affair a year before they married but didn't have the courage to call the wedding off and so he simply carried on with the relationship once they returned from honeymoon. He left most weekends saying he was going diving with the boys and she never suspected. As the evening progressed Kate opened a second bottle of wine and with coffee they had a couple of decent slugs of Remy Martin in big brandy balloons.

The stack on the record player lifted and shifted down into position and Lesley Gore's hit record *It's My Party* boomed out and filled the lounge room with sound.

'It's our tune,' shouted Cheryl and pulled Kate to her feet. They started to dance, twisting unsteadily at first, their voices raised raucously as they sung the chorus.

> *It's my party and I'll cry if I want to*
> *Cry if I want to, cry if I want to*
> *You would cry too if it happened to you*

Eventually tiredness overcame them and they staggered up the stairs. Kate threw sheets and pillowcases at Cheryl as she disappeared through the guest bedroom door. Kate stood at the door of the nursery and tried to focus on the sleeping forms of her children. Giggling she made her way unsteadily to her bedroom. She couldn't be bothered taking her clothes off and just lay on the bed. But the room did laps around her. She got up went into the bathroom to splash some cold water on her face. She sat in the armchair in her room putting her feet up on the bed. She stretched out trying to keep the dizziness at bay, humming the line *it's my party and I'll cry if I want to*. Memories of another time came in like an old friend to meet her.

She was in the coastal town of Estoril on the Portuguese Riviera, with its streets dotted with medieval and glamorous pastel coloured hotels. Greg had booked them in for two nights at the Palacio Estoril hotel, it was their first stop over on their journey to Australia. The elegant suite was spacious with ornate plastered high ceilings and long oak framed double glass doors leading out onto their balcony. In the centre of the room were two double beds dressed in white, armed with piles of fat pillows, the beds separated by a cedar side table. On the writing desk there was a writing stand displaying gold embossed stationery.

After the porter left, with a couple of escudo pressed into his hand, Kate went to explore the marble bathroom. A floor to ceiling bevelled mirror reflected the glass walled walk in shower with its shiny showerheads at either end of the walls and at the other end of the room a pedestal bath. A high marbled wall separated the toilet and bidet. Greg opened the doors onto the balcony and stood looking down at the panorama of the harbour with its fishing boats and people on the beach who were still swimming and sunbathing in the late afternoon sunshine. They dressed for dinner, she in her apple green silk dress that flattered her figure and Greg handsome in his lightweight grey suit with a white shirt and grey tie. They had made reservations for dinner on the flagged terrace overlooking the sea, where the tables were formally dressed in crisp white linen set with gold rimmed white china, silver cutlery and gleaming crystal. Each table lit with a stout candle protected in a glass holder. They were shown to a table on the edge of the terrace with a view of the ocean. As the twilight descended, the lights of the city sparkled. She had heard of a balmy night but this was the first she had experienced. They were looking at the menu debating what to have when she became aware that a white-jacketed waiter was staring at her. As she looked up his brown eyes met hers and he clenched his fingers to his lips and blew her a kiss. 'Are you flirting with the waiter Katie? ' Greg smiled.

'Maybe I was, does that make you jealous?'She stretched her foot out under the tablecloth and touched his thigh with her toe. His hand reached under the table to rub her ankle. He smiled again, focusing on the menu.'Oysters I think,' he said and Kate laughed. After dinner they sat in the lounge in large stuffed and studded brocade armchairs to take their coffee. The waiter bearing the silver tray smiled with appreciation of a pretty girl, his brown eyes boldly meeting hers as he placed the tray in front of her. She poured the coffee into the demitasse bone-china cups while Greg read about the history of the magnificent building.'Palacio Estoril was built in 1930 and it became a favourite bolt hole for European

Royalty and many British and German spies as Portugal was neutral in the war.'

'Oh the intrigue, the romance,' she replied softly as she looked around the gold leaf corniced room, the background music in the lounge was playing *The Way You Look Tonight*. The radio stations in England had broadcast it non-stop that year before their wedding. She sat back in her chair enjoying the mellow voices of The Lettermen crooning life into the hit ballad. Greg looked up from his brochure and smiled remembering the song and mimed the chorus to her.

Yes you're lovely, with your smile so warm And your cheeks so soft, There is nothing for me but to love you, And the way you look tonight.

She remembered the pristine white damask bedspread on one of the double beds being kicked aside as they made love. Romance had been her foreplay and she was as ready to be loved as much as he wanted her.

Within no time Cheryl was out more often than home. Kate became more and more disenchanted waiting on the crumbs of her company; the odd shared late night cups of coco where Cheryl confided details of her different dates and the frequently rushed meal before she dashed to meet friends. When Lucy suggested Kate and the children stay overnight on the night of the general election Kate jumped at the invitation, not because she was interested in election results but simply to have adult company.

'Have to be realistic, the odds are not in the Tories favour,' Frank said as he carved thin slices of roast beef. 'The public has lost faith in them. Douglas Home doesn't present well as a leader and coupled with that dammed Profumo business.'

'I never understood what happened with that, Daddy,' Kate said.

'He had an affair with a woman who was the reputed mistress of a Russian spy.' Frank's voice rose in anger. 'This man was the Secretary of State for War, for God's sake and he beds a prostitute with dubious connections. To top it all he lies about it in Parliament. We just have to hope that people can see beyond this.' But it wasn't until the following morning that it was confirmed that Harold Wilson and the Labour Party had won by just four seats. Frank stabbed a square of toast soaked with egg yolk onto his fork. 'Maybe we could have held on if more of the right people got off their backsides to go and vote. I put it down to apathy. We should make voting compulsory like they do in Australia. But the blame can be laid well and truly on the sex scandal. People can forgive all manner of political blunders but when it comes down to morals it's a different story.'

Kate spread marmalade onto her toast as she listened to him. He's right, she thought even in this so called liberated era people still make harsher judgments about people's sexual peccadilloes than their other failings. I wonder what they'd think of mine?

'There must be something about these colonials that attracts us,' Cheryl said to Kate as she left on Friday evening for a weekend away with John, a New Zealand vet from work. As the front door closed on the sounds of Cheryl and John's laughter Kate went to the lounge window and discreetly watched as John's car drove away.

I'm like the proverbial wallflower she thought. I'm housebound, duty bound and moribund. I want a man to make me laugh and drive me away for the weekend. With nothing to do except have sex, eat and drink. Without having to worry about the responsibility of Ally and Ben.

She closed the curtains and switched on the side table lamps. She picked up the *TV Times* and flicked to Friday programming.

Good, she thought. I'll just have time to make a quick bite of something before Coronation Street. How pathetic getting your kicks from watching a character like Elsie Tanner's sexual exploits.

On Saturday Kate made three batches of mince pies to store in the freezer ready for Christmas. The children rolled out the leftover scraps of pastry with Ally's toy rolling pin, placing these offerings of very grubby looking pastry shapes on a baking sheet which Kate put in the oven to bake until crisp. They had these for tea with a little raspberry jam. It was the evening when the children were in bed that time really hung. It was as if the silence had an aura of its own beaming endlessly out into space. She put on the television, more for company than to watch. Benny Hill was chasing scantily clad women around a park. She curled her lip and switched it off. She wandered round the lounge aimlessly, picking up a book and laying it down. She opened the lounge curtains to look out into the dark night. It had started to rain and watery smudges ran down the windowpane, her breath on the windows created misty patches.

I hope it's raining in Brighton she thought and Cheryl and John get soaked and land up with colds.

Jane phoned just after breakfast on Sunday and asked them to lunch. Ian opened the front door and the sounds of Roy Orbison's *Pretty Woman* burst through the greyness of the day.

'Turn it down kids,' Ian yelled as Ally and Ben ran down the hall to join their cousins.

'Feels like a party, love the music,' Kate said as Jane took her coat and hung it on the oak hallstand. In the lounge replica antique furniture and swag of velvet curtains reflected Jane's taste. Kate sat in the warmth of the kitchen as Jane and Ian prepared lunch. She could see the bare trees through the window and on the patio the white wrought iron outdoor setting looked wet and forlorn.

'What can I do?', she asked.

'Nothing, just sit.'

She watched as the couple peeled and cut vegetables on the other end of the large kitchen table. They worked as a team, checking with each other every now and then to see what they needed to do. When Ian threw the last peeled spud into the pan on the bench and a spray of water soaked Jane, they laughed. He put his knife down and wiped her face gently with a tea towel and kissed her cheek.

Kate sighed.

'Are you okay, Kate?' Jane asked, noticing her sister's vacant stare.

'I'm fine Jane. Are you sure there is nothing I can do?' Over lunch fortified with a large glass of red wine she told her sister how lonely she felt, even though Cheryl was there and that many friends who had once been regular visitors to the house when Greg was alive no longer called.

'Well let's face it Cheryl is hardly ever home, she's making up for lost time, you can't blame her after what's she had to put up with that shit of a husband. You see Susan don't you?'

'Yes, we often meet for a coffee.'

Kate's white linen napkin lay untidily on the table in front of her. Jane's eyes followed as Kate smoothed and carefully folded it back into the ironed creases before tightly rolling it to slip inside the serviette ring.

'Look, Kate, it's hard on people many do not know what to say and worry they may upset you. Maybe people rationalise that it's a process you have go through on your own and nothing that they can do will make it any different.' Jane squeezed her sister's hand. 'Have you seen Tom lately?

'Just once since I've been back, but now he also seems to have gone to ground.'

'Don't read too much into it, Kate, you set the boundaries of that relationship.'

'Yes I know. I'm just a bit low at the moment. It will pass I'm sure.'

On a leaden day in mid December the phone rang. Kate scooped up the receiver. 'Valentine 2846.'

'Hi Kate, my name is Jack Williams, you don't know me but I met Greg at university and only just heard of his passing and wanted to pay my respects.' His voice was deep and pleasing to the ear.

Kate's face flushed. They chatted easily for some time about the children, her trip to Australia and she learned that he had recently relocated to London from Hong Kong. He was born and raised in Queensland, was a dentist like Greg but a couple of years younger than him and he was touring the world doing locum work. Finally he asked if he might drop by to say g'day as he was working in a suburb close by.

'Of course I would love to meet you. Any friend of Greg's is a friend of mine. But give me a call before you drop in so you can make sure I'm home.'

'Yes, yes, yes,' she punched the air as she jogged back to the kitchen.

For days she checked the phone frequently to make sure it was properly on its cradle and when it did ring she rushed to answer it. It was over a week before he called to ask if it was convenient to drop in later that day. Kate bustled around tidying the house. She changed the children's clothes; scrubbed their faces with a warm flannel and brushed their hair. She decided to wear jeans and a blue sweater and piled her hair into a bun leaving soft wisps of hair to frame her face.

Dressed and waiting, she put out cups and saucers,

filled the kettle and put it on the hob. The doorbell rang and Kate peeped through the lounge window before going to the front door. Parked at the curbside was a red, late model Austin Healey. Like the rest of his compatriots she knew who worked for the National Health Service, it appeared that he too was generously recompensed for his services to British dental health. She opened the door to greet him. He was tall, taller than Greg but similar features, a thinner face but the same jutting chin, blue eyes and dark hair. The difference in their heights was a good icebreaker.

'My God, you are tall!', Kate exclaimed, hoping her nerves did not play out in her voice.

'No it's you who is short,' Jack replied, laughing.

She took him through to the lounge where Ally and Ben were playing. 'Tea, coffee?' Kate queried.

'Tea would do nicely, thanks.'

Kate noticed when he smiled how white and even his teeth were. He followed her into the kitchen where Kate, with trembling fingers, warmed the pot and put out some biscuits on a plate.

'Kate I was really sorry to hear about Greg, he was great bloke and it must have been a terrible loss to you and your family.'

The familiar tightness around her chest came. 'Thank you, it was a difficult time.'

She paused pouring the boiling water into the teapot waiting for the moment to pass.

'How did you like Hong Kong?'

'I loved it and the people. I was there just after Typhoon Wanda and it was a mess when I arrived, but the Chinese are hard workers and they soon got everything back on track. Their economy is textile based so practically wherever you went you saw women and men working their little Singer sewing machines, in houses, in shop windows and even out on the street,' Jack said.

As the conversation progressed she relaxed, there was a familiarity about him that appealed. A couple of hours passed easily before Kate realised it was past the children's bath time.

'Perhaps we can catch up again, babe,' he said. The term babe excited her.

'That would be great,' Kate replied, as she closed the front door. Doing a little jig as she went up the hall.'No two ways about it these colonials are definitely attractive,' she said out loud.

'He is really nice,' Kate said to Cheryl that evening as they ate dinner.

'How did he get your number?'

'I don't know. Presumably in the telephone directory.'

The conversation moved onto Cheryl's work that day but Kate was only half listening, she was wondering how long it would be before he phoned again. The days passed slowly as every phone call she anticipated hearing his voice.

When Jack called in mid January, Kate had given up the notion that he would call at all and his voice caught her by surprise when she answered the phone. He asked if she would like to go into town that evening. He was a member of a couple of clubs and they could have a drink. 'Won't be a late night as I am working.'

'Sounds good to me. Look forward to seeing you.' She grinned as she dialled Cheryl's work number. 'If you're home tonight can you baby sit? Jack-the-lad phoned and asked me out.'

'That's fine, I had no plans. I'll try and get home a bit earlier so you have more time to get ready.'

Kate put down the phone. She giggled as she stretched her arms wide and slowly gyrated her hips. Ally tugged her skirt.

'I'm hungry Mummy.'

'Peanut butter sandwich?' Kate smiled at her daughter. 'And maybe a chocolate biscuit later if you're good.'

Ally clapped her hands.

———

They managed to get a park on Wardour Street. They weaved their way through the crowds milling around the entrance to the famous Flamingo Night Club. Clusters of young people gathered on the pavement. Boys in smart suits with thin neck-ties, winkle-picker shoes and their girlfriends wearing ballet flats and tiny mini skirts, short mannish haircuts and darkened lashed eyes gazing out sullenly from their pale faces and white lips.

She had to almost run to keep up with Jack's pace all the while drinking in the swirl and sounds of coffee bars and pubs. Soho was buzzing and her eyes blazed with excitement as they went down the basement steps to the

Berwick Street club, Dave Clark Five's latest track *Glad all over* was pumping out of the loudspeakers. Brass wall lights highlighted the embossed gold and scarlet wallpaper while multiples of coloured bottles and red leather banquettes were reflected in the mirrored bar that ran the length of the room.

'Gin and tonic?' he asked. She nodded sliding onto one of the barstools. Jack sat next to a couple of men wearing business suits.

'Kate meet a couple of fellow Queenslanders and my good mates,' he said as he slapped one of the men on the back. A girl with Titian hair joined the group. As Kate watched he kissed her full on the lips and caught her hand as she stepped back.

'How're you, gorgeous? Meet Kate. Kate meet Red, big party girl, she's from Melbourne but we won't hold that against her.' Red flicked at him with her scarf.

'You,' she said.

He swung round with his back to her and talked to his friends. Red kept her company and Kate listened while Red did the talking. She told her that Jack was a great bloke but as mad as a cut snake. Kate nodded. Red flicked her hair back from her face and dipped her finger into her champagne coupé half full with a creamy looking liquid.

'Brandy Alexander, don't you just love them?'

Kate shook her head but Red did not notice, she was busy tracing her finger round the inside of the glass and sucking her finger clean. 'I love London it's just one long party, I've just spent a year backpacking around Europe,

I had a ball, an absolute ripper, be hard to go home and start work again,' she said.

'Right we are off,' Jack said as he downed his drink and steered her out of the club. 'Good blokes those two,' he said as they motored to the second club in Berkeley Square. 'Think you'll like the Club Tropico, all the birds I know seem to love it.'

Jack was right Club Tropico appealed to all her senses. A subtle scent of frangipani and coconut oil greeted them as they entered the vast room fringed with palm trees, frescos of tropical island beaches and bamboo cages hanging from the ceiling, home to live parrots. A simulated tropical storm raged with thunder and lightning crackling all around them and the dominant feature wall, supposedly of black lava rock, became a cascading waterfall.

The front desk seemed to know Jack and showed them to a table. A waiter wearing a Hawaiian shirt brought them the menu.

'Plantation Punch?' Jack asked.

'Sounds good to me.'

Kate felt like a child on Christmas morning as she stared around her. A towering meringue and raspberry sauce confection was delivered to a neighbouring table by a waitress dressed in a frangipani-patterned sarong.

'This place is incredible,' she said.

He ordered a t-bone steak she a bowl of fries, saying that she was not that hungry. She was nervous and didn't want to eat anything using a knife and fork. Over the past weeks she'd noticed that her left hand trembled as she lifted her fork to her mouth.

The Plantation Punch arrived looking very edible. It had a big wedge of fresh pineapple jammed over the rim and three maraschino cherries speared on a plastic cocktail stick.

As she sipped her punch and they talked she relaxed and began to enjoy herself. She spoke about her time as a hostess and embellished the Nairobi story of the thief who ran off when he saw her white face and headgear.

Jack chuckled. 'That's a corker if I ever heard one.'

His steak arrived and she was more than ready for her bowl of fries and wished she had ordered something more substantial. She picked at her fries while she watched him eat. He cut the meat from the bone, with the precision of a surgeon and when he finished the last mouthful the bone was clean and white. He did not touch the salad that came with it. When he finished he pushed the plate across the table and snapped his fingers to the waiter. 'We'll have another round,' he said his fingers indicating the empty glasses.

They talked, her body half turned towards him as she rested her chin on the back of her hand. They talked of his high-rise apartment in Hong Kong, the night-lights of Kowloon and laughed at the description of his first attempt of using chopsticks. When he excused himself to go to the bathroom her eyes followed his angular gait across the restaurant. She waited by the front door of the club and watched while he paid the bill. The cashier said something to make him laugh, he looked her way briefly and said something in reply and they laughed again. He caught her arm as they made their way back to the car.

'That cashier fancies you,' he said.

'That's nice,' she said. He smiled. She tried to walk in unison with his steps but hadn't the length of stride.

'You need longer legs my girl,' he said. She grinned, she liked the way he said 'my girl.'

It was close to ten when Jack drove up to her house and helped her out of the car and to her front door. 'Thank you,' she giggled, 'I had a ball and I could easily become addicted to Plantation Punch.'

He laughed and snatched a kiss to her lips before striding down the path.

'I enjoyed it too babe. Let's do it again sometime.'

She watched as his car roared down the road, her ring finger tracing the outline of her mouth. 'Babe,' she whispered.

Cheryl was still up. 'The kids are fine, not a peep out of them,' she said.

'Thank you, you're a brick,' Kate replied.

'Did you have fun?' Cheryl asked putting on a saucepan of milk to warm. 'Hot chocolate?' Kate nodded. 'Well come on spill the beans, what was he like?' Cheryl said.

'He's gorgeous, Cheryl, and I had a great time. At first he was a bit distant, spent most of his time at the first club talking to his friends, he might have had some business I don't know but when we went to the second place, it was good, well more than good, bloody terrific.'

'Well when are you going to see him again?' Cheryl asked

'Not sure,' replied Kate, 'he just said let's do it again

sometime, but I hope its soon.'

Cheryl sipped on her hot chocolate. 'Why don't we have a party? That gives you the perfect excuse to invite him around?'

'I love that,' Kate leapt up and put her cup in the sink. 'Tomorrow we'll plan it.'

<hr />

She had dropped Jack's invitation to the party into his surgery but she still had not heard from him the day before the party.

'I'm so disappointed that he hasn't called. I must have got the signals wrong I thought he liked me,' she said to Cheryl as they stood waiting in line to pay for the booze at the off license.

'Look he still might call you never know. But it'll still be a gas. I'll get John to round up some friends. It'll be okay you wait and see.' Jack phoned on the morning of the party to say that he would be there and he would be bringing a friend.

Cheryl was sorting through the collection of records.

'Jack's coming,' Kate said racing into the room.

'Perfect,' Cheryl said picking out the Beetle's *Please Please Me* album from the pile.

'But he's bringing a friend. I bet it's that girl I met in the club.' 'Not so perfect but if he does, we'll get John's New Zealand pals to chat her up.'

<hr />

Kate pulled on her black patent boots and looked at herself in the mirror. She was wearing a black and white plaid mini skirt with fishnet panty-hose and a white satin shirt that showed a bit of cleavage. She had her shoulder length blonde hair styled in a fashionable geometric cut. She clipped on her earrings, black shiny plastic orbs and undid another pearl button on the shirt and lent forward and tweaked her cleavage again. With a last check in the mirror and a practice flick of her hair she went downstairs to start plating up the nuts and crisps. The doorbell rang as Dusty Springfield's record *Wishin' and Hopin'* was playing. John and his friends carried in cases of beer and a large bag of ice and stowed them in the sink in the utility room. John introduced Kate to Dan and Jim, both meteorologists on leave after a yearlong stint in Antarctica. Dan wore brown corduroy pants and Jim a beige corduroy jacket with leather elbow patches. Neither man said a word and she smiled remembering that her sister had once said that men who wore corduroy, especially with leather patches, were guaranteed to be totally trustworthy but incredibly boring.

'So you were in Antarctica. How was that?' Kate asked.

'Cold,' Jim said

'Now that's the biggest understatement I've ever heard,' she laughed nervously but getting no response continued. 'It must have been freezing.'

'Yes, it was pretty cold,' said Dan.

'Did you see polar bears?'

'Yes lots of polar bears,' said Jim.

'Really and I suppose you saw seals.'

'Yes plenty of seals,' Jim replied.

'Must have been terrible for Shackleton,' Kate said

running out of conversation.

Dan stared at Kate in disbelief. 'Terrible,' he replied.

God how lame I am she thought. But these two boffins are bloody hopeless. Why don't they make an effort to make conversation?

Dan and Jim shuffled their feet and opened another can of beer. She's out of our league Jim told John later adding don't forget mate we've only had blokes to talk to for the past year.

———

Kate looked at her watch nine o'clock and no sign of Jack.

'Bugger it,' she said to Jane and Ian, 'Lets dance.' She downed her glass of wine, turned the record player up to blast out the Beatle's number *Love, love me do*. Within minutes furniture was pushed aside and the whole party was twisting with her. Kate was in full dance throttle when she saw him enter the room. She missed a beat of the music. She mouthed hello before picking up the beat again.

'Go, girl, go,' Jack murmured before going out to the kitchen to find a beer.

Kate flicked a strand of hair behind her ear and followed him.

'Hi babe,' he said. She was trembling as he kissed her cheek, her face turning hungrily to be kissed on the lips like an infant searching for milk. He stepped back and with one hand caught her shoulder and turned her full circle. 'Meet Roger my flat-mate he's another Australian dentist but studied in Brisbane so he didn't get to meet Greg.

'I'm really pleased to meet you Roger,' she smiled. Really pleased her thoughts echoed the sentiment

'There is something about Jack,' she whispered to Cheryl later in the kitchen as they plated up the trays of sausage rolls hot from the oven.

'Yes I can see what you see in him, he reminds me of Greg.'

As she handed round the hot sausage rolls Jack took the plate and set it down on the table and led her out into the hall. The light spilled from kitchen casting shadows down the hall. They sat on the bottom step of the stairs.

'How're you doing, Katie? You liked the Plantation Punch eh?'

'You could say that,' she giggled like a fifteen year old on a first date.

'Would you like to do it again?' Jack asked, slipping his arm around her shoulder.

'Yes I would love to. I had a good time,' Kate replied looking up at him coyly through her blackened eyelashes.

He kissed her, his lips were a promise, warmly opening over hers. His grip tightened pulling her hard into his chest. Her fingers pressed into his back. His tongue pushed into her mouth exploring and darting. She almost moaned with pleasure and wanted to say now, upstairs, this instant. But Jim came down the hall and they pulled apart. The meteorologist oblivious to the sexual tension between them started chatting to Jack about Hong Kong. Kate's heart was hammering when she slipped away. She sucked her lower lip she could still feel the bloom of his lips. In the lounge she poured herself another glass of wine.

'Now where were we,' Jack appeared at her side and took her glass. 'Come on Kate this music is too good to miss.' *My Girl* by The Temptations was playing. He pulled her close to him and sang along to the chorus. 'Well, I guess you'll say *What can make me feel this way? My Girl, My Girl, My Girl, Talkin' about My Girl.*'

Kate joined in the chorus '*Oooooh, Hoooo. Hey, hey hey. Hey, hey, hey.*' With each move of the dance his thigh pushed against her body. Her pelvis ached to be touched and she pushed hard against his leg. She closed her eyes and cleaved to his chest. He smelt of aftershave and mouthwash. She fingered the button on his shirt where it pressed into her face and she softly sang the lyrics. '*What can make me feel this way? My girl, my girl, my girl.*'

Cheryl grabbed Kate's arm. 'Sorry you two but people are leaving we need to say good-bye.' Cheryl and Kate stood at the open door. Kate shivered, impatient to return to Jack in the warmth of the lounge. Their departing guests, wrapped in topcoats ran down the frosty path to their cars, their thanks disappearing into the wind.

She turned to go in but met Jack and Roger.

'It was a ripper of a night thanks Kate,' Roger said stepping out into the cold.

Kate turned to face Jack. 'Surely you are not going?'

Jack put his arms around her. He kissed her, his tongue parting her lips and filling her mouth for a teasing instant before pulling away.

'It was great babe, we'll do it again soon.' He turned to wave as he got into the car. Kate turned and went in, a trickle of tears made her mascara run in black dots down her face. She went upstairs and changed into her dressing gown and in the bathroom she savagely wiped her face with a warm flannel.

John was staying the night and the three of them cleared as much away as possible before they went to bed. Kate scraped the plates and piled them on the kitchen table ready for washing up. She put away the leftovers of the supper into the fridge.

'How about we leave the washing up for the morning? We'll do it first thing before the children get home from your parents.' Cheryl said.

'Yes, we'll do it tomorrow, you and John go up, I'll be up shortly.'

Cheryl put her arms around Kate. 'Maybe he was protecting you. You know—from gossip.'

'Yes, maybe,' Kate looked pale and tired, her body felt as though she had been in a car wreck.

She switched off the record player and picked up the *My Girl* single and put it back into its sleeve. Her arm was aching and she pulled it across her chest. She was grateful for the warmth of her bed, which soothed her soreness. She switched off the electric blanket and lay awake listening to the sounds of Cheryl and John's lovemaking before drifting off to sleep. She dreamt about Greg again that night. She was walking through a clearing on a desert island and suddenly there he was. He looked at her directly and she called his name but he turned away. She ran after him. He turned round to face her and told her to go away, that he didn't want her. Her tears woke her, she got up and went to the window it was just getting light.

She pulled on a pair of jeans and a sweater and went downstairs to wash up and clean the party away. When she finished and everything was, as it should be, she put on the kettle on the hob and stoked the boiler.

By the end of the week she was exhausted, her arm felt strangely limp and her head ached from all her punitive ramblings about Jack to Cheryl and Jane.

The following week Jack called. 'How about another Plantation Punch at the club?'

Without a flicker of hesitation Kate responded. 'Love to, when?

'Tomorrow evening, I'll pick you up at seven.' Jack replied. Both Cheryl and Jane told her to be careful.

'You're playing with fire, Kate, and you are going to get burnt.' Jane said when they were out supermarket shopping.

'No, Jane, you always think the worst. I think Cheryl was right when she said he was protecting my reputation.' She chose a box of cereal and dropped into the supermarket trolley. 'Both you and Cheryl said you thought my expectations were a little unrealistic.'

'Stop watering things down, Kate.' She caught Kate's hand and pulled her closer and spoke softly. 'This man is out for what he can get, I recognised the type instantly and he'll use you, why can't you see this?'

'Stop it, Jane. Just because you didn't like him, you only met him once at the party, you don't know him. He has not used me as you put it. I know he likes me. You don't kiss someone like that unless you're keen. I just have to be patient, not come on too strong.'

Jane sucked in her breath sharply. 'Be it on your own head,' she said and pushed the trolley past her.

The low car was a challenge to get into wearing a short skirt. She sat sideways before swinging her legs into the car and as she did so her skirt rose to expose her thighs. As he changed gear he ran his hand down the side of her thigh.

'Nice,' he murmured.

Kate coughed. She put her hand to her throat and could feel her pulse beating ferociously and a tightening deep in her pelvis.

It was the same routine, first the Soho club where he chatted to all his friends while she sat and stared at her gin and tonic before moving on to the tropical night of splendour club in Berkeley Square. She had waited all evening for him to give some sort of explanation as to why he left the party so early but none came.

Buoyed by her second Plantation Punch she asked, 'What happened last Saturday night, the party...' her voice trailed off.

'Yeah, what a great night. Roger and I went on to the Soho Club with Red and had a ball.'

If Jack had been looking at her instead of looking around to see whom he knew in the club, he would have seen Kate's face grimace.

Her voice was shrill when she announced she needed the bathroom. In the quietness of the toilet stall she silently coached herself. It was difficult for him with Roger, obviously he felt responsible for him, couldn't just dump him after all they came in the same car. Would he have been so open about going to the club if he was seeing Red? I don't think so. When she got back to the table she was smiling once more.

On the drive home he said 'Time for a coffee I think.'

She smiled. 'Yes, coffee it is.'

When she took the coffee into the lounge Jack was dressed only in his underpants and socks and sitting on the rug in front of the fire. His trousers and shirt were flung across a chair; his shoes still laced had been kicked off under the settee.

Her mouth dropped open as she stared at him. She could hear the tick of the clock on the shelf. She slid the tray on the table and stood beside him.

'Coffee?' Her eyes sparkled.

'Come to poppa, babe,' he ran his hand up her leg.

***

'Yes we did', she replied in answer to Cheryl's cocked eyebrow as Kate made the children's porridge the following morning at breakfast.

'So,' Cheryl said softly

'So it was wham, bam, thank you mam. He said thanks babe that was great, will call you, and he went.'

'That's pretty awful. How do you feel?'

'Don't ask me that, I know what you and Jane think

and you're probably right but I'm besotted with him, even last night's quickie doesn't turn me off.'

Kate stripped her bed and washed the sheets. The weather was freezing and when she put the sheets and pillowcases out on the line they froze moving stiffly in the breeze and she wistfully remembered the punkah fans in Africa. Next she tackled the nursery with Ally and Ben in tow. With a cloth and a bucket of warm soapy water she washed and wiped the furniture, pulling out their beds, she cleaned walls and skirting boards. They had morning tea with fruit and biscuits in the warmth of the kitchen. Next it was the kitchen's turn, cleaning what she could of the Aga, the stove and the sink. Ally and Ben both had cloths and their job was to wipe the stair treads. The fun of cleaning lasted all of five minutes before they went back into the playroom creating mayhem as they pulled out all the toys indiscriminately. After she fed the children their lunch and put them down for a nap, she wandered the house her mind would not be still. Like a movie in her head she replayed scenes with Jack over and over.

He called three days later mid afternoon to see if she was in that evening. She gave the children an early tea and bathed them. Neither child would be still as she tried to nappy them and dress them for bed. Ally ran naked through the upstairs rooms thinking it was a great game. Kate caught her and managed to dress her in her nightclothes but Ally was wired alert and sleep was not going to be her friend that night. Kate's heart was racing as she put them in their beds and told them a story. Ally had calmed but she demanded a second story. Kate shook her head but Ally persisted and Ben added his demands for a second story.

'No more, I said no more,' she shouted and slammed the nursery door shut behind her. She could hear Ally kicking the nursery door above her screams. She closed her bedroom door and the sound was muffled. With trembling hands she changed her clothes and fixed her make up.

She tip toed out to the landing all was quiet, She carefully pushed the nursery door open Ally was asleep on the floor and Ben in his cot. She put her into bed and tucked her in. They both looked so vulnerable when they slept, innocent faces, long eyelashes touching their mound of pink cheeks and mouths that twitched occasionally. She was overwhelmed by guilt. Jack kissed her cheek. Instantly she wanted more, especially tonight, but she moved away. Give him space, she thought, don't rush him. She took the bottle of scotch he offered and got her good crystal glasses from the cupboard.

'Are you hungry.' She blushed. 'I mean do you want some food?'

'No babe, I'm fine.'

She poured them both a whiskey. 'I love the Berkeley Square club, how did you find it?'

'I was introduced to the club by a friend, Tom Appleton, I think you know him.' Kate lowered her gaze and bit her lip.

His face was impassive as he continued speaking about his home in Queensland. 'Rockhampton, billed as the beef capital of the world, but really just a big country town.'

'I remember those country towns in Queensland when Greg and I drove up to Brisbane, we stayed overnight in a couple of the small towns and I was always amazed at the size of the breakfast that they served, a T-bone steak that overhung the plate, rashers and rashers of bacon, two eggs, mushrooms, tomatoes and bake beans all with half a loaf of toast. Could have fed a family of four.'

'Yes babe, Queenslanders have big appetites,' he winked at her. 'Ever been to a B and S Ball?' He did not wait for an answer. 'B and S, stands for Bachelor and Spinster. Yeah they're great, everyone goes feral, they're held in the bush and we drink Bundy.'

Her eyes quizzed.

'Sorry babe, Bundaberg Rum, lots of it and when we can't stand up we sleep it off in our utes.'

'Yes, I know what a ute is.'

But Jack wasn't listening his thoughts fourteen thousand miles away remembering the bush bashes of his days before dentistry.

'God, I get horny just talking about these parties, we used to shag everything on two legs.'

As he finished his sentence he lent towards her and put his hand up her skirt and caressed her thighs clumsily before his determined fingers started to work their way under the lace leg of her panties. His breath was hot on her face as he whispered 'Oh babe you're so ready.'

He unzipped his fly.

'Yes, but not here', she murmured her voice throaty.

'Cheryl will be home shortly.'

She looked at her bedside clock. It was nine o'clock when he removed his pants. But not his shirt, nor his tie, nor his socks and it was twenty to ten when he stood up and put his pants on again.

'That was great babe. Must away, I am meeting Roger in town.'

'God, Jack, do you have to go, why don't you stay awhile?'

'Sorry babe, have to go I'll call you.'

She went back into the lounge and cleared the glasses, plumped the cushions and went into the kitchen.

She washed the glasses and sat down at the kitchen bench her head in her hands.

Cheryl threw her car keys down on the hall table and walked into the kitchen.

'So, how did it go?' she asked, seeing Kate in her dressing gown.

'Don't ask me, I'm so disgusted with myself but it is like an obsession. I'm a grovelling mess wanting more and more of him.'

'Well, love, you are the only one who can sort this out. You have a good head on your shoulders you will work it out. Now, I think it is time for bed as we both need our beauty sleep,' there was a hint of exasperation in her voice.

The long winter days passed with no call from Jack. Each day was an agony as she waited for the telephone to ring. When she couldn't stand the tension any longer she would call him at the surgery but his nurse always told her he was unavailable. She ate little and sleep deserted her. The days turned into weeks with Kate hardly leaving the house in case the phone rang. She got Jane to ring her daily to make sure the phone was working.

Jane called Cheryl at work and asked her if she had noticed that Kate was holding her arm up across her chest and was constantly rubbing it as though in pain. Whenever either of them asked about it, she dismissed it as a muscle strain. John had stayed over with Cheryl and as they breakfasted they observed Kate standing desolately at the kitchen door as she watched her children play in the sunroom. Her face was like chalk, her hand rubbing her left arm that rested across her chest. When they went upstairs to Cheryl's room, John said quietly to Cheryl 'I think we need to do something about your friend, she looks very depressed.'

'Yes and I think she is really not well, have you noticed how she is protecting her arm? But I just don't know how to help her.'

'I think she needs to know where she stands with this fellow, without a doubt he is not interested but the opportunity presented itself and he took it. I really don't think he has the slightest understanding how vulnerable she is,' he said.

Cheryl answered, 'More so because Kate consciously or unconsciously sees Greg in him and that's what this is all about.'

'I think we should talk to her as she can't go on like

this,' John replied.

That morning as Kate watched her children playing she saw Ben being comforted by Ally. The little girl not much bigger than her brother put her arms around him and gently patted his back. She saw Ben put his head on her shoulder. She watched as Ally helped him race his cars along the linoleum, 'How could I?', she whispered. 'How could I have lost sight of my children?'

After Cheryl and John had spoken Kate thanked them and told them that she had decided that she wanted to see Jack and ask him face to face where they stood.

'Are you sure that this is what you want?', asked Cheryl.

'Yes,' said Kate, 'I know the answer but I need some sort of completion, which I think this will be.'

'I think we need to come with you Kate' said John.

'Thank you, I do feel a bit wobbly but I really need to do this.

It was late morning when they arrived at the block of flats. John and Cheryl waited in the car. Bile rose in Kate's throat as she knocked at the door. Roger opened the door. She asked to see Jack.

'He's asleep, Kate,' Roger said, closing the door.

Her whole body was shaking as she pushed the door open wide and asked Roger to wake him, as it was important she should see him. When he came back he told her that she could go in. Jack's room smelt like a dirty pub bar, a combination of stale alcohol and cigarette smoke. Strewn across the floor was a half eaten peanut butter sandwich its greasy filling smeared through the fibres of the cheap beige carpet. Jack sat in the middle of his crumpled bed unshaven and irritated by her presence. His face was puffed and red, angry that she insisted he should wake when he had a major hangover from his all night partying. The contrast between them was dramatic. Kate was dressed neatly, her hair brushed and her skin fresh and clear. As she looked around the room any anxiety that she had dissipated. She said simply and clearly 'Jack, I just need to know where we stand. Rather, what I am to you?'

'What you are to me?', his voice rose in anger.

He shook his head and angrily flicked the bedclothes back to expose his naked body. He cupped his fingers openly around his purpling testes and rubbed his flaccid penis like a pastry maker might rub fat into flour.

'Babe, you missed a great night last night, I had a skinfull at the club and shagged a couple of the barmaids.'

Her face showed no emotion as she stared at him. 'Poor girls, that must have been a disappointment for them,'

'Nice one, Kate,' Jack replied his voice gravelly. His eyes narrowed meanly as he pulled the covers over him.

'I would be more generous about your sexual inclinations. Did you know your friend Tom said you were gagging for it. Sex without obligation were the words he used, and so I obliged.'

Her heart was beating so hard she felt he would have heard it across the room. How could I have been so infatuated with this slob, this pig of a man? Of course it was Tom. Jack's words 'gagging for it,' echoed over and over in her ears. She wanted to slap him. She imagined her fingers stinging his cheek over and over and leaving a crimson mark of shame.

'Oh, did I miss something? Was that your idea of giving the poor little widow a good time? You are so fucking deluded about your sexual prowess. Trust me, Jack, girls prefer blokes who take their time—and their socks off.'

'What a crock of shit. You wanted it, you used me,' Jack scowled.

'No, you used your alleged friendship with Greg to get an easy and convenient lay. You're despicable.'

For what seemed an age they faced each other. Hostility was printed on his face but Kate's anger was spent.

'Thank you, Jack,' she said. She turned on her heel and walked out of his room, his flat and his life.

***

The pale sun on that March day was trying to push through the clouds when she walked out of the block of flats. The wind cooled her flushed cheeks and blew the remnants of the seedy encounter away. When she got to the car she was smiling.

'So?', asked Cheryl.

'Why didn't you tell me what an arsehole he was?'

Cheryl shook her head and smiled.

'We did but you weren't listening. Are you okay?'

Kate nodded. 'More than fine, I saw him for what he was an arrogant, despicable...' she paused searching for the right word to vilify him.

'Prick is the word you're looking for,' John said, his

eyes smiling at her through the mirror as he started the engine, released the handbrake and put the car into gear.

Cheryl repeated 'Definitely a first class prick.'

She wrote to Greg that evening when the children were in bed, her writing pad open on the green leather tooled desk.

My dearest,

When you were alive I never thought of myself as lustful, more lacking in libido than dissolute. But within months of losing you my mind and body longed, ached and demanded intimacy. Why am I sanitising my behaviour by using the word intimacy, I wanted sex. At first masturbation satisfied the longing but soon I was starving for everything masculine.

The drive so strong that I brazenly asked some one I hardly knew for sex. Sex with Tom was simply sex and the arrangement was fine I had no attachment to him and strangely not much guilt either. But it was naive of me to think that he would be discreet.

Fred was different and as well as being a great lover he was a friend. It was an honest relationship, no games, no agenda except when I got off in Sydney it was over. My only regret being that you and I did not have the chance of developing our lovemaking into an art form like I enjoyed with Fred.

Jack Williams walked into my life when I was most vulnerable. I was starved of tender loving moments that others shared and my fear of being on my own was devouring me.

Cheryl said that Jack bore a resemblance to you. I'm sure she was right he was an Australian, a dentist and had a certain wild colonial thing that I loved in you. But added to this was that he reconnected me to a world outside my mundane life. He was a powerful, heady concoction. I can see all the psychological why and how. I understand that this is the way I avoid facing the pain of grief but knowing it intellectually does not stop it when I'm in the grip of its fever. Today my fever broke; I had been in its grip for too long.

I suppose the whole shameful, unhealthy episode could be seen as a catalyst. But I'm just grateful that he was such an arsehole today as it made it all so easy to walk away.

I have been feeling pretty rough these last months but I think I might sleep well tonight. The exorcising of Jack feels like a cool wind blowing through my mind and spirit.

Still and always will, love you. Katie xx

Chapter 8

•••••••••••

An Epiphany

Jane put three measures of coffee in the plunger and waited for the kettle to boil. The sisters and their children were making the most of the warm weather. It had been a month of extremes, with the lowest temperature on record for a March day in the first week of the month and three weeks later, the highest.

Kate was seated at the wrought iron table on Jane's patio watching the children play. The garden beds, alive with daffodils, framed the pathway running down to the children's play area. The children played in the large sandpit, their jumpers and fleecy jerkins dumped on the grass beside them. Jane carried the cafetière to the table and pressed the plunger slowly down into the liquid.

'Okay, so what else did the bastard say?' she asked.

'Oh can you believe that he said that Tom had told him about our arrangement and that he was just doing me a favour. He is just a first class prick,' Kate said.

She seemed to have difficulty with the final word of

her castigation of Jack. The insult 'prick' became 'purr-ick.'

Jane's eyes widened with each detail of the account and nodded encouragement to continue the story but what was becoming more noticeable was Kate's manner of speech, each word becoming more difficult to understand.

'What's wrong with you, Kate, you're slurring your speech,' she leant forward accusingly to smell Kate's breath. 'Have you been drinking?'

'No, don't be bloody ridiculous, Jane, it's ten o'clock in the morning.' Even with the spur of irritation Kate's speech was ponderous. Jane's brow furrowed.

'Your speech is slurred. What's going on Kate?'

'You can hear it? I just thought it was my imagination. I must be tired.'

'What about your arm that you've been nursing for weeks now? Cheryl and I asked you what was wrong with it and you gave us some weak excuse about a pulled muscle?' Jane asked

'Look I didn't want anyone to worry about it. It's just a bit of numbness and tingling in my left arm that's all.'

Jane raised an eyebrow. 'More like you didn't want to deal with it. So do you have any other symptoms that you don't want us to worry about?'

'Look the odd headache, and my eyes feel blurred at times, but Jane I have been through a lot recently I put it down to stress.'

'How long have you had this?'

'I got the odd twinge in Australia but living with the

Sinclairs is enough to make anyone feel sick.'

Jane stood up her hands on her hips as she looked down at her sister.

'Kate you cannot bury your head in the sand over this, you have to do something about this straight away,' her voice was tinged with exasperation. 'I wonder if this has anything to do with the Bell's Palsy you had when you had Ally and the paralysis on your left side when you were pregnant with Ben?'

Kate bowed her head, her hands covering her eyes 'For God's sake, Jane, don't try to scare me,' Kate said rubbing her brow. 'They said that Ben must have been lying on a nerve.'

'But the doctors didn't say that about the Bells Palsy, in fact they said they did not know what caused it,' snorted Jane. She softened her tone. 'Kate you must go to the doctors, you need to know what you are dealing with.'

'I will in my own time.' There was an edge of defiance in her voice. 'I will okay?'

Jane shook her head and got up from the table. She went back into the house and dialled their local doctor's number. Kate was standing close to the sandpit watching the children play when Jane joined her. 'I have made you an appointment with the doctor tomorrow at half past nine,' Jane put her arm around Kate and kissed her cheek. 'Please don't argue, just do it for me.'

'Jane, it's probably just stress. Looking after two toddlers tires me out, as you well know.' She picked up the children's clothes and folded them over her arm. 'But okay, I'll go to put your mind at ease.'

She noticed Dr Singleton's white coat sleeves rode high on the cuffs of his tweed jacket, probably shrunk from regular laundering she thought as he placed a thermometer, tasting of Dettol under her tongue. He held it up to the light to read it and grunted. He asked her about her health in general, did she get fatigued easily, was she depressed or anxious? Did she get muscle spasms? Did she have difficulty focussing? He wound the blood pressure sleeve around her forearm and pumped the black bulb in his hand. He pursed his lips as he recorded the results in his notes. He shone a bright light into each eye. Obediently she followed his finger direction with her eyes as he moved round her head. Using a small rubber mallet he tested her reflexes. Finally he stuck a pin into various parts of her arm and leg while her eyes were closed.

'I will make an appointment for you to see a neurologist, Kate. It will be in the next few days and I will let you know when it is arranged.' He smiled and patted her shoulder reassuringly 'Probably nothing much to worry about but needs to be checked out.'

'Do you think it is serious?' Kate asked, her fingers twisting her wedding ring.

'As I said, Kate, probably nothing but we just need to get these symptoms checked out.'

The appointment with Mr Ian Marfane, Consultant Neurologist at the Institute of Neurology was made for the following week at the University College Hospital in central London. Frank and Lucy took her to the appointment while Jane minded the children. The examination seemed no different to the one she had with Dr Singleton, maybe a little more intense questioning and extra attention to the reflex testing, which took an age as did being prodded with a pin. Mr Marfane's grey head was bowed over his writing pad scribbling his case notes while Kate looked out of the window onto the tree-lined streets. 'I would like to get four of my students to examine you, Mrs Sinclair, do you have any objection?', Mr Marfane asked, peering over the top of his reading glasses.

Kate subjected herself again to probing and questioning by each of the nervous students. When the last student finished and had left the room, she asked if he knew what it was. Mr Marfane avoided her question saying that he would be reporting to her doctor. He stood up to show her to the door. It was late morning by the time Kate and her parents left the hospital and lunch became their priority. They found a small café nearby where they had a sandwich and coffee.

'I can't believe that these specialists are so arrogant, it's like your health has an identity of its own, only to be discussed amongst the medical world,' Kate said as she bit into her ham sandwich. 'God anybody would think I had a brain tumour with all the extra attention from his students.'

'Don't think like that, Kate, he probably does that with all his patients. Just try not to upset yourself,' Lucy said giving Frank an anxious look.

Frank was silent before putting his hand on Kate's

arm. 'Lets take this one day at a time.' He paused. 'A day at a time and don't let your imagination run riot.'

'Sorry just voicing fears that we probably all have.' Kate squeezed his hand.

Dr Singleton called her the next day and asked if she would be home in the afternoon for him to visit. Kate and Lucy sat together on the settee in the lounge as he told them the news. 'The results, Kate... I am afraid it is not good news.' He cleared his throat noisily. 'You have multiple sclerosis.'

'What is it, I mean what exactly...?' Kate's voice trembled. Lucy put her arm around Kate's shoulder.

Dr Singleton cleared his throat again. 'You've probably heard it more often called MS.' Kate and Lucy nodded. 'Basically it's a disease of the central nervous system. We don't know the cause or how this disease will affect an individual patient. What we do know is that you can expect to suffer ongoing episodes of your symptoms in varying degrees,' he frowned and shook his head. 'Sorry, Kate not the news any of us wanted.'

Kate's face was pale and her breathing shallow. 'I'm sorry doctor but I just don't believe it, I think I've had some sort of breakdown, you know the shock of Greg's death and trying to cope...'

The doctor's voice cut across her words. 'Kate, it is not easy to diagnose MS but your case is fairly clear-cut. The neurological damage that's been identified on your left side clearly indicates the progression of the disease. I am really sorry, Kate.'

Lucy shivered and pulled Kate closer. 'What's the

prognosis?'

'Lucy, that's not easy to predict. No two cases are ever the same but Kate does appear to have an aggressive form of the disease, so you should be prepared for Kate's ongoing disability.'

'And the treatment?' Lucy asked.

'Medication for pain and as much rest as possible. Diet is important, high protein and good quality leafy green vegetables. Kate, I can see this is too much for you to take in at the moment but I suggest you come into the surgery in a day or two where I can answer any questions and we can discuss your treatment,' he said.

A vivid slash of red patched Kate's cheeks. 'I want a second opinion please. Can I do that through you?', she asked.

'Of course, I'll organise one and get my secretary to notify you.'

Kate stared intently out into the garden while her mother went with the doctor to the front door. It was a warm afternoon and she could hear the comforting sound of her children's voices as they played out in the back garden. 'God, I need a cup of tea, I'm sure you must,' Lucy's voice sounded hollow like she was putting on a brave front.

'Well at least it's not a brain tumour,' Kate said. Lucy tutted.

'Sorry, I don't mean to be flippant. It's just that I will not buy into any label they want to give it. I truly believe it's my body's way of saying enough is enough.' Kate said.

'I'm sure you're right darling, the shock of Greg, and having just given birth, who knows whether you suffered post-natal depression as well. Sometimes doctors make mistakes, let's wait and see what the second opinion is,' said Lucy patting her hand.

'But I know I need help, I think I'd better give Aunty Joyce a quick call to see whether it's possible to get another live-in unmarried mum.'

Lucy was pouring the tea when Kate came back into the kitchen. 'Well?'

'She said it's finding the right person and at the right stage of their pregnancy,' but to leave it with her and she will do her utmost,' Kate said.

'Well in the meantime we will all just to have pitch in when you need us,' Lucy patted the bench beside her 'Come and have your tea, it'll work out, Try not to worry.'

The second opinion differed little from the first, except the female neurologist was more communicative than Mr Marfane.

'Not good news I am afraid, Mrs Sinclair. You would appear to have significant scarring and damage to your left foot and arm which, when taken with your previous history of episodes of paralysis indicates that it is fairly aggressive. If this continues you will more than likely be in a wheelchair within two or three years. Down the track brain surgery may be an option if you were suffering debilitating tremors.'

Kate sat rigid in her chair. Brain surgery, she thought, In a wheelchair. Christ.

Kate's vision blurred and she bent to pick up her

handbag. She thanked her and went into the reception to finalise the paperwork. Her mother waited anxiously to hear the news but Kate made light of it as they walked to the car. 'Same diagnosis as Marfane but at least she told me. She did not hide behind our GP to give me the news.'

'I'm so sorry darling, are you okay?' Lucy said

'I don't know what to think, Mummy. It's too much to deal with. I just hate labelling it a disease. You know, if I accept what they say about it being aggressive and being in a wheelchair and everything else, then what chance do I have. I don't want to believe it.'

Her arm was useless and ached continually and she now wore it bound in a sling made from one of her scarves. Her left leg was weak and when she was tired she dragged her foot.

Dr Singleton suggested that she join an MS support group who could help her through these first months as she came to terms with her condition. No, bloody way, she thought, I don't want to know.

She woke one morning in September to find the fight had gone out of her. The children were up and around but she could hardly open her eyes and floated between sleep and consciousness, her limbs heavy and unwilling to move. Cheryl phoned Lucy, fed the children their breakfast and waited for Lucy to arrive before leaving for work.

Lucy tucked the blankets in around her daughter and pulled the curtains. 'Sleep Kate, don't worry about anything.'

Kate slept until mid evening. Frank arrived and helped Lucy with the children's evening ritual of bath, tea and bedtime stories. They made Kate some dinner and washed up before they left. Kate sat in the lounge trying to concentrate on the television. Absent-mindedly she rubbed her arm with the warmth of the palm of her hand. While it did not relieve the ache her touch was comforting. With her good arm she pushed herself off the chair and switched off the television before dragging herself up the stairs to bed. Curling herself into a ball and with her arm wrapped around a pillow she slipped back into a deep welcome sleep. Lucy and Jane took it in turns to help for several hours each day with the children. Kate or Cheryl would give them breakfast and by mid morning Kate was exhausted, her head hammered and her arm and leg swung uselessly. She climbed gratefully back into bed to sleep intermittently until mid afternoon when she got up and took over the responsibility of the children for a couple of hours until Lucy returned to bathe, feed and bed the children.

The passing days and weeks blended into one but the gentle routine was a healing balm to Kate's aching body and by Christmas, she was feeling stronger and spent Christmas at her parent's home. Most of the day she lay rugged up at one end of the dark red velvet settee.

'Like Lady Muck,' Jane tucked blankets over Kate's legs. 'Let's hope it's more like Lady Luck next year.'

When the primroses, on an early February day, broke through the hard brown soil in Kate's front garden Jane had taken the children to play at her home. Kate was resting, lying on the settee in the lounge with the gas fire radiating warmth. She was listening to Rimsky-Korsakov's Scheherazade. She loved the piece, the dramatic opening bars and the aching purity of the solo violin before the echoing crescendos of violins filled her mind. She had played it non-stop during those first months following Greg's death.

She concentrated on every note, at one with every decibel, every distinct instrument. The record finished and the gramophone clicked off. The music still echoed in her mind. Her tension had left her and every part of her body was relaxed and sank heavily into the settee.

She became aware of her breathing; even her breath seemed to have a rhythm, a natural rhythm. She imagined her breath flowing into her body and out. The grey chatter of her mind had become quiet.

She opened her eyes. The orange tweed of the settee which she lay on, so dull before by comparison, was vibrant like a Buddhist monk's robes. Cha-ching, cha-ching her thoughts spun, tumbling to give her clarity

I see myself as powerless, but am I? I have been ruled by fear. My body is simply creating my fears of loss, being not enough, not capable to shoulder the burden of responsibility.

She examined her hands, flexing her fingers of her right hand. She tried to do the same with her left hand, it was sluggish but there was movement.

I said I refuse to buy into the disease and yet these past months I have focused on nothing else.

She sat up, slowly swinging her legs onto the floor. The normal blurring that jiggled and juxtaposed her vision had ceased and as she stood she saw the sharp clean images of her belongings. She stared at the furnishings and contents of the room their colours were fresher and shapes more compelling than she had ever remembered.

She walked over to the large bay window. The sky was grey and heavy as though it was going to snow and patchy sunlight was trying to find loopholes in the grey. As she watched random golden pin pricks of light pierced through the dense cloud.

I need to put my focus on something positive, like being creative. Yes that's it, a creative project. I need to create something new each day. It doesn't matter what I just need to focus on the planning and joy of creating.

Almost on cue the clouds parted and shafts of pale gold fanned out and reached up into the sky. She laughed; all I need now is the full symphony orchestra.

But Kate knew without doubt it was her epiphany, Epiphany with a capital E.

That first evening when she sat with her pencil poised ready to layout plans for her creative episode, she did not know where to start or what she would do. But as she concentrated she saw that it did not matter what the creative vehicle was, the power of the exercise was in her attention to the task. She realised she should not set the bar too high, as the pressure of trying to achieve would defeat the purpose of the joy of creating, purely for creating sake. As she sat on the settee that night her legs folded under her, she remembered that she had always wanted to go to the opera. She had heard of *La Boheme* and knew that it had a beautiful aria. The name of it escaped her but here was her opportunity to make this her first project. She began to write. The following day she took the children to the library to get out the boxed long playing records and the English translation of the libretto of Puccini's *La Boheme*. That evening with the children in bed, she took herself to the opera having made herself comfortable on the settee, a balloon glass of Remy Martin on the table beside her. She followed the English translation in the libretto as she listened to the first two acts. As the soaring tenor and soprano voices filled her living room, she warmed and sipped the golden elixir. When the hero Rodolfo sang *Che gelida manina* she cried but her tears were simply a joyous appreciation of the magnificence of the music. The following evening she lay listening cocooned on her lounge to the final two acts of the opera. As the curtain came down on Mimi's death, she was in awe at the majesty of the talent of Giacomo Puccini vowing to add the opera *Madam Butterfly* to her list.

Over the next couple weeks the library became the small family's second home, a treasure cave of inspiration. She now referred to her daily creative missions as her DCMs and felt it was serendipitous when her father told her it was the acronym for the Distinguished Conduct Medal. Three times a week in the children's section the assistant librarian sat perched on a low stool, her skirts billowing out around her as she read to her young audience. Giving time for Kate to gather craft books and magazines to augment her ideas. It was the library assistant who suggested she start a book club.

'Don't say it, everyone already has made digs about retirement homes, but although it makes my arm ache if I do too much, it's most therapeutic,' she said when Susan visited.

Kate clumsily manipulated the knitting needles tugging the cobalt blue wool round and through the stitch. As she and Susan chatted, the ribbed square of woollen promise grew little by little.

She had determined to make her numb arm work regularly taking off her sling to grapple with shiny steel knitting needles and odd coloured balls of wool to slowly knit neatly ribbed squares. Her progress so slow, that she reckoned one square equalled one DCM. One day when she had sufficient squares, she planned to blanket-stitch these together to make a patchwork blanket.

'Kate, I'm thinking of joining a meditation group and wondered if you'd like to go with me. They are into guided meditations, the more experienced ones of the group lead the meditation and gradually as we become more into it we can put up our hand to lead the session, I mean that is if we want too.' Susan said.

'Qu'est ce que c'est, guided meditations?' Kate said. She had been toying with setting herself a task of improving her school girl French upon discovering a French

phrase book on top of a carton of paper backs still waiting to be unpacked.

Sue grimaced 'Je le comprends, it's when someone
through their words, guides you into the desired trance-
like state. I suppose its more appealing to me rather than
repeating a mantra over and over.'

'I like the sound of it. That would make an excellent
DCM. So I'll come to the group with you but the deal
is you have to join my book club,' Kate said ,putting her
needles down and rubbing her arm.

'Sounds like a good deal, providing I don't have to
speak French, where do I sign?'

Chapter 9

• • • • • • • • • • •

The Power of the Mind

Eighteen-year-old Julia the youngest child of a publican from Somerset came to live with them at the beginning of March. She had been discharged from the WAAF when the camp doctor confirmed her pregnancy. Her stomach was massive and her back splayed. It's a big baby thought Kate knowing that she was at the beginning of her second trimester.

The children warmed to her as she was childlike herself, happily taking part in all their play. They squealed with laughter when she told them she was born in *zommerzet*. Julia's accent and expressions were infectious and Ally's lips mirrored Julia's excited exclamations of ooh aye. They gazed intently at her face, round as a full moon with wide set coffee brown eyes and thin black hair dragged back off her forehead. Her affectionate term 'my lover' became standard in the house. She was simple in the best sense of the word, without guile and as though she was seeing the world afresh with each experience.

Her lack of enthusiasm about domestic chores did not faze Kate. Julia's accord with the children meant she had more time to focus on her DCMs.

'They still believe I'm in the Air Force,' Julia answered when Kate asked about her parents as they ate lunch.

'How do you manage, what about your mail, don't they send it to the camp still?', asked Kate.

'No we don't write letters, I phone them once a week. I have to be careful what I say. They'd kill me if they knew I was pregnant,' Julia said taking a bite of a pickled gherkin. Her mood lifted as she ate. 'My boyfriend's a mechanic in the Air Force. He's lovely, beautiful blue eyes and blonde hair,' she said.

She took another pickled gherkin and whispered 'He was so cheeky you know, he kissed my hand and said how about it.' Julia beamed as she remembered. 'We met behind the hangar and did it that night.'

'Does he know about the baby?', asked Kate

'Well my lover, I told him, but he said it wasn't his, couldn't possibly be his. How could he after we did it?' She pouted, her fleshly lower lip almost touching her chin.

'What exactly do you mean? You did it?'

'Well you know he put his fingers into my private place,' she blushed brick red. Just then Ben fell and let out a huge wail, so the conversation was dropped.

—

The meditation group met every Tuesday at a small community hall less than a ten-minute drive from Kate's home. The plain brick hall with its flat roof was used for all kinds of community activities including a weekly playgroup that left the children's paintings, like cheery paper bunting, around the walls for all to enjoy. On winter nights when the electric bar heaters, hung high overhead, were needed you could smell the chalk dust. At the rear of the hall was a small kitchen, its yoke yellow painted cupboard doors were fastened with stout brass padlocks as though they may hold something more valuable than the assorted selection of cups, mugs and plates that had been donated by the community over the years. A large stainless steel urn was placed on one of the Formica benches with a small bowl under the tap to catch the drips.

The members of their group took it in turns to act as tea monitor. Their job was to fill the urn, assemble the cups and set out the corporate supplies of a range of teas, coffee and biscuits. While other early arrivals swept the floor, set up chairs in a semi circle and lit the calming lavender candles.

Like the hall's chinaware, the eight-fold group, five women and three men, were equally varied with a disparity of ages, creeds and social backgrounds but united by their imagination and joy of meditation. The meetings consisted of three meditations prefaced with a short warm-up relaxation exercise, before the first of the thirty-minute meditations. Each meditative journey included methods to relax the body and calm the mind before the leader guided them deeper into a state of peaceful consciousness.

A woman named Maggie joined them in the coffee break. She wore heavy silver earrings that dragged upon her earlobes and spoke with a soft Scottish brogue as she welcomed them to the group and asked if they were enjoying the evening.

'How do you still your mind? I found my mind chattered non-stop,' Kate asked.

'I find rather than trying to push the thoughts away I simply let them float on past. Think of yourself as the observer. But I agree it is hard at first you need to persevere and practice,' Maggie said.

Kate practiced at home sitting comfortably in a chair, closing her eyes and focusing on her breathing but found the thoughts of domesticity and vague feelings of unease chased demandingly through her mind. But one morning as she gazed out of the window and saw the blueness of the sky fringed with the grey green of the silver birch trees moving gently in the breeze, she closed her eyes and the imprint of nature gave her a peaceful starting point where she was able to let thoughts drift past like clouds in the sky.

She looked forward to each Tuesday meeting. Susan and Kate appreciated each member's leadership but both particularly loved the meditations presented by the large unconventional man called Bob. He had long hair, tied back into a ponytail with a black ribbon. Besides his ability to weave imaginative stories he was blessed with a similar sounding Cary Grant tone and pace to his voice. Soon Kate and Susan did not notice the studs in his ears or the contrast to all the short back and sides manicured men that they had known as he ferried them down to deep joyful places.

Early one August morning, before it was light, Julia, in her thirty-seventh week of her pregnancy, tapped on her door.

'Kate, I think I'm having my baby.'

Kate tumbled out of bed pulling on her dressing gown and sped down the stairs to find Julia sitting in the kitchen looking very frightened. Suddenly her eyes squeezed tight and she let out a low moan. Kate looked at the clock on the wall it read ten past five.'How long have you been having contractions?' Kate asked, as she put her arm around Julia's shoulders.

'I don't know but I can't abide them. I lay there for ever wondering if I just had stomach cramps.' Julia said.

'Well I think we had better start timing them, have you had any bleeding?'

Julia shook her head. Kate found a pad and pen and wrote down the time of the last contraction. Kate sat with her as they waited for the next one.

'It's coming again,' Julia's face crumpled and her knuckles turned white as she gripped the edge of the table, moaning loudly.

'Ten minutes between the two,' said Kate, 'we'll just keep monitoring them for the moment.' As the daylight filtered through the kitchen windows Julia had her last contraction and no more for the next half hour. Kate put the kettle on. She needed a cup of tea.'I think they might be Braxton Hicks contractions,' she said.

Julia looked puzzled.

'Bit like warm up labour pains but not the real thing, but to be on the safe side I think we will ring the doctor's surgery as soon as it opens.' At eight o'clock the pains started again, still ten minutes apart. At half past eight Kate rang the surgery and spoke to Dr Singleton who agreed to come round shortly. Just before nine they stopped.

Kate was preparing the children's breakfast when the doctor arrived. Kate took him into Julia's room. She listened out for his footsteps on the stairs as she fed the children but it wasn't until she was washing up the breakfast dishes that Dr Singleton came into the kitchen.

'I am truly perplexed Kate as I can't make any judgment on this. She has so much adipose tissue I can't feel the baby. She seems to have stopped the contractions at the moment. But to be on the safe side I will organise a bed for her at the maternity hospital and an ambulance to take her there this morning. Never seen anything like it, best left to the obstetricians to sort this one out,' he said.

At the hospital Julia was taken into a curtained cubicle to wait for the obstetrician. Kate visited the cafeteria and got herself a coffee in a cardboard cup.

In the waiting room she picked up a copy of the *Good Housekeeping* magazine. As a bride this magazine was her bible. It gave her information on home décor, fashion and food. One of the articles that she especially liked was the monthly beauty and fashion makeover. She harboured a secret fantasy of being chosen to be one of the capable and competent career women who got a new hair style, make up and a working wardrobe, with captions under their transformation pictures like office smart, evening glamour and bandbox fresh. The label bandbox fresh caught her imagination. She had researched the origins of the expression and found it came from Tudor times when the starched Elizabethan neck ruffles called bands were stored in custom-made boxes now it had evolved to simply mean stylish and well groomed.

Kate scrutinised the woman of the month's makeover featuring a blonde matronly looking librarian. But the makeover images showed her to be much more glamorous. Her hair softly curled, chic in her burgundy woollen pant suit with a polka dot silk scarf as she took her children to school and for a night out on the town she wore an alluring black velvet evening gown with pearls. She smiled as she read the caption: *Starry night bandbox fresh.*

A nurse poked her head round the door of the waiting room. 'Mrs Sinclair?' she queried. Kate closed the magazine. 'Dr Eccles would like to see you.' She led the way through the warren of green corridors to the obstetrician's office.

Dr Eccles was a man in his forties with a thick head of sandy brown hair. He stood and pumped her hand.

'Thank you for your patience, Mrs Sinclair, your charge Julia Digby is an interesting case. I hasten to add she is fine. Do not be concerned. She has had a false pregnancy, the medical term is pseudocyesis.'

'A false pregnancy?' Kate's hands rose and emphasized

her disbelief as she talked. 'No. How can it be? After all her pregnancy was confirmed by a RAAF doctor and she was even discharged from the WAAF because of it. I can't believe it she looked and showed every sign of being pregnant.'

Dr Eccles, ran his hands through his hair and nodded rapidly, 'Yes quite remarkable I agree. The symptoms of pseudocyesis mirror the symptoms of pregnancy and are hard to distinguish and it fools a lot of health professionals, especially when returning a positive pregnancy test. She tells me she had morning sickness, cessation of menstruation, tender breasts, cravings and of course the indisputable weight gain.'

'Why wasn't this picked up in her pre natal visits?'

'I'm sure it would have been if we had access to the latest scanning invention that is being developed in America but...'

'But she had contractions, I mean to all intents and purposes, real contractions.'

'Yes,' Dr Eccles voice rose in excitement. 'Yes, that's really interesting as only one percent of woman who have a phantom pregnancy actually experience labour. You see this woman believes that she is pregnant, well was and with this condition will display all the characteristics of pregnancy and as we have now seen, even going into labour.'

'Is this condition rare?' Kate asked.

'Yes it's rare today, but pseudocyesis has been reported as far back as 300 BC in fact it was widely believed that Mary Tudor, Queen of England, in the sixteenth century experienced more than one of these phantom pregnancies.'

'What causes it?', she asked.

'We're not sure. There are a few theories around that seem to make sense, such as a woman's intense desire to become pregnant or conversely an intense fear of becoming pregnant, but the general thought is that emotional conflicts or depression may be a contributor. We will keep her in to observe her over the next couple of days and get a psychotherapist to speak to her. If he is satisfied we will let her go home when we think she is fit,' Dr Eccles concluded.

Julia had been taken to a one-bed ward after her examination. She was sitting up in bed when Kate, carrying a box of chocolates, came through the door of her room.

'How do you feel Julia? Are you okay?'

Julia blinked back at her.

'The doctor said I had a false pregnancy and there is no baby. But I can't understand it, the doctor at the camp said my pregnancy test was positive.'

Kate explained what Dr Eccles had told her. Julia's eyes widened as she began to understand.

'Well that's a relief, I don't have to give my baby away, cause there is no baby.'

Kate asked her directly 'Tell me Julia, what did happen behind the hangar shed that night?'

'I told you what he did.'

Kate pressed again. 'Is that all he did, nothing more?'

'Listen, my lover, I've told you what he did, isn't that enough?' Julia gave a sigh and rustled through the top layer of her chocolates taking a bite out of a caramel before exasperatedly returning it, half eaten, back onto the tray.

'No, my lover, it is not enough to get you pregnant, but it's been a busy day how about we talk about it tomorrow?' Kate replied.

Jane's mouth opened and closed several times like a goldfish when Kate told her.

'I can't believe this I've never heard of a phantom pregnancy. But not only was it a false pregnancy but it was a virgin false pregnancy.'

'I know, it's bloody amazing, I mean she had the whole kit and caboodle ate pickles non stop, could feel the baby's movements and Jane I swear she was in labour.'

'You would never believe it in a month of Sundays.' Jane replied.

'Just shows you what the power of the mind can do.' Kate said as she bundled the children into the car.

Julia phoned from Somerset to tell Kate she was working as a barmaid at her parent's pub and walking out with a nice young man, this one had brown eyes and was the son of a local farmer and no she hadn't done it yet. Kate smiled as she cradled the phone to her ear.

'You make sure, my lover, that you use a rubber if you do,' she said before ringing off.

With the passing months Kate's energy was returning, the children still had a daytime sleep when she could indulge her own creative pursuits. Each day was an adventure whether she was repainting the children's nursery furniture, teaching the children to make paper-mâché puppets or creating floral arrangements using greenery and flowers from the garden. As she became more daring with her challenges she even chanced her hand at recovering her dining chairs with pleasing results. The old covers of the second hand walnut dining chairs had faded and were starting to fray, now they shone with new green and cream Regency striped sateen covers. Her promise to listen to Puccini's *Madam Butterfly* made six months earlier was fulfilled one September evening. It was still light as the soprano's voice pure and haunting sang the aria *One Fine Day*.

Closely following the libretto Kate spoke the words her mouth rounding and flexing effortlessly with each consonant and vowel.

One fine day we'll notice, a thread of smoke arising on the sea.

With each phrase she realised her mouth, tongue, and larynx had been working as one. She looked down at her arm, it rarely ached and she had no need of the sling.

Christmas 1966 erupted in the Taylor household. For the first time since Greg's death they held the traditional morning cocktail party. Family, friends and neighbours sipped Frank's traditional Pimm's served in tall glasses and topped with a sprig of mint and cucumber while nibbling on canapés of Scottish smoked salmon.

Later when the last of the cocktail party guests left Cheryl and John washed and dried the glasses and dishes while Ian, hands encased in padded oven mitts took the heavy bird out of the oven. The fragrance of roasted turkey, thyme and sage stuffing billowed through the house. Carefully he lifted the twenty-pound bird onto the carving board. Jane covered it loosely with clean tea towels. The roast vegetables still needed a good half hour of cooking and the oven was turned up to make sure they crisped and browned. Jane checked the water levels under the steaming Christmas pudding and Lucy made the gravy. Kate set about laying the table. First the table blanket and then the white linen cloth edged with lace, starched and ironed to within an inch of its threads. With precision she set out the silver cutlery, napkins, crystal and her homemade Christmas crackers for the children and a holly table centre piece.

As the turkey was bought to the table for Frank to carve, she lit the candles and turned off the overhead light. The stout alter candles spilled random soft splashes of light around the table. As the last bite of pudding and mince pies were eaten Frank stood and raised his glass. Looking at Kate he said 'To absent friends, to Greg.'

'To Greg,' Kate responded softly, her voice lost in the swell of enthusiastic toasting.

The three glasses of Pimms and the frequently topped up glass of vintage port, had made Lucy relaxed and talkative.

'You see, Cheryl, we had been into the city, to check out the wedding caterers at one of their functions. Greg was driving us home and as usual he was taking, yet another,' she lifted her pencilled eyebrows, 'shortcut through the back streets when the car made a coughing noise. Oh dear, he says I think we've run out of petrol.' She shook her head and pursed her lips. 'Again?, I asked him. He was always running out of petrol.'

'You're right I'd like a pound for every time he ran out of petrol in the five years I knew him.' Cheryl said.

'Exactly, you know what I'm talking about. Well the car spluttered to a stop outside a very dark and bleak graveyard in what I would only describe as an unsavoury neighbourhood.'

'Unsavoury, as in tasteless?' said Jane laughing.

'Shush, Jane, they all know that I mean disreputable, anyway where was I?'

Lucy took another sip of port.

'Greg went off to find a petrol station leaving Kate and I in the car. No street lights, just the light of the moon. You can imagine how frightening it was. Suddenly through the gloom we could see a figure of a man coming out of the graveyard and shuffling slowly towards the car.'

She paused and placed her hands dramatically around her throat. 'We were terrified.'

'We locked all the doors and tried to find something to defend ourselves but all Greg had in the car was a book of maps so we just clung to each other. Suddenly he rapped on the window and yelled whiskey, give me whiskey. Must have been the town drunk. It was such a relief when he took off weaving his way down the road.'

Cheryl and John clapped.

'No applause yet I haven't finished,' Lucy said taking another slurp of port. 'As you can imagine I gave Greg the rounds of the kitchen when he returned with the petrol can. So the following day he turned up on my doorstep to apologise and gave me this plant.'

She took the long green spiky plant from the sideboard so all could see. 'When I asked him the name of the plant, he gave me a cheeky smile and told me it was called Mother-in-law's Tongue.'

As the laughter eased Frank said with a broad smile 'Well that just about sums him up doesn't it?'

This was the first time Lucy had told the story since his death. Her retelling was not tinged with muted voice and cautious phrase that people often did when speaking of some one who had died. The story liberated all at the table and gave them license to speak of him irreverently and honestly.

In the new year Cheryl and John announced that they were breaking up. John was going home to New Zealand. Neither of them would talk of the end of their relationship except to say that they both felt that it was the time to go their separate ways and that they would always be friends.

An old friend persuaded Cheryl that she had a future managing the front of house for his new restaurant in Cornwall. She gave the same response to all those that probed about her move to Cornwall. 'Its simple living in Cornwall and being a maitre d' of a fancy restaurant, beats the heck out of being a veterinary assistant in the 'burbs.'

To Kate she confided, 'John is lovely but it never was going to go anywhere. I'm desperate to get away, start afresh.'

'I'll miss you Cheryl,' but Kate knew it was the right time for them both to lead their own lives.

One evening after the children were asleep she got round to a project she had been putting off ever since she had moved houses. She intended to create an album for the children as a keepsake of their father. In the lounge she opened the cardboard box that had been skulking in the back of the hall cupboard. Memories tumbled out. Black and white pictures of Greg at his graduation wearing his gown and mortar board, strips of photo booth pictures with both of them giggling, sepia pictures of him as a young boy in scout uniform around a campfire. Slides in full colour taken on their honeymoon one of them wearing towelling robes snuggling together on their balcony in Estoril and a shot taken on a Sydney harbour beach both looking tanned and happy. She took a deep breath and continued collating them putting to one side those that would go into the album and slides that needed to be made into photographs. It was painful work and she decided that it would take more than one night to go through them all. She ran her finger over a shot of them taken when they got engaged, his smile was expansive and she kissed the tip of her finger and gently touched his mouth.

In April 1967 Kate asked Dr Singleton to set up an early morning appointment with Mr Marfane the following week. She had been clear of all of her debilitating symptoms for six months.

She had to stand in the tube in the early morning rush hour, hanging on to the roof strap by her arm and by the time she got to Euston Square station her arm was trembling. She was apprehensive as she walked from the station to the hospital.

Mr Marfane was his thorough self and his examination of her took the best part of an hour. Each tap of his rubber mallet and each pinprick of needle was more intense than the previous examination. When he had exhausted all of his testing he said 'Thank you Mrs Sinclair, your doctor will contact you with the results of my consultation.'

'Mr Marfane, I would like you to tell me what you found.'

The neurologist didn't respond instead he pushed his chair back from his desk and was about to show her the door. She did not get up.

'Mr Marfane I'm not leaving until you give me the results.'

He frowned. 'Very well Mrs Sinclair, if you insist. I can find no trace of your previous symptoms and I can only conclude that you are in remission. However, I will send a full report to your GP.'

The rain that had threatened earlier in the morning had gone. She half skipped and walked to Russell Square tube station, pausing on the way to ring her mother from a call box. She simply told Lucy that the specialist had said emphatically that he could find no trace of her previous symptoms. She did not add the medical caveat of assuming she was in remission. Lucy was over the moon.

'Sweetheart that is the best news, I will phone Daddy and your sister now to let them know. The children are fine and having a great time. Have a wonderful lunch. See you this evening.'

Smiling she stepped out of the phone box and a passer-by said 'Good to see someone has something to smile about.'

'You are so right,' said Kate over her shoulder as she disappeared into the tube station. She caught the train to Knightsbridge Station, just a short walk to Harrods where she was meeting Prue for lunch.

'A celebration for my return to health and for your return to Old Blighty. I can't believe you're home.', Kate said as she ordered a bottle of bubbly.

'Darling, thank God you're better, I reckon those dry old in-laws had a lot to answer for,' Prue's voice bounced around the small restaurant.

The waiter popped the cork and poured the fizzy liquid into champagne coupes.

Prue raised her glass 'Good health.'

'Amen to that and welcome home,' Kate said.

'Did you ever hear from Fred?' Prue asked. Kate shook her head.

'No sadly, he really was a friend as well as the best lover I've known. What about Leo?'

'You're joking aren't you but I did catch up with Paul, you know the quantity surveyor from Melbourne, while I was backpacking around Australia, it would never have come to anything, he was a bit too conservative for me but nice man.'

Prue told her how she and a couple of English friends had hired a yacht and spent a couple of months sailing around Great Barrier Reef and exploring the Whitsunday Islands.

'Everyday we snorkeled. The ocean was turquoise and the colour of the coral and the millions and millions of reef fish it was absolutely amazing, darling.'

'I've always wanted to do that but we never got that far north,' Kate said.

'Maybe one day you will,' she leaned forward. 'But let's get to the meat and potatoes. Back in Sydney I met a man, a publisher with lots of money. Absolutely gorgeous by the way, and we got very close. We moved in together and all was perfect for a few weeks until he started staying out all night. Said he was working, complete bollocks of course. It got very nasty as it turned out he was also screwing the girl who lived in the apartment next door. Really, darling, he was an absolute prick.'

Champagne sprayed from Kate's mouth as she laughed.

'We must be soul sisters as I recently had one of those.'

Prue listened intently as Kate told her about Jack and

when she came to the punch line, shagging two bar-maids, all Prue could say was 'What a prick, what an ab-solute prick.'

The two women raised their glasses again.

'To us,' they whispered and winked at each other.

They hugged and parted at the door of Harrods. Prue to catch the train back to her home in Gloucestershire and Kate the tube to Essex.

Chapter 10

● ● ● ● ● ● ● ● ● ● ●

Self-Mastery

The wind blew Kate's hair across her face. She brushed it back with her hand, stirring a distant memory of lying on a beach in Australia. Greg had smoothed her windswept hair, framing her face before he kissed her tenderly on the lips. He kissed her cheeks, her eyelids and forehead, his kisses soft and undemanding. Instantly his face came alive in her mind. For a while now she had found it hard to conjure up his face and it had saddened her that she could not remember it at will. The framed black and white images of him that she carried with her offered no insight into the complexity of him.

She recalled the way he had smiled at her as he turned to watch her progress down the aisle on her father's arm on their wedding day. Her memory leapt to his love of spoonerisms and the predictability of him saying that's a trucking fig buck, each time they drove past a truck or a lorry. His unpredictable gifts—the lurid pink baby doll pyjama set that had saved her in Nairobi, the blue mini car sitting in the garage when at long last, with his coaching, she passed her driving test and her prized green suede coat that he had bought her on their honeymoon.

It was the last day of a week-long holiday in Sussex. The small cottage in West Wittering had two small bedrooms with sash windows that rattled in the wind, a pink tiled bathroom and sitting room come kitchen with a small overgrown garden. It was leanly furnished but that didn't matter as the weather had been unseasonably good for May and she and the children had managed to spend most days on the beach.

Ally waved her spade at her mother before getting down to the business of filling her bucket with sand. Kate had found the turreted bucket in the local corner shop. Ben shovelled and whacked the upturned bucket with his spade and Ally carefully lifted it up leaving a circle of almost perfect turrets. She watched as they played wondering how two children from the same parents could be so different. 'You can't pull the wool over that one's eyes,' her father once said as Ally reasoned, being a year older, that she need not go to bed at the same time as Ben. Ben was the calmer child, more content with his own company leaving the battles to his sister.

'Mummy, Mummy,' Ally called, 'come and build a sandcastle with us.'

They piled the mound of sand high and flat so that they could place the final glory of the turreted sand pie on top.

Can't have a sandcastle without a moat,' said Kate as she took Ally's spade and dug a deep trench around the impressive mound of sand with its turreted crown.

Ben tugged at her hand, pulling her to the water's edge, insisting that they fill the moat with water. They filled bucket upon bucket full to pour in the neatly dug out trench around their sandcastle. No sooner had they spilled the water into the moat, the sand sucked it up.

'Never ending job, bit like you two,' she said to them.

Ally, her fine fair hair blowing across her face, looked up at her with her customary what do you mean expression. Kate laughed and scooped the pair of them up in her arms

In the local fish and chip shop in the village she considered the large menu above the counter. 'Cod and chips I think, kids.'

Ben did a little jig, 'Fish and chips, yes,' he said. The shop owner handed him a chip hot from the fryer and Ben tossed it from hand to hand before blowing on it noisily.

'Won't be long love,' the man said to Kate. A recording of The Temptations belting out *My Girl* was playing on the radio and Kate immediately thought of Jack. It had been over two years since the Jack episode and she rarely thought about him but today the memories of his bizarre behaviour made her smile. Tom had phoned to ask her out a few weeks after she said sayonara to Jack and she remembered how good she had felt when she said—no thanks I'm washing my hair tonight.

The seven days had rolled into one joyful meditation of ocean, sandcastles, play, ice cream, fish and chip meals and sunshine. They left early on the Sunday. Kate closed the front door and replaced the key under the flowerpot on the front step. She drove the car slowly through the narrow lane of hawthorn hedgerows abundant with delicate white blossoms before reaching the main road for the homeward journey.

Kate rehearsed her guided meditation each day. She remembered Maggie's advice and visualised each step she would take them on, seeing where she needed to pause and allowing them to imagine the scene fully before starting again on the journey. She decided to keep it fairly simple making use of symbols to take them on their forest journey to the valley below. She had recorded Chopin's *Concerto No. 1 Romance-Larghetto* to play in the background.

'It's so cliché, I've used all of the predictable symbols', she said to Susan on the way to the meeting, 'but it's a start.'

Kate was a little nervous as she commenced with the introduction of directing the group into a comfortable relaxed state focusing on the breath. As she closed her eyes and spoke her visualisation to them, the shapes and colours of the meditation flowed easily. Her voice like silk as she took them down the forest path to the clearing of purple flowers in the centre a crystal temple. Gently easing their passage into a deeper state. Gradually she bought them back to wakefulness and the group stood and stretched, they applauded quietly before in turn they congratulated and embraced her. Susan was the last to reach her.

'It was beautiful, I loved it,' she said.

⌐———⌐

Kate had signed up to do a one-day Self Mastery workshop with Bob and Maggie. She looked up the directions in the A to Z street map and mapped out her route to Hadonstone a few suburbs away. It was a smooth run through and she found the Church of England parish hall easily. The hall had been designed in an arts and crafts style that was popular in the early 1900s. The smell of beeswax and coffee filled the small hall, a glory of hand hewn timber craftsmanship and art deco stained glass windows.

Maggie and Bob were already there and greeted her with a hug. Bob poured her a coffee from one of the large plunger jugs and topped it up with milk. She looked around and saw that the hall was already set up with chairs arranged in a 'u' shape around a lectern. A blackboard and easel stood to one side. Behind the easel she could see a stained glass window, the plain glass offset with patterns of bold swirls and scrolls of apple green and purple. On the blackboard was the chalked quote:

> *Knowing others is intelligence; knowing yourself is*
> *true wisdom. Mastering others is strength;*
> *mastering yourself is true power*
> *Lao-tzu (6th century Chinese philosopher)*

As they chatted a tall well postured man who looked to be in his mid to late fifties approached them. Wearing faded jeans and a black leather jacket over a crumpled grey shirt his white hair stood in irregular tufts where it had defied the comb. He greeted Maggie and Bob like old friends.

'This is Kate Sinclair, one of the members of our meditation group. Kate, Liam Russell, our course facilitator today.' Maggie said.

He clasped both his hands round hers, breaking into a broad smile as his dark blue, almost purple eyes met hers. 'It's good to meet you Kate. I hope you enjoy the day.'

Someone began clapping and calling them to be seated.

'Better we don't sit together Kate, you will get more out of it seated next to someone you don't know,' Maggie said as the three separated around the horseshoe of chairs.

Liam stood to one side of the lectern as he welcomed them and ran through the logistics of the day, timing of morning tea, lunch and that he hoped to bring the day to a conclusion at four. He told them that notes would be given out at the end of the day.

'If you like to take notes yourself, feel free but try not to get too bogged down in the note taking, better you are present, in the moment.' While there was an element of raspiness to Liam's voice, each intonation generated a tread of authority.

A pen clattered to the floor and Liam smiled sympathetically as a woman bent to retrieve it.

'Now I would like you to close your eyes for a second and make a choice about what you would like to take away from the day.'

A woman wearing a brightly coloured caftan with her hair pulled tight off her face put up her hand.

'But how do we know what we want to take away, when we are here to learn?'

'Good question,' said Liam his eyes searching for the woman's name badge pinned to the shoulder of her dress. 'But presumably Nola you came today for a reason, something resonated with you.'

The woman nodded in agreement as Liam continued. 'And that may be the choice that you may want to make.'

Kate closed her eyes. I hate ambiguity, she thought. But I'm here to learn so what is it I want to get out of today? It came easily—a growing awareness of who I am. She let out a deep breath and opened her eyes.

'Self-mastery in one day, you may say is an overly ambitious proposition and of course you would be right but the decision and acquiring the tools to master yourself can easily be achieved in a day. Self-mastery is about living the life you were meant to live rather than one formed by patterns of negative beliefs formed from the cradle and carried through to adulthood. Self-mastery is understanding that your thoughts and emotions create your reality.'

Kate's eyes were drawn to the glass window beyond, escaping into the sweeping colour and its beauty. She felt Liam's eyes upon her and she turned her attention back to him.

'Let me repeat that. Your thoughts and emotions create your reality. I see some of you struggling with this but as the day progresses I think this premise will make sense to you.' Liam paused and looked around the room to the upturned faces.

'It takes courage to change your life, to be accountable to your true nature because the act of change demands a great deal. My background is osteopathy. I have been a practitioner for thirty plus years. An osteopath's training and philosophy centres on viewing the body in a holistic manner, as a self-contained, self-healing unit. As a young man I suffered substantial injuries in a car crash that left me hospitalised for the best part of eight weeks. It was while I was immobilised, my body encased in plaster, that I really came face to face with my core values as an osteopathic practitioner. It was a seminal moment. I made a decision to use all of my senses to heal myself. Meditation had always been a daily habit but now I added self-hypnosis, self-visualisation and I began to read all that I could find on the power of the mind.'

Kate gazed intensely at Liam; previously his message had been academic, mere words that she tried to dwell upon like a child learning poetry at school. Now his language connected at a deeper level, an easier level where she did not have to direct her concentration to follow what was being said, instead she knew quintessentially what he was saying.

'Where conventional medicine had predicted that my recovery would take at least four months I was back doing my normal working week in just under two months. It was through this exploration and reading that I really began to understand the power of consciousness.'

Kate stared at Liam, thoughts and emotions create our reality, have I not lived it myself, have I not seen it at work in Julia she reflected. Liam stopped and took a sip of water from the glass on the table beside him.

'But before we start going into this more deeply if you want to change your life, there is one fundamental decision that you have to make. This decision is that there has to be a structural change in the way you live your life. Instead of living your life by reacting to factors outside of yourself, you have to be guided by whom you truly are, to know your own heart. Finding your passion. Living from here,' Liam paused and pressed his hand to his heart. 'Living from your heart rather than living your life reacting to the outer world.'

Kate doodled on her pad, sketching a heart with an arrow through it and underneath the word passion with a run of fiercely drawn question marks. It was as though Liam sensed her anxiety. 'Be assured that between us all we will find each and everyone's innermost holy grail, your compass to living your life joyfully and fruitfully.'

'First take out your pens and paper and I want you to consider what your unique talents and gifts are.'

Nola's hand shot up. 'I am not sure I understand,' she said.

Liam smiled at her. 'What things you are good at, that you love and come easy to you? What are you passionate about? What do you love Nola?'

Kate smiled grateful to Nola for asking for clarification. She got out her pad and pen and started to write but wondered if making a good Coq au Vin constituted a unique talent. The list looked fairly uninspiring when she completed it. My children. Good cook—especially Coq au Vin! Loved being an air hostess. Love travel. Love learning. Appreciating nature—a beautiful garden, mountain views or the ocean. Love colour. Dreaming / planning and working on my creative projects. Meditating.

Liam had started talking about how the universe is created in the mind but Kate's mind was elsewhere. She was grateful that she didn't have to share her jottings with anyone as she considered her list disappointing in its brevity and scope. Liam seemed to have an uncanny knack of knowing when Kate was not attentive and he paused smiling down at her.

'The seventh century Indian philosopher Shankaracharya said whatever a person's mind dwells on intensely and with firm resolve, that is exactly what he becomes,'

He touched his forehead. 'So what I'm saying is nothing new. Buddha said *All that I am is the result of all that I have thought.* More recently Edgar Cayce the American physic said *The spirit is life, the mind the builder and the physical is the result.* They all taught whatever thoughts we actively give energy to we create'.

Liam took the chalk and wrote on the board as he spoke.

The mind is key to all creations.

'Time I think for a tea break, twenty minutes should pull us up. After that we are going to give our intuition an airing as we read others beliefs and passions.'

At the break, she and Bob went outside to the freshness of the day; it was a little overcast but the temperature was warm. Kate was pleased to be out in the fresh air. 'A lot to take in,' she said.

Bob nodded. 'How do you find it so far?'

'It made sense to me, especially when he talked about his recovery from the accident. I know that focus on my creative projects have changed my life. But I was disappointed when I wrote down my list of unique talents. They were pretty pathetic,' she paused looking for the right word. 'Pretty pedestrian, I was hoping that I might get a flash of insight that I was the next Picasso or Jane Austen.'

Bob laughed. 'Ah the ego is never satisfied. I think it was the Indian guru Sai Baba who said, *When you try something above your capacity that is conceit. When you do something less than your capacity that is theft.*'

Kate's face pinched in exasperation. 'Bob, I have no idea why you have to talk in mystic riddles why can't you just say what you bloody mean in plain language?'

'Ah, but it makes you think,' he said with a wink.

Maggie joined them at that moment slipping her arm through Bob's. A classic red head, her pale ginger brows and lashes made her green eyes more compelling in the span of milky skin. There was a perceptible intimacy about the way she took his arm and Kate understood in that instant that they were lovers.

'Are you enjoying it?' Maggie asked, Kate nodded.

'We always get so much out of Liam's workshops,' Maggie said.

'I have always believed that the mind's focus or energy creates our reality or destiny, whatever you like to call it,' Bob said.

'Yes I certainly get that focusing on what I love is the way to outsmart the tired old negative tape that runs in my head.'

Bob nodded 'Yes that's true. But Kate you also need to be aware that your beliefs about being good enough and I sense, self worth are a constant companion and will always, with the right trigger, shadow your reaction to the outside world. You need to make choices to focus on what gives you joy and allow the negative bits to float on by, like we do in meditating.'

Bob's voice was a comforting link as Kate stared at the cars rolling past on the road below them.

'Kate, simply focus on your heart let it lead you to your happiness. For me I love building things and so I am at my most productive and creative when I have a trowel and tray of mortar in my hand or finding rocks to craft a dry stonewall.'

The traffic was busier now that it was later in the morning. She imagined the Dads driving their children to sports meetings and as her thoughts took shape she felt jealous and rejected. Jealous of what they had, imperfect because she did not have the 2.5 family life. She felt self-pity rise in the back of her throat. Her bitterness at Greg's death enveloped her for a moment, but as quickly as it came she saw clearly that this was what Liam and Bob meant when they talked of living life through reacting to the world outside. She understood that she was perpetuating a story that reflected her own warped rules of life. Feeding into her fears about being alone and how children without a father to guide them and show them the ways of the world, would always be lacking. But her thoughts were an observation rather than a bone to take down on the mat and chew, as she would have done before.

After morning tea, the quote on the blackboard read.

The only real valuable thing is intuition.

Albert Einstein

She found that she was more capable than she had ever imagined when called upon to simply trust her intuition working in groups with people she did not know.

To her amazement people could, without knowing anything of another, offer a snapshot of who they were by simply trusting their intuition. Each of them somehow blessed with compassionate words to open sealed and scarred wounds and allow the tears to fall without trying to soothe them. No sooner than the tears were wiped away, they intuited a vision of each person's magnificence and were rewarded as the person joyfully blossomed.

Kate loved this level of connection with people and thought wouldn't it be wonderful if I could have this deep and honest relationship with everyone instead of being who I think, they think, I should be.

True to his word Liam finished on the dot of four and handed out the notes of the day. The group lingered not wanting the day to finish, going round and hugging each other in turn before they left.

Frank and Lucy had taken the children fishing for the

day. Ally and Ben were in the playroom looking intently into their jam jars where a few sticklebacks swam desolately around and around. When Kate walked in they screamed with excitement both tripping on their words trying to tell her how they had caught them with their nets. Two new white nets on bamboo poles stood proudly by the back door.

They had fish for dinner, fat, fresh perch that Frank had caught. As they ate Kate tried to explain the day's workshop to her parents.

'Not quite sure about that love,' Frank said shaking his head.

Lucy's face puckered. 'It sounds to me like this man has found an easy way to take money from the gullible. It's nonsense, Kate. Where was he during the war, I would like to know. I can tell you that my mind certainly did not dream up being bombed out of two homes.'

Frank reached across the table and patted Lucy's hand.

Kate stood up and cleared the plates away from the table. 'I don't have the answers Mummy, but for me it makes sense.'

I shouldn't have told them, she thought, as she washed the dishes. I should've known Mummy would have found it threatening. She hates considering any thing different. Since the war security has been everything. To her it's all about a roof over her head, her position in the pecking rung of the bloody class system, the way she and her home look and her family's wellbeing, anything else is not only superfluous but also could threaten the very fabric of who she believes she is. When Kate got into bed that night she remembered childhood picnics in detail sitting by the river or on the beach somewhere in East Anglia where Frank and Lucy had fished and where she and Jane had either searched for tiddlers in the shallows or hung from jetties close to the water to catch small crabs on a hand line. She knew that her parents would never understand her need to look beyond the formative tissue of the family and she knew that whatever her quest their love for her would remain solid. She was their daughter and they were her parents.

She thought how they had suffered during their lives, living through two world wars, coping with the deaths of family and friends and the loss of everything they owned. But how, despite all of this, they had a joy and generous enthusiasm for life. She thought once more of the fishing nets by the back door and Ally and Ben's faces pink from the fresh air of the day out and smiles so wide. She clasped her hands tightly together in supplication and closed her eyes.

'Thank you God, Universe or whatever for my parents, I am truly grateful.' She said softly.

How was the workshop, was it just as challenging as we imagined?', asked Susan when she rang.

'Yes totally challenging. But it was a remarkable day. I took notes; I'll give them to you tomorrow. You'll have to do it you'd love it.'

'I'm keen to do it and would love to read up about it first. But the real reason I rang is to invite you to dinner on Saturday evening. You think Jane or Lucy would baby sit?', she asked.

'That is great thank you, can I confirm?'

'Oh do try and make it, we have one of Charles' clients coming, a lovely man and I want you to meet him.'

Jane was enthusiastic when she called. 'Of course we can have the kids. Kate, you sound a little unsure, what's the problem?'

'Just a little anxious not sure I want to meet a new man.'

'Stop thinking like that, it's just a dinner party. Go and enjoy yourself. You know it'll be a good night as both of them are great cooks.'

Susan was waiting at the front door with a glass of wine as Kate paid the taxi driver.

'Eminently sensible catching a taxi,' she said as she took her coat and led her into the lounge.

'Well, drinking and driving is not something I do well, especially with Charles' generous top ups of my wine glass,' she said kissing Charles cheek.

'Just being a good host Kate,' Charles said. 'Let me introduce you to Jim Benson.'

His hand was warm to the touch when they were introduced. It was difficult trying to put an age on him, he could have been anywhere between mid thirties and early forties. Of medium height, he was a man with an air of correctness from his smoothly shaved face, tweed jacket worn over a cream viyella shirt, a red paisley tie, oatmeal coloured slacks to the mirror shine on the toecaps of his shoes. His voice was pleasant and confident as he talked to them about his base in Geneva.

Charles handed Jim a glass of 1961 Burgundy from Bordeaux. Holding the glass comfortably with his thumb and forefinger, he gently rotated it before putting his nose deep into the glass and breathing deeply the complexity of the wine. He spoke knowledgeably about the vintage and region to Charles. Susan winked at Kate as she offered her a dish of spiced nuts.

'Spiced nuts, Kate? Do try, they have a delicious hint of curry powder from Bengal, or is it Bombay?'

Kate laughed and began to relax.

'Behave,' she said softly.

'Melon boats with prosciutto but lets give it it's proper Italian name—Prosciutto e Melone,' Charles said in his best Italian accent as he placed the entrée plates on the table. They ate in comparative silence, with the odd murmur of praise.

'Try the black pepper with it. It seems to bring out the flavour more,' said Susan.

'Just delicious,' said Kate.

'Truly delicious.' Jim said and they smiled shyly at each other across the table. His eyes, she noticed were brown, not velvet brown that you could drown in but a safe tawny brown. He must smile often, she thought, already fine creases marked the skin around his eyes.

Susan and Charles cleared the plates and went into the kitchen to assemble the main course. After filling her wine glass Jim asked politely about her trip to Australia.

'Australia's wonderful. When Greg was alive we travelled through the outback and up to Fraser Island in Queensland. It's remarkable really, so wild and the colours of the landscape are unbelievable. This time I stayed in Sydney with my in-laws so that the children could meet their grandparents. That was hard, mixing three generations and really two different family cultures so it was good to be home.' Kate paused. 'Enough about me what about you?'

Jim took another sip of his wine. 'I have an engineering business based in Geneva and am divorced and have no children.'

'I'm sorry I didn't mean it to sound so direct,' she said.

'No, I didn't take it that way. But it only seemed fair, I already knew a fair bit about you from Charles. But it's all good we were too young and not ready for commitment.' He took a deep breath. 'We're great friends now and it works well. I think sometimes you have to make mistakes to grow.'

At first he had seemed a formal, conservative man but now Kate found him more human. He is a nice man she thought as Charles carried in the crown roast on a large platter. Jim and Kate applauded.

'What a feast! Johnny and Fanny Craddock had better look to their culinary laurels,' Kate said, watching as several dishes and tureens were set on the table.

'Has anyone seen colour TV yet?' Kate asked cutting into her lamb cutlet.

Jim nodded as he wiped his mouth with his napkin. 'Saw a couple of things, not a great deal to get excited about especially the televised games from Wimbledon,' he said. 'Couldn't imagine it would be all that dramatic, seeing as everyone plays in whites but I suppose the courts looked fairly green. Probably need to get the players to dress in different colours so it would have more impact,' she said playfully.

'Kate, you know that will never happen. Good God, woman, it is almost as radical as thinking that cricket teams will play in colours.' Charles winked at her.

'Oh you men are so precious about your sport, I think it would spice up a cricket match to have teams wearing different colours,' Kate said while Susan nodded enthusiastically.

'Kate, this is blasphemy. It never will happen, well not in my lifetime,' Jim laughed.

During the lull between main course and dessert Kate found out that Jim had boarded at Roxall Public Boys School. Just when she had decided that he must have been born into a position of privilege she was proved wrong.

'Would you believe Mum cleaned other people's houses and Dad took a second job to pay for my fees,' Jim said. There was something wistful about the way he said that, as though somehow he did not quite believe he was worth the effort. As they drained their coffee cups and liqueur glasses he asked if he could drive her home.

Susan winked at her as she got her coat. 'Call me about Tuesday's meditation,' she said, as she closed the front door.

He opened the car door and escorted her to the front door. 'I enjoyed your company tonight Kate.' He kissed her cheek.

'It was lovely meeting you,' she called as he went down the path.

She was weeding the front garden mid morning when a bouquet of pink roses was delivered. She read the card. *Hoping to persuade you to join me in search of the perfect restaurant. Will call later. Jim.* She cut the long stems of the tight pink buds and trimmed the leaves. He's a nice man and he's only here for a few weeks and it would be fun she thought.

'There's an Italian restaurant that I want to try out, evidently it is supposed to be very good, but I would love a second opinion,' Jim said when he called in the afternoon.

'Well if I am able to get a babysitter that would be lovely,' Kate replied.

Tuesday evening Susan presented her guided meditation. She wove a story of far away lush tropical islands with a path that led down through the rain forest to stand beneath the warmth of the waterfalls.

'Well tell me what do you think?' Susan asked she drove home.

'Your meditation was..,'

'No not the meditation, Jim.'

'He is a very nice man,' Kate said

'But no chemistry?' Susan sounded disappointed.

'No, but he is very nice man and your meditation was

perfect,' Kate finished.

Jim took her out several times in the next couple of weeks to different eating houses in his quest to find the perfect restaurant. He told her about his favourite restaurant in Geneva, a small very French styled restaurant that only served steak with café de Paris butter and pommes frite and lashings of green salad.

'You can't book and you always have to queue to get a table but believe me it is the best steak and chips you could ever have.'

'Sounds wonderful, I wish there was that type of restaurant here. That's the problem so many chefs believe huge menus will attract customers. Instead if they concentrated on fresh seasonal produce they would do much better. Yes, a small menu and do it well,' she said.

Jim listened attentively as Kate told him how she had made changes in her life through her daily creative practice and meditation. He told her about his love of skiing in the winter.

'I go to the French ski slopes Chamonix Mont Blanc which is just a short journey from Geneva, you'd love it Kate. I play tennis in the summer. My method of switching off,' Jim concluded and smiled at her, happy that they appeared to be bonding.

One day when he called he met Lucy and was introduced to the children. Jane said Lucy had told her he was a most charming man and that he bought the children small presents and although he was a little formal with them, Lucy could tell he made an effort to get to know them more.

'So have you slept with him?' Jane asked.

'No he is a perfect gentleman and anyway I don't fancy him in that way,' Kate replied.

'But that wasn't always a prerequisite was it?'

'True,' Kate replied with a smile.

Three weeks after they met Jim took her to Simpson's in the Strand for lunch.

'I took your comments on board about a small menu and Simpson's immediately came to mind, they specialize in roast meat and make a bit of theatre of it, I think you'll like it. It may well become our favourite.'

Kate read the menu, there were a few starters, side dishes and desserts like buttery sweet treacle pudding but its reputation was built mainly on rare roast beef and Yorkshire pudding.

Sipping gin and tonic in a padded red leather booth they watched a waiter in a long white apron trundling a gleaming mahogany trolley to a nearby table. Lifting the cover of the silver dome a rib of beef, rare and succulent was revealed. Kate watched the waiter carve thin slices of dark pink beef dripping with juices onto the plates.

Jim took her hand and she turned to look at him, expecting him to say something light and frivolous. 'I know this is probably too soon, but I believe we could have a future together,' he said.

Kate's cheeks flamed and she pulled her hand away. Jim

took her hand again, cupping it softly between his hands.

'I just wanted to put you on notice it is a question that I hope you will consider, I believe we would be very happy and I would be honoured to be a father to Ally and Ben.'

He leant towards her and kissed her cheek.

'Anyway enough about it today, let's decide on what we are going to eat.'

'Thank you,' Kate murmured as she took her hand from his clasp.

'Darling, he is so nice, such a charming man. You and the children would be well looked after.' Lucy said.

'Mummy, sorry to spoil your dream, he is the loveliest man, I like him but do not love him.'

'Well maybe that would come in time you and the children need security darling. After all maybe you've had the great love of your life and to find a decent man who is willing to take on another man's children is going to be hard, you said yourself what a lovely man he is. Think seriously about it darling it would be the answer to all our prayers for you.'

The long ribbons of skin fell onto the board before she halved and cored the apple. 'Applesauce and pork chops for dinner. I wonder if he'd like that,' she said out loud to the empty kitchen. 'I'm sure he would. I know he is a good man and Mummy maybe right, in time I might grow to love him.' She sliced the apples into the pan and put them on to cook.

She took the children down to the coast the following day. Too cold to go on the beach they sat in the car eating their sandwiches watching the white tipped waves whipped into a fury by the wind, crash onto the shingles. The Sai Baba quote that Bob had told her, came into her consciousness. When you try something above your capacity that is conceit. When you do something less than your capacity that is theft. That's it she thought I do not have the capacity to love him and that to marry him would be wrong however tempting the security and lifestyle he offered.

She called into her mother's house on the way home and told her of her decision. Lucy caught Kate by the shoulder as she walked out.

'Before you ring him and tell him no, I want you to consider this more fully.'

Her voice was more strident than Kate had ever heard before. 'Kate, you're a woman who needs a man, you've said so yourself many times since Greg's death how hard you find coping on your own. Jim as you've said is a man of substance and integrity who you like and value and who is prepared to raise Greg's children and you dismiss it saying you do not love him like some young girl with romantic notions.' Lucy was trembling as she concluded. 'Surely to God Kate you could learn to love him for all of our sakes.'

Kate's nose pinched as she stared at her mother.

'I won't marry him because he seems the perfect solution Mummy. Have you thought about him, don't you think he deserves more than someone who would be with him only for the emotional and financial security and acting as father to my children. You're right the thought of being on my own for the rest of my days is frightening but you know Mummy I'm doing okay and I'm proud of how I'm managing the children on my own. What the future will bring I don't know, maybe I was meant to be a single parent but I do know that if I ever get married again it will have to be for love.'

She rang him when she got home and asked him to come round that evening. He arrived carrying flowers. She was anxious, she poured them a drink'

'I'm sorry Jim, I like and enjoy your company immensely but I am not in love with you and without love it would not work for either of us.' Jim was gracious saying he understood and left the proposal open.

'Perhaps if we had had more time I could have convinced you,' he said at the front door. But his step was firm as he went down the path and she sensed he too felt relieved.

When she met Susan for coffee that week, she was relieved that her rejection of Jim's proposal was not a high priority for discussion as Susan had news of her own. Charles had just been accepted as a partner with an international accountancy firm in Nassau, Bahamas.

'We leave the second week of December. The firm has rented us a house on the beach that backs onto a golf course. Can you imagine Christmas on the beach?' Kate shook her head.

'Charles is in seventh heaven a golf course on the doorstep,' the excitement quickened Susan's words.

Kate had a farewell dinner party for Susan and Charles three days before they left for their new island life. Lucy, Frank, Jane and Ian made up the party. She had included the couple's favourite dishes for Charles a starter of French onion soup and chocolate pudding that had a gooey luscious centre in honour of Susan.

'And the condemned pair ate a hearty meal,' Charles joked as he raised his glass to Kate. 'We had better return the meal, within the not too distant future. How about you come out and have a decent holiday with us when we get settled?' 'Now that sounds like an invitation you can't refuse,' said Frank beaming.

'Here's to Nassau and you two having a wonderful life, but I'll miss you,' Kate said raising her glass again.

Chapter 11
• • • • • • • • • • •

Maggie's Galactic Guided Meditation

Kate missed Susan's companionship when she went to the final guided meditation meeting of the year. Maggie took the lead role in the meeting that night and retold one of her more popular meditations. Kate had never heard it before and she wished that Susan had been there to enjoy it as it was whacky and completely different to the traditional water, forest, crystal caves style of journey that most of them employed.

Instead Maggie's narrative put them into a green velvet lined womblike spaceship and shot them upwards through the deep blue vastness of space, travelling faster and faster until all reached the birthplace of new stars where anything and everything that they had forgotten about their true nature and purpose was accessible to them. Maggie's voice was soft as she painted the story.

'The spaceship slows, slows and gently stops. You open and step out of your pod. You are weightless as you slowly float through the brightness of the zillions of twinkling stars. As you float through space you come face to face with yourself. Face to face with who you ever wanted to be, who you know you are.'

Kate could feel the bubble of a smile erupting on her face, she felt free, like a child. And when Maggie bought them all safely to terra firma again and told them to open their eyes and come back into the body of the room at their own pace, the room rippled with people's laughter and pleasure. At the coffee break Kate managed to take Maggie aside. 'That was so good, you have an incredible imagination, I wish that Susan could have heard that. I wonder if you are doing it again because maybe I could tape it to send to Susan, that is if you are happy for me to record you?'

'I last did that two years ago and I think it will be maybe another two years before it's heard again. But I am happy to record it myself and get it to you. Why don't we use it as an excuse to have coffee? I have been meaning to catch up with you after Liam's workshop.' Maggie said

'That sounds great, can I call you in the New Year?'

'Sounds good, I have a clean diary for 1968 so far, just give me a ring when it suits.'

Kate made the coffee date in early January on a day when the children were at playgroup. Maggie arrived as Kate was wrapping the last of the Christmas decorations to store away for another year. It was sleeting outside and Maggie's coat had absorbed the cold and dampness. Kate kissed her wintery cheek, hung her woollen coat on the hallstand and bustled her into the warmth of the kitchen.

She poured boiling water into the coffee plunger and set out some leftover Christmas cake as they talked. Maggie's elegant fingers pushed the boxed tape, with its handwritten label Maggie's Galactic Guided Meditation, across the table.

'How on earth did you dream it up?' Kate asked.

'Did you see the movie *The Angry Red Planet*?'

Kate shook her head. 'It was pretty laughable, a 'B' grade horror movie with a spaceship being sent to Mars only to bring back man-eating plants and creatures like giant cockroaches. It was so ludicrous that it stuck with me. And when I was trying to think up a different script for a meditation it came up, just a bit of fun really. But delightfully the meditation worked on so many levels for different people.' Kate pushed the plunger down slowly in the glass jug and poured the coffee into their mugs. They sat companionably sipping their coffee and feasting on Lucy's homemade fruitcake.

'What did you think of Liam's workshop?', Maggie asked. Her open countenance and intensity of her gaze demanded nothing less than an honest and candid discussion.

'I loved it, well you know my story so you can imagine how much it resonated with me.'

'Are you completely cured?'

'Yes. According to my specialist I'm now free of all of my symptoms—so in my view I'm cured, in his, I'm in remission.'

'So what made you dream up MS do you think? 'Maggie

rested her chin on her hand and waited expectantly.

'All I can say is that when I had the road to Damascus moment on my settee in the lounge,' Maggie smiled. 'I saw that I had been focusing on loss and feeling powerless, which I suppose answers your question.'

'Makes sense doesn't it?' Maggie said.

'But all the same, Maggie, it's very hard to get your head around that disease is not random and that you actually play a part in it. Certainly it was easy for me to see that mine was in the making for a few years before it was diagnosed. I think my immune system simply had enough. Either that or it was some sort of divine intervention to get me back on track.'

'What about Julia and her phantom pregnancy then?' Maggie asked.

'Okay, so we are both saying what other conclusion can you come to?'

'That the mind is a powerful creator, especially when you're faced with evidence like Julia. Just incredible, did they have any clues as to why?' Maggie asked.

'Well she didn't get any feed back from the psychiatrist but she was very frightened that her parents may have found out, so maybe that played a part in it. But she was incredibly naïve. I just think that she had a strong conviction that if a man touched her in what she saw as her secret, sacred place, then it was all over and she was impregnated. She was amazed when Jane and I told her the facts.'

'Poor Julia, lack of sex education is part of our era don't you think. I had no knowledge of menstruation when I first had a period. It was up to my sister to tell me and go out and buy the sanitary pads from the chemist and show me what to do with them.'

'I know, I came into puberty knowing so little, only what I learned behind the toilet block in primary school. I remember the headmaster caned us for our smuttiness as he called it,' Kate said.

'I reckon the swinging sixties is our generation's defiance at the ridiculous values of our parents era,' Maggie replied

'Yes but that doesn't mean everybody out there is enjoying free love. By free I mean joyful sex without reservations of guilt and shame.'

'I can't imagine you were ever ashamed of sex,' said Maggie.

'I think my sex life with Greg, as short as it was, was affected by my hang-ups, and after he died I used sex, well, lust really—I was obsessed—as a consolation for love, and that really made feel ashamed.'

'Kate, lust and obsession are a bit strong.'

'Well whatever you like to name it, it was not honest,' Kate's face reddened as she determinedly continued. 'The longing for sex was agonisingly painful, it burned me up.'

Maggie listened intently as Kate told her about her sexual liaisons. Maggie smiled and said 'When I was first divorced I think I had over ten different men in those first couple of years of being single.'

'Maggie it's not about the numbers of men, if the opportunity had arisen I probably would have gone with a battalion. Forget the fun of a sexual romp, the longing for a man devoured me and trust me it is different when you're a single mother of two small children.'

'Kate are you saying that single mothers don't deserve to have a sex life?

'No that's not it Maggie, it was the guilt that my babies were coming in a poor second to their mother lusting after men like a dog on heat.'

Maggie picked up the cafetière to pour Kate more coffee but Kate shook her head and placed her hand over the cup.

'Do you enjoy sex?' Maggie asked.

'Well with Tom, Max and Jack it was an insatiable hunger and the act was a means to an end but with Fred it was different. Mind you he was very experienced in knowing what turns a woman on.' Kate replied.

'What about Greg?'

'Not brilliant, I think we were both pretty inexperienced and I probably had unrealistic romantic expectations and having two babies so close together wouldn't be ideal for anyone's sex life. Probably given time we could have worked things out.'

Maggie listened as Kate confided her feelings of guilt that she had denied him sex the night before he died.

'God, how crass,' said Maggie.

'Crass, yes,' Kate nodded, 'but I still I regret that I didn't show him that night that I loved him. Wouldn't you have felt the same if it were Bob?'

'Bob would never have put me in that situation.'

'Yes but you have the advantage of being much more enlightened than we were. I know that Greg was not perfect, nor was I, but I loved him and it saddens me that I never showed him. I think that was the only way he knew how to show love.'

'Sorry Kate, I should know better than making sweeping judgments.'

'It's okay. I understand intellectually so much more now but still the emotional acceptance of some of my stuff, I suppose it's guilt mainly, is hard to come to terms with.'

'Have you tried facing the pain allowing it to be instead of trying to avoid it?' Maggie asked

'No, maybe I should.'

'If you never face it how can you accept it? Maggie licked her finger and picked up the last of the crumbs of the fruitcake from her plate. 'But Jim, is a different matter. Yes?'

'Yes I am really fond of him, he's such a nice man and yes, no sex. Not long ago the desire for sex would have driven me even if the chemistry wasn't there. That's progress, don't you think?'

Maggie smiled. 'Yes, if you think it is.'

The Aga popped and hissed. Kate looked at the clock it was nearly one. 'Where did the morning go? I'll make us a sandwich. Are you okay with ham and tomato?'

Kate got out the makings and put the kettle on to boil. She layered the ham and sliced tomatoes onto the buttered bread while Maggie made the tea.

'There have always been decent men in my life, my father of course, but he was not around for the formative years, just coming back into my life after the war when

I was eight. But what really just came home to me as we talked is that I'm sexually attracted to men who have the capacity to hurt me in some way.'

'Were you abused as a child?' Maggie asked as she bit into her sandwich.

'Well if you count my grandfather's withdrawal from me or telling me in so many ways he really did not care for me, the answer is yes,' Kate replied.

Maggie pressed. 'Yes, I understand but do you ever think you were sexually abused?'

Kate wiped her mouth with her napkin and took a sip of tea. 'Not to my knowledge but who's to say what happened in wartime.'

She dreamt that night. She was in a garden of large cabbage roses. It was a summer day and the sky was cloudless. She was drawn to admire a particularly large petalled blossom. As she stared at the white rose it morphed into a gigantic butterfly that angrily buzzed around her head its menacing antennae trying to claw her face. She ran but it kept chasing her until she could run no more and fell. The winged horror settled its fat body over her face its acrid smell suffocated her. She tried to fight it off but she could not move or breathe.

She woke in a sweat, her heart beating hard as though she had run a mile and the fear so palpable in the darkness that she had to turn on her bedside lamp. Stumbling out of bed she switched on the landing light and went into the nursery, both children were asleep sprawled across their beds, their bedclothes pushed aside. She pulled the covers over them and went back to bed in the darkened room. As she lay the smothering fears returned and she switched on the bedside light again, her eyes resting on her book that lay open on the table beside her. Determinedly she witched off the lamp and slipped back down under the covers. The darkened room was pitch black but soon woolly shapes of furniture played fearsome tricks with her eyes in the darkness. The quickening dull thump of her heart beat in her ear and she felt a band tightening around her chest making her breathing shallow. Her panic shortened each breath until she could hardly breath. She focused on her breathing, breath in, breath out, breath in, breath out. Slowly her racing heartbeat slowed and settled. She became aware of a dull ache that spread down from her lower stomach until it centred in her pelvis. The dull pain pulsating deep into her body. Powerless to stop its gnawing waves she lay still, at one with its rhythm. It faded and she slept.

The second post landed with a thud on the hall mat. Ben heard it and skidded down the hall to get it. Besides the gas bill there was the familiar blue square of an aerogramme but this time the postmark did not read Australia. Eva Sinclair wrote infrequently. Her letters fleshed with local news, the monthly rainfall and the results of the bowls competitions. At the conclusion of each letter she enquired about the children. Kate's letters in response simply focused on the children's growth and development.

But this one was postmarked Nassau. The children were drawing sprawled across the kitchen floor with paper, pencils and crayons everywhere. She settled down on the bench seat with a cup of tea to read Susan's letter.

Dear Kate,

How are you? Hope all is well with you and the children and that you are still doing the guided meditation. Please give my love to them all, especially Maggie and Bob. We have settled in well and the house is gorgeous, the house and pool back onto the golf course. We have four bedrooms all with their own bathrooms! Also there is an enormous outside entertaining area, two large reception rooms and a separate dining room. The kitchen is huge and you won't believe this but we have a maid, yes you read it right we have our own maid. Willa Mae is a native Bahamian and I love her. I gave our first dinner party last weekend; I really needed to repay the amazing hospitality we have received since arriving here and it was just so easy with Willa Mae's help. It is sheer fantasyland here the sky is the most amazing blue and the sea turquoise. I regularly swim off the private beach here in the estate. I have to keep pinching myself to know that it is I living the dream! Charles is working hard but he plays golf once a week but aims to play more now we are starting to get the lay of the land, so to speak. I have taken up bridge I can almost hear you laughing from here. All of the partner's wives play so I stupidly said yes when someone asked if I would like to have lessons with her! Do I like it, not sure yet I am hard pressed knowing what I should be bidding or which card to lay down.

Anyway the whole purpose of the letter is to ask you out for an extended holiday. The Easter period is a beautiful time of year they tell us, does not have the dreadful humidity of summer. So if you could come towards the end of February and stay through March before the rainy season begins in April that would be perfect. Please write back immediately to say yes, I miss you and I know you and the children would have such a great time with us. Willa Mae loves children and says she will baby-sit so you and I can hit the town (well Bay Street, bit of a one horse town, but the shops are wonderful.) Give the kids a big hug and kiss. Love Susan xx

Two days later she phoned Susan.

'Nassau here we come. I provisionally booked our flights from Heathrow to Nassau 28th February and Nassau to London on 1st April, does that suit you?'

'Kate that is perfect and now I can start planning,' Susan said.

Chapter 12
• • • • • • • • • • •

Bahamas

From the aircraft window Kate and the children could see the confetti of Bahamian islands fringed with white in an otherwise cerulean sea. The plane touched down smoothly onto the tarmac runway and taxied to a stop in front of the small Nassau airport building. Bougainvillea vines in vibrant pinks, corals and purples made a dramatic splash against the faded pink render of the airport walls.

Kate's arms were full of bags and topcoats now jettisoned by the children in the heat and her shirt clung damply to her back. A steel band was playing led by a fellow in a broad brimmed fringed straw hat. As the music ebbed he spoke over the microphone

'Welcome to the beautiful island of New Providence,' his voice so deep Kate felt he might launch into a rendition of *Ol' Man River*.

Ally and Ben were red faced and little beads of perspiration dotted their top lips as they dragged their feet wanting to stay close to the sounds of the steel band. At the entrance to the customs shed, women dressed in bright flowing muumuus greeted the passengers with drinks of pineapple juice in paper cups. Ally tugged at her arm, they were in a line and needed to move on. She handed Ally and Ben their coats to carry while she searched in her handbag for her passport and Customs form.

'What's the reason for your visit?', the large Bahamian officer asked, the brass buttons of his white uniform straining across his midriff.

'Holiday,' she replied happily. He stamped her passport, smiling broadly at Ally and Ben who were staring unashamedly at this large coal-black man.

Trailing their winter coats they moved through to an open area where the suitcases were being unloaded. Kate could see Charles and Susan waving to them in the distance behind the security fence. They waited patiently until the Custom Officers checked and chalked their luggage and with a porter carrying their bags, they were through the last barrier and into the welcoming arms of their friends. Charles went to get the car as they stood with Susan on the airport forecourt laughing and chatting. Charles pulled up to the curb beside them in an American white convertible with red leather seats.

'What do you think Ben? 1964 Mustang, its the same model they used in *Goldfinger*,' he said as Ben ran his small hand over the duco.

'Goldfinger?' Ben said inspecting his fingers.

'Sorry Ben, *Goldfinger* is a movie, probably too much

for you at the moment but you'll have to get Mum to take you to see it when you get a bit older,' Charles said.

He packed two of the larger cases into the boot before the family with the rest of the luggage squeezed into the back seats of the car.

'It's only a thirty minute drive so not too long kids,' said Charles as they moved out into the traffic heading back into town.

The road into town ran along the coast. They drove past the fine pale sandy beaches that edged the open lagoons of turquoise blue waters fringed with palm trees.

'The island is surrounded by a coral reef which means no nasties like sharks or barracuda,' said Susan turning her head to speak to them. Soon the road turned inward slightly from the coast and ran through some residential areas with their weathered pastel timber buildings and past the magnificent buttercup yellow turreted Lagoon Hotel.

'Pretty expensive to stay there but it has the most incredible pool and beach front.' Susan yelled back again to them, her dark hair blowing in the wind.

To their right a golf course came into view, the grass greener than Kate would have imagined in this heat and peppered with small groups of golfers.

'Look at the little buggies the golfers drive,' Kate nudged Ben excitedly.

'They're called golf carts Ben and we have a magnificent one, you wait and see,' said Charles as he changed gears and slowed as they came to the gatehouse of the Nassau Beach Gated Estate. Ahead of them they could see grand homes with white rendered walls and well tended lawns that ran down to the sidewalk.

'The Country Club is at the end of this road Kate and backs onto the beach and we'll go there tomorrow,' Susan said.

The Mustang turned into the driveway of number thirty-three where one wall of the house was splashed with coral bougainvillea, it's vine tentacles spreading upwards and sideways to catch the sun. Willa Mae was waiting for them with refreshments, slices of buttered date loaf and a large pot of tea. She was round and solid, she walked slowly her shoes hanging off her heels flip-flopping as she moved across the wooden floors. There was an easy grace about her as she bent down to greet the children taking them in a generous embrace saying their names as though she had known them for all of their lives. Ally and Ben stood looking up at her before Ben slipped his small hand into hers and Ally took her other hand and the three walked through to the kitchen.

'I know,' Susan said meeting Kate's delighted gaze. 'She has ten of her own and just adores children and they adore her.' Susan suggested that Kate unpack while Willa Mae took care of the children, giving them their morning tea and taking them to explore the house and the garden. Susan bought her a cold drink and showed her how to operate the air-conditioning. 'When you've finished come through to the patio we'll be sitting out there,' said Susan closing the bedroom door.

Kate's room was a vision of an English garden, the walls covered in a profusion of chintzy motifs of white daisies, pink roses and sprigs of bluebells, which offset by the blue and green Regency striped fabric used for the curtains and the bedspread, the floral motif continued in the bathroom with matching towels. The children's room was an unrelenting nautical theme with tall ships under billowing sail, anchors and legends of sailor's knots in boxed frames. Kate knew the children were going to love having their own bathroom. The first thing both wanted to explore was the bathroom wherever they went. It always amazed Kate that given the right environment, which was anywhere apart from home, they could successfully be counted upon to visit the bathroom at a steady rate but at home they were like camels and could happily go all day without. Ally was the worst, she would cross her legs and jiggle her body off and on as she played but would always deny that she needed the bathroom. Kate took the children's clothes out of one of the suitcases and piled them on her bed ready to take into their room. She hung her clothes in the wardrobe and took the children's into their room and put them away in the drawers of the dresser. Finally she placed her toiletries on the bathroom shelf before splashing her face with cool water, brushing her hair and renewing her lipstick.

Charles and Susan were leaning over the balcony as she joined them on the patio.

Susan turned to greet her. 'Here come and watch. The children have discovered the pool. Kate, a swim will have to be on the agenda this afternoon.'

Kate had heard their squeals of delight as she came through the large elegantly furnished reception room onto the patio with its white cane furniture.

'Wonderful. It'll help tire them out so that they can get a good night's sleep,' she said watching them with Willa Mae. Clipped hedges and flowerbeds ran the length of the rectangular pool. At the far end of the pool the dividing wall of the property had been transformed into a waterfall with cascading water splashing down over it's cobbled face.

The house, rented by Charles' firm, was completely furnished down to linens and silverware. The reception rooms reflected the elegance of North American décor, big sumptuous couches and chairs, side tables with large bulbous lamps and deep shades, the timber floor polished to a shine and laid with Persian rugs and runners with patterns of ochre reds and dusty blue weaving. The dining room was substantial. Two wrought iron chandeliers spot lit the long mahogany table that seated up to fourteen guests in blue brocade upholstered carver chairs. A mahogany sideboard displayed, what Kate could only describe in a letter home as a robber's haul from the London Silver Vaults. Surprisingly the large kitchen was plain white and quite utilitarian. No modern American high gloss treatment here Kate reported, no batteries of shining electric equipment, it was simply designed as a place where the maids did all the work of the household. The children were ready for bed after an afternoon in the pool. Willa Mae had left their meal ready for them before she left for the day to start all over again with her brood of ten. The heavy curtains in the children's room were a godsend and they were sound asleep before it got dark. Charles poured her a gin and tonic as she came into the lounge. Dusk was just starting to tinge the sky as they sat out on the patio. Susan had lit several mosquito coils and was burning citronella candles to keep the mosquitoes away. Charles chatted to them about his work as they watched the last red rim of sunset leave the sky.

'You're incredible, Charles. I'm hopeless with figures. I'm amazed that you love balance sheets and tax laws,' Kate said as they walked inside the house.

Charles laughed. 'Well it's not work to me but I suppose it helps that I like numbers but don't discount my other interests.'

Kate smiled. 'And talking about wine, which we weren't but I'm sure we are going to, does this magnificent house have a wine cellar?'

'Now Kate you would know I would never have rented the house without a decent wine cellar.' He was wearing a yellow and blue checkerboard shirt, more suited to an arts graduate than an accountant.

'Yes, Charles, but just open a bottle without all of the nonsense that goes with it, so we can have a glass while I finish off dinner.' Susan said.

Charles winked at Kate before walking out of the room. His voice echoing as he walked through the hall.

'You women have no understanding of the finer things of…,' his words fading as he disappeared into the wine cellar.

In the kitchen Susan clicked open the door of the refrigerator.'I am horribly spoiled. Willa Mae did most of the meal preparation for me. She set the table before she left, so all I have to do is pan fry the chicken, dress the green salad, put out her delicious potato salad and we are done.'

They sat at one end of the spacious dining table. Eating, talking and drinking chilled Chablis from large wine glasses until Kate found it difficult to keep her eyes open. 'Time for bed,' she said, kissing her friends good night.

~

The Sinclair family slept till after eight the following morning. Charles had already gone for his morning swim, breakfasted and was on his way into work when the family eventually made their way onto the patio for breakfast. Willa Mae brought out a stack of pancakes not finicky thin crepes but fat round dollar pancakes piled high on a plate. Under her arm was a bottle of maple syrup. Ally was helping and carefully carried a large bowl of fresh fruit and Ben followed bearing a bowl of yoghurt.

Susan joined them as they were finishing the last of their meal. She was wearing a sleeveless orange linen shift and her long dark hair, still wet from the shower, was tied back at the nape of her neck.

'Wow you look gorgeous, Susan, Nassau obviously agrees with you. You're positively glowing.' As Kate said those last words it suddenly clicked. 'You're pregnant aren't you?', she shrieked.

'Yes, just twelve weeks, we thought it would never happen and all we needed to do was come to Nassau,' Susan said laughing.

Kate embraced her and smoothed her hand over Susan's taught stomach.

~

The electric six-seater golf cart was quiet as a whisper as they ran through the roads of the complex. Its dark green bodywork gleamed in the morning sun. A scalloped valance trimmed the metal roof almost hiding the leather straps that held the neatly rolled up plastic weatherproofing. Kate sat with Ben in the passenger seats and Ally in the front with Susan.

Glossy allamanda vines studded with yellow trumpet blossoms tumbled over brick walls on either side of the driveway of the Country Club. Three pink-washed pavilions linked with pergolas heavy with climbing bougainvillea housed the clubhouse, a restaurant and the locker rooms.

Along the cream walls of the reception area were framed pictures of the past and current Club Commodores. Susan signed in at the reception desk and received a key on a large wooden key ring and a pile of white fluffy towels. As they came out into sunshine again they saw to their right an Olympic size swimming pool, the blue water alive with splinters of light dancing across its surface. Bordering the pool on the far side were small terraced beach shacks. Susan led the way across the flagged pool deck past the rows of beach chairs to the gabled-roofed shacks each painted a different pastel colour, their one, sky blue. Inside it was equipped with everything they might need for a day by the pool or the beach including a bathroom with a shower, a large basket containing extra towels, deckchairs, a couple of comfy armchairs and a daybed with a soft throw over should a nap be in order. At either end of the cabin were French windows, one end opening onto the pool and at the other the doors led onto the fine pale sand of the beach with the sea green water of the lagoon beyond.

Ally and Ben wriggled out of their towelling robes, Kate managed to put on their cotton sun hats before they picked up their bucket and spades and ran down the beach to the water's edge.

'It's okay we can keep our eye on them from here,' said Susan unpacking the children's bottles of juice and putting them into the small fridge.

Kate erected two deckchairs outside the cabin. She slipped out of her shift dress and removed the straps to her swimsuit so that her shoulders would get an even tan. Popping on her large sunglasses, she sank back into the chair beside Susan and watched the children on the beach. 'This is unbelievable. Now all we need...,' her words stalled mid-sentence with the arrival of a waiter who asked if he could get them something to drink.

'Coffee?' Susan asked.

Kate nodded her face a picture of amused delight. 'I was going to say someone to fan us but a coffee is infinitely better.'

'We have been trying for nearly five years and we really had given up hope, the move to Nassau was part of trying to put it behind us, so at the end of August I will be a Mum,' Susan said as they sipped their coffee.

'I'm just so thrilled for you. You never spoke about wanting children and I never wanted to pry but I did wonder,' Kate said.

'Yes look I just felt I might jinx things if I ever spoke about it, but it was a hard few years, well nothing compared to you.'

'It must have been heartbreaking for you both,' Kate said quietly, reaching over to touch her friend's arm. 'I wonder if meditating worked its magic?'

'You know, Kate, I honestly think that you have something there, when I first started meditating I was still desperate to have a child. It was agonising waiting to see if I got my period each month. About six weeks into the meditations, I began to let go and accept that I probably would never have a child of my own. We decided on the Nassau job and you know what, with all the upheaval of moving here I never even realised that I had missed two periods. Fancy not even missing them, after all those years of hating them. It was the nausea that made me go to the doctors, I thought I had picked up a tummy bug.'

From the beach came the raised voices of Ally and Ben. Ally struck out at Ben and angrily tramped over their sandcastle as Ben tried to pull the spade from her hands. Kate jumped up from her deckchair and ran down to placate both children who began to howl loudly.

'Enough, that's enough,' she said to them. 'Shake hands and make up, now.'

Reluctantly they shook hands but not before Ben pulled Ally's hat off and Ally stomped hard down again on what was left of the sandcastle. Susan wandered down to the group carrying a couple of towels.

'Are you sure this is what you want?' Kate pointed to the two warring children.

'Couldn't think of anything better,' Susan laughed as she draped a towel around Ally. 'Anyway, time to come up kids, it's lunchtime.'

'What the heck is a BLT sandwich?' Kate asked as they studied the menu.

'Bacon, lettuce and tomato, very American and very good,' Susan replied. 'We've a strong American influence in the islands although it's a British colony. Bound to be I suppose because we are so close to the States,' she said.

With Ally and Ben sitting on towels at their feet, facing the lagoon they ate their BLT's and a large bowl of fries, devouring every last crumb. After their lunch settled, Kate took the children into the shallow end of the pool. Neither of them was afraid of the water and wanted to play on their own but the water was still too deep for them.

'You two need swimming lessons,' Kate said.

'They do one-on-one swimming lessons here. We could get them swimming before you go home.' Susan said, sitting on the edge of the pool.

The first week of the holiday sped past so quickly. Each morning Kate drove the children to the pool giving Susan some time to sort out her domestic issues and their entertainment schedule. Their swimming instructor was a young white Bahamian named Mariah who was born and raised on Eleuthera, one of the out islands. She told Kate her island was long and narrow being just over a mile wide. With the beach and ocean being so accessible it was no wonder she was more at home in the water than on land. Within the first week Ally, was already swimming underwater unaided a short distance, while Ben wearing his flotation arm bands was happily splashing his way around the pool.

Willa Mae looked after the children the day Susan and Kate went into town to meet two of Susan's bridge buddies for lunch. The Ivy restaurant and bar was located off Bay Street, in a quieter part of town, close to the business houses. Groups of expatriate accountants, lawyers and bankers jostled around the central bar before moving into the restaurant to eat. Susan's friends were already seated at one of the white clothed tables.

'Has Kate tried conch yet?' asked Rose a mother of four and wife of one of the managers from Charles' firm as she looked at the menu.

'No not yet I was saving it for today, they do the best conch fritters and chowder on the island,' Susan said

Kate eyes followed the conversation between the two women. 'Conch?' she queried

'Conch is the signature dish of the Bahamas. It's a large sea snail, doesn't sound appetising I know but trust us you'll love it. They have the most distinctive shell, I'm sure you would seen it, Kate,' said Clair, sitting opposite.

Her fair hair was short cut in a Mia Farrow pixie crop that accentuated her dark brown eyes.

They ordered, conch fritters to share and for Kate a

small bowl of chowder while they settled for salads.

'The whole work permit thing is ridiculous,' said Rose timing her statement between the roars of approval from male diners as they watched a live broadcast of a baseball game being shown on a screen hung from the ceiling.

Rose's sunglasses were used as a headband keeping her tangle of tawny hair off her face. She took another sip of her gin and tonic and looked up to the screen. 'You know Kate the only way a wife of an expat can get a work permit is if she is a teacher or willing to teach.'

As the roar followed a huge hit clearing the outfield fence, she leaned closer to Kate and spoke quietly. 'I work illegally managing the affairs of a Canadian industrialist who has interests in the Bahamas. All very hush hush, we could get thrown off the island if the authorities found out. But truly, Kate, I would go mad if I didn't have something to do here, other than playing bridge and ladies lunches like these,' she said.

Clair popped another conch fritter into her mouth. 'It's not too bad for me as the twins are only three which keeps me pretty busy and of course the odd game of bridge and one day a week I do yellow birding.'

'Yellow birding?' Kate queried.

'They call hospital volunteers here Yellow Birds. Maybe 'cause we wear yellow uniforms,' she laughed. 'But once the twins are old enough I would love to get a job. But as Rose said the only guarantee of getting a work permit here is teaching,' she added 'the island is desperate for teachers.'

'Well I can tell you,' Susan said.

At that moment another excited roar filled the air.

'I can tell you,' she shouted. 'I am not morally fazed simply doing nothing. I'm enjoying every precious minute of my hedonistic lifestyle made possible by our lovely Willa Mae.' Susan smiled as the noise level dropped.

'So you're happy to let Willa Mae have the major input in raising the new baby?' Rose asked.

'You are so cynical, Rose, where would you be without your maid to help manage your four unruly chickadees.' Susan said.

Clair groaned 'Sorry Kate, we are so tactless.'

'I'm sorry too, how on earth Kate do you manage on your own?' Rose asked.

'When the children were babies I had a live in help for a while. Now I'm so used to being on my own I just see it as my way of life but I'm lucky to have a mother and sister who come to the rescue when I need it.'

There was another roar as the game came to an end and the conversation was lost in the dissonance of men's voices and chairs being scraped back from tables.

They made their farewells out on the pathway promising to catch up again before Kate returned home. She and Susan walked down to the harbour edge to watch the young boys dive deep into the clear water for conch shells. Kate, camera at the ready, waited for the boys to pop up like corks their arms out stretched with their prize. On a nearby stall she purchased a large deep pink tinged conch shell. The woman who sold it to her said the one she had chosen was a rare right turned Queen Conch and was a Buddhist symbol of good luck.

'I expect she says that to all her customers,' Kate said to Susan.

'I think I've heard that a right turned shell is rare in these waters so it's bound to be lucky,' Susan replied.

The Straw Market was set close to the dock and it was busy with American tourists from the large cruise ship berthed for a few hours in the harbour.

Kate bought sets of plaited palm frond placemats embroidered with blue raffia shells and a straw letter rack with an image of the archipelago of the Bahama Islands stitched in turquoise raffia. Bay Street was the main street through the town and it was busy with tourists all hunting for a duty-free bargain. The stores with their square paned bay windows and wrought iron hanging signs showcased the very best of luxury items that money could buy.

In the elegant Treasure Island Shop, Susan and Kate gazed wide-eyed at spectacles of fine china, sparkling crystal, table linens and lamps. The smell of perfume enveloped them as they approached the perfume counter with its display of bottles and vials. They sniffed endless strips of cardboard sprayed with perfumes. Finally Kate opted for the light and floral Quelque Fleurs by the French perfume maker, Houbigant as it reminded her of a visit to the south of France with Greg.

'We went to Grasse and the smell of the flowers and perfume was amazing,' she said to Susan as the assistant wrapped her purchase.

The chintz curtains lifted in the gentle breeze from the open window and she lay gazing at the night sky alive with stars.

She didn't want to sleep. It had been such a good day, an indulgent day. She reflected that it was fascinating that one women's paradise is another's prison. The island life-style is perfect for Susan, she thought, supporting Charles in his career, entertaining and especially now she is having her first child, it's a dream come true. That was me once, marriage and babies equalled happy ever after. But I understand Rose wanting something more.

She realised that she was no longer jealous of what these women had. Still fragrant with Quelque Fleurs lingering on her wrists, her last thoughts before she turned on her side to sleep were—I'm free to be my own person and I like that.

She had a dream that she was flying. In the dream she simply waved her arms up and down and arched her back lifting off the ground effortlessly. As she rose above the ground she could propel herself easily along with her arm movements. It was so real, just stroke the air and float along in the breeze. She rose to just above the tree line and below could see the incredible vista of beaches and the outline of the coral reef.

***

The alarm clock was ringing, she heard it from some distant place but did not stir, the shrill of the bell was persistent and she reached out to silence it but missed the button and on it rang relentlessly. She remembered the swimming lessons.

'Shit, shit, shit,' she said as she clambered out of bed and ran to the children's room.

Both were up, Ally drawing in her notebook and Ben sat on the floor vrooming his matchbox Mustang across the carpet.

'Okay you two, I overslept and we're horribly late so I need you to help me,' Kate said. She pulled out their swimsuits from the chest of drawers and grabbed their towels from the bathroom. 'Put your swimsuits on and Ally have a look for your goggles, they're probably somewhere in your bathroom, find them please while I find my costume.'

In her room she scrambled through the drawers to find a one-piece suit but remembered it was still on the line. She took out the new bikini and a scarlet lace jacket that Jane had encouraged her to buy. Clutching the lace edges of the jacket together she took the children to the kitchen to pick up some fruit to eat before their swim.

Susan was up already, sitting eating toast and reading the paper. 'That bikini looks fabulous why haven't you worn it before?' she asked.

'Because it is an age since I have worn a bikini and I feel extremely self conscious,' Kate answered tartly.

'Oh and by the way no point holding the jacket like that it's lace and see through. Just enjoy the admiring looks you'll get at the pool today,' Susan said as she crunched down on her toast and went back to reading her paper.

Ally wearing her goggles, which she had found in the linen basket, was in the water first. Her feet, pointy toed and kicking forcefully as she pushed deep to swim the width of the pool under water, her hair streaming back and her arms close to her sides. She looked like a little porpoise the way she suddenly came up for air spraying out water before diving down and kicking off the remaining distance.

'When does she learn to swim on top of the water?' Kate asked.

'She will, now that she is completely water confident we'll try and get some techniques into her style,' Mariah replied.

The orange inflatable armbands that had assisted Ben as he paddled across the water, lay beside the pool deflated. With each lesson Mariah had gradually blown less air into them until today. But without them he had not acquired any natural buoyancy and directly Mariah's supporting hand was removed he sank. But he loved the small cork flotation board, his legs thrashing the water wildly as he propelled it around the pool.

'He'll do it, you wait and see,' Mariah said patiently, 'they all learn in their own time.'

'See you at six,' Kate said to Mariah after the lesson finished and they left the pool. Mariah was babysitting the children that evening. She had wanted to take Susan and Charles out to dinner and both agreed they wanted to eat at the Country Club.

'You'll love the restaurant. The club always does a great meal and it's such a good atmosphere. We'll have a drink at the bar first and book a table for half seven,' Susan said. Both children were hungry and fractious. To stop the argument that was rapidly building between them Kate had let Ally come in the front seat with her while Ben was relegated to the back seat of the golf cart with strict instructions to hold on tight. As she was turning right into the road from the narrow driveway that led into the club she was distracted by Ben who was pulling Ally's hair. Taking her eyes off the road for an instant she took the corner too sharply and almost ran into the path of another golf cart, which was turning into the driveway. Both carts braked sharply and stopped in the middle of the road. Kate was shaken, but the children were fine and still fighting.

'Enough is enough,' she said and snatched Ally's hand away as she was about to lean over and pinch Ben. 'You two behave or you will be walking home.'

Her hand tightened on the steering wheel, she knew that the near miss was her fault. She couldn't see the driver as he had the sun behind him but his cart was blocking the road.

'Are you alright? Children alright?', he called, his voice was deep, with an English accent.

'Yes we are fine thank you. So sorry, but if I can get you to move we can get out of your way.' She was embarrassed and wanted to get away from the incident as quickly as possible.

'No problem,' the man said as he reversed the cart and waved as she drove away.

The children were quiet as she continued the journey

home and she drove cautiously, her foot arched over the brake pedal and only relaxing once the green executive cart was safely parked in its small garage.

The club that night was busy when they arrived. Charles led the way into the softly lit bar. Comfortable wicker armchairs with fat cushions were grouped around the room and the midnight blue bar shone in the light of the myriad of lit candles in glass holders that dotted the room and the bar.

'I think you should have a cocktail Kate, they do pretty good cocktails at the club.'

Charles ordered a Mango Daiquiri for Kate and a non-alcoholic cocktail of fruit juices for Susan. The women went over and took a table by the window that overlooked the pool where a few swimmers were still enjoying the remainder of the day. Charles stopped and chatted to the group on a near-by table.

'I think they live a few doors up from us, I have seen the couple out and about a few times, not sure who the man is though,' Susan said to Kate.

As the waiter delivered their drinks, Charles left their neighbour's table and joined them. 'Sorry girls, didn't mean to leave you but was just talking to Karen and Andrew who live in number thirty-nine. You know them Susan, the nice couple, he's with the Bank of Nassau, she's a teacher.'

'Yes I do remember them just couldn't put names to their faces, but who is he?' Susan asked.

'I think that's her brother but anyway we will soon find out as they have asked us to join them for a drink,' Charles replied.

Karen and Andrew made them very welcome and set about the introductions and moving extra chairs into the circle. Kate took a seat next to Karen's brother Colin. He stood and shook her hand when they were introduced.

'How are you enjoying Nassau?' he asked as she placed her glass on the table beside her.

'Unbelievable, well after the grey skies and suburban life of London, it's simply heaven. Do you live here?'

'No, I live in the States, in Miami,' he said.

The sun was setting and through the windows Kate could see the staff lighting torches around the pool.

'Pretty isn't it?', he said and she nodded.

'Tell me did you get home safely this morning?'

She had thought his voice was familiar. 'Oh I had hoped I would not run into you again,' she said laughing as a broad smile lit his face.

'I'm really sorry, I'm normally a very careful driver.'

'I would imagine you would be and especially driving Charles' flash cart,' he said drinking the last of his beer. He called the waiter.

'Would you like another daiquiri? Susan, what's that you're drinking? Andrew, Charles another drink?'

Kate looked around. Susan was happily discussing education prospects with Karen while Charles and Andrew were deep into money and tax matters.

'An Englishman in Miami? What's that like?', she asked.

'Well obviously same climate offering a similar life-style but bigger and brasher with more luxury hotels, more shops and definitely more traffic lights,' he replied.

'That's interesting, now you mention it I can't remember seeing any traffic lights in Nassau,' Kate replied.

'You're right, not even one at the new Paradise Island Bridge, have you been over there yet?'

Kate shook her head.'Heard of it but not been there yet, we plan on taking the children over to the beach there, what is it called?' she asked.

'Cabbage Beach, it's an incredible beach you'll love it,' he answered. 'How old are your children?'

'Ally is nearly six and Ben nearly five.'

'Have they started school yet?' he asked

'No. They start this year. Ally starts when we get back and Ben at the beginning of the winter term. Do you have children?' Kate said.

'No I'm not married which probably makes it easier with my lifestyle. I'm a pilot with Pan Am, based in Miami.'

Kate leant forward excitedly in her chair. 'I was a hostess with British United Airways,' she said.

'When?' Colin asked.

'About seven years ago. I flew Viscounts,' Kate replied.

'Ah, Viscounts, you could never hear yourself speak over the sound of the turbo props but beautiful aircraft.'

Kate nodded.

'But I wanted to fly jets, and not just any jet, I wanted to fly Boeings and BOAC was in bed with VC 10's only getting Boeings into service in 1960 whereas Pan Am had them two years earlier.'

Their conversation progressed easily as they shared their flying experiences. Colin had just asked Kate about the East African sector work loads when Charles interrupted, the waiter had just told him that their table was available.

'Well it seems our table is ready.' He turned to Andrew. 'Are you eating?' Andrew nodded.

'Shall we see if they can manage to seat us all together?' Charles asked

'Splendid idea,' said Andrew.

While Charles and Andrew went to the dining room to see if they could get a table large enough to seat them all, Kate and Susan went to the powder room.

'I love the euphemisms for the lavatory that Americans use,' Kate said.

'Yes but I much prefer Powder Room to the more commonly used John,' Susan replied.

As Kate entered she saw the frilly curtained dressing tables bearing all manner of aids to restore any damage that a woman's time in the bar may have done. Perfumes, hand cream, hairpins and body lotions neatly lined up across the glass counters.

'I stand corrected now I see why they call it the Powder Room. Oh I love the excess, you never see anything like this in England.'

Susan and Kate put on a fresh coat of lipstick and tidied their hair. Susan asked softly 'Are you totally fine with this Kate, you seem to be enjoying the chat.'

'Susan, it's more than fine, I'm having a great time,

they all seem very nice,' Kate replied.

With a last look in the mirror they walked arm in arm across the bar into the dining room.

The rest of the party was seated and the men stood when they arrived. Charles took charge.

'We are doing boy, girl so Kate you are at the head of the table and Susan you are next to Andrew. Kate went to the end of the table where Colin pulled out her chair.

'And you are next to me,' he said quietly to her, his tone was conspiratorial and instantly she blushed.

In comparison to the sultry dimness of the bar the dining room was ablaze with lights so there was no hiding her reaction. She picked up the large leather bound menu and studied it intently waiting for her cheeks to cool. She stole a look at him over the top of her menu. His face was reddened from the sun and he wore his hair slicked off his face but it was his eyes that she was drawn to; even in the dim light of the bar she had seen they were unafraid to hold their gaze. Where others, when talking to you, may have met your eyes for an instant and looked away his steadfast gaze was unnerving. As she watched him reviewing the menu he pulled the side of his cheek as a man might do with a sidebar moustache. Suddenly he looked up and smiled, his eyes, now she could see in the light, were a bluish grey, the colour of slate. She knew she had been caught and quickly she lowered her eyes back to her menu.

'Kate, you should try crawfish with black-eyed peas and rice if you want a real taste of the Bahamas—you'll love it,' Andrew's voice broke her reverie.

'Eleanor, our maid does the best Red Snapper with black-eyed peas and rice. We get her to cook it for us at least once a week.'

Once their orders had been taken and wine poured, Colin asked 'So how do you know Charles and Susan?'

'Charles was our accountant and we were all friends, good friends,' her breath tightened, she didn't want to speak about Greg. 'Susan and I joined a guided meditation group, which both of us just love.'

Colins' eyes widened and his body shifted in his chair to face her. 'Guided meditation. I have never heard of that. I did a transcendental meditation course a couple of years ago, have you heard of that? But guided meditation sounds interesting. What do you do?'

'Transcendental meditation is where you use a mantra right?' she asked. Colin nodded.

'You'll have to tell me more as that's about the extent of my knowledge. Neither of us had meditated before and when Susan heard of this group it appealed to us. Short story, the group is led by one of the members through the various stages, becoming aware of the body and the breath, relaxing the body all the while they are taking you on a beautiful journey to the levels or states of consciousness. They do this by creating a story line, an imaginative story possibly using symbols or other elements.'

'But how do you still the mind without a mantra?' he asked

'Well, I suppose it is because of where you put your attention, if you are focussed on the words of the journey.'

Colin interrupted again. 'Sorry Kate, but that means

your mind is not still, it is imagining the journey.' He smiled broadly as though he had won the point.

'Well, not disputing that, but is the mind still when you are ohming or whatever your mantra is?' Kate parried. Their meals arrived at that moment.

'We'll have to continue this debate later,' he said.

Her meal of rock lobster, spicy peas and rice lived up to Andrew's promise. As they ate Karen asked her about Australia and whether she had seen Ayers Rock. 'No I didn't get there but I saw a lot of the outback and that was such an experience seeing kangaroos and koalas in the wild. But you know Sydney is such a beautiful city with such an amazing harbour,' she said.

'It is a stunning place. I went to Sydney a couple of years ago. I was considering applying to Qantas, it has the best safety record and they had Boeings in service very early in the piece for their long hauls. I was very tempted but Pan Am meant I could get a base closer to home,' Colin said.

'Where are you from?' Kate asked.

'South West of London, close to Richmond.'

Karen rejoined the conversation 'Oh, are you two talking about home?' They both nodded and turned towards her.

'Do you miss England?' Kate asked.

'Yes and no, we love it here but after a couple of years on the island you need to get off and go to the big smoke. We go once a year to London but with free accommodation in Miami we try and pop over every couple of months for a weekend.' Karen said

'But not for much longer as my contract with Pan Am is up at the end of July and I'm thinking seriously about going back to England.' Colin said

'Won't you miss the American lifestyle?' Kate asked.

'Yes I am sure I will but there is something about the English way of life that can't be replicated.'

The party decided to have coffee on the patio. Kate took a seat between Andrew and Karen. Colin sat with Susan and Charles.

'It's a beautiful clear night we should be able to see the Milky Way,' said Karen. The night sky was vibrant with stars and as their eyes adjusted to the inky blackness they could see the scimitar of stars carving a luminous band of light across the sky. Kate had seen it once before in the Australian night skies when she was on honeymoon.

'Never seen this in England,' Andrew said 'too much cloud cover.'

Charles drained the last of his coffee and brandy.

'Home I think, early start tomorrow, Susan has to come into town with me and Kate has to get those children to the club by eight thirty for their swimming lesson.'

'I enjoyed our chat about flying, hope we can catch up again before I leave,' Kate said to Colin exchanging a courteous kiss on the cheek.

'Well that is definitely on the cards because I need to straighten you out about your meditating techniques,' he grinned.

Susan had already left with Charles when Kate rallied. The couple had papers to sign at the office before Susan went on to her prenatal check-up.

Kate grabbed the beach bag and her purse as she ushered the children into the golf cart. She was going to buy breakfast at the club after their swim.

At the poolside Kate stretched out on the sun bed and closed her eyes. She was tired and as Mariah put the children through their paces, she pulled her sunhat over her face contenting herself that she could still hear their voices. Gradually the noise faded as sleep overtook her, breathing gently into her sunhat. Colin's voice woke her 'Are you meditating or sleeping?'

She scrambled to sit up.

'Good morning, just relaxing,' she said as she pulled herself untidily into a sitting position.

He was wearing cream shorts and had a towel round his neck. He sat on the edge of her sun chair and watched Ben kicking his board across the pool.

'He's doing well.'

'He's working at it.'

'Are you swimming?'

'Not sure, I'm still half-asleep.'

'Well you should definitely have a swim, that'll wake you up.' She watched as he walked to the end of the pool. The shape of the calves of his legs round and smooth reminiscent of her window cleaner's legs. Maybe five foot ten or eleven she thought noticing the stretch of his shoulders brown against the whiteness of the towel around his neck. He left his shorts and towel on a sun bed and dived into the water. He came up spraying water and grinning broadly.

'It's great come on in.'

She removed her turquoise shift and searched in her bag for her big hair clip to hold up her hair. She lowered herself cautiously into the water. It was surprisingly cool. Her daughter suddenly popped up beside her.

'You're like a little fish, Ally,' she said.

Mariah shouted. 'I want to see you curving those arms, Ally, swim back to me please.'

Kate slowly swam the length of the pool and stopped at the end. Floating on her back, with her arms outstretched along the tiled edge she watched the children at the other end. Colin finished his swim and sat on the edge of the pool beside her.

'They're very good, especially Ally', he paused, 'Is that her name?'

'Yes Ally it is, she is like a little porpoise. Mariah has a job to get her to swim on the surface, but Ben is a plodder, he'll get there,' she replied.

'Have you had breakfast?'

'No but I have plans,' she replied.

'That's a shame I was going to invite you to join me for breakfast on the patio by the beach, they do a great breakfast there,' he said.

'Well why don't you join us because that's exactly what I intended to do,' Kate replied.

'You really are quite an independent woman aren't you?' he said.

She watched as he towel dried his hair. As he scrubbed

at the thick dark flicks of wet hair they lightened in the morning sun.

'Yes, thank you I take that as a compliment.'

Mariah shouted to her 'All finished Kate.'

Kate got out of the pool and walked back to where the towels and beach bags lay on the sun bed. 'Thanks Mariah for everything see you tomorrow morning,' Kate called, as Mariah headed off to the club change room.

Kate bent down and gave the children a hug. 'Well done both of you.'

At that instant Colin joined the family group. 'I want you to say hello to Colin, he is one of aunty Susan's neighbours and we are going to have breakfast with him here at the club.' Both children stared up at him and Ally recognised him straight away.

'You're the man who nearly ran into us yesterday with your cart.'

'Yes clever girl, how did you know?' he said.

'Cause you were wearing those big shiny sunglasses and have the same voice,' Ally replied.

Ben was shouting, trying to be heard 'No, no Mummy nearly ran into him.'

Colin bent down and shook Ben's hand 'Well done lad.'

He picked up Kate's big beach bag as she slipped her dress over her one piece and gathered the towels.

'Shall we eat?'

The small patio only had a couple of beach-goers enjoying breakfast, which meant they virtually had the pick of the white painted wrought iron tables overlooking the beach. The sun was high in a clear blue sky and the beach was smooth no footprints on it yet; she imagined the staff raking it at dawn. The still waters of the lagoon beyond glistened in the morning sunlight. They were grateful for the shade of the large umbrella over the table.

They all had the Beach Club Breakfast Plate with the children sharing one serving between them. The breakfast special was made up of rashers of thin crispy streaky bacon, sausage links, two fried eggs 'over easy' and potato rösti with buttered toast, a jug of freshly squeezed orange juice and coffee. As they ate the children discovered that Colin was a pilot. He was patient as he answered their questions. He explained in simple language about the engines, how the plane stays up in the sky, why it rattles so on take off, why so much noise on landing, where they got the food from but found it hard to keep a straight face when Ally asked innocently.

'What happens to the number ones and twos when you flush the toilet? Do they fall out of the sky onto somebody's head?'

'Yes what does happen, Colin, instead of cats and dogs does it rain poo? Kate gave Colin an exaggerated wink.

The children jumped up and down waiting for him to answer.

'Well children sorry to disappoint you but it's not like trains where everybody's business is dumped onto the tracks and that's why they say don't use the toilet in the station but planes collect it all in a big tank which gets emptied when they land.'

'What do you mean a big tank, like the soldiers have?',

asked Ally.

Colin chuckled. 'Love the literal thinking.'

'That's enough now leave the poor man alone. I think you could take your buckets and spades onto the beach.'

She held Ally back.

'Ally? Are you listening? Do not go in the water. What did Mummy say?'

Ally mumbled her reply and shot from Kate's grip running to catch up with Ben. The waiter filled their coffee mugs and they added the half and half.

'It takes a bit of getting used American coffee but I love the half and half,' Kate said. She stretched out in her chair turning her face upwards to the warmth of the sun. 'This place is just so beautiful,' she murmured.

'Yes it is, but I'd like to show you and the children a beach that is hidden away and that tourists never visit.'

He paused watching her reaction before continuing. 'As we are both flying solo I thought it would be nice to get to know each other more. Maybe we could take a picnic.'

Kate interrupted, 'That is so naff and sounds like a typical pilot's pick-up line and how do you know that I'm solo as you put it?' she demanded.

He laughed 'My apologies it just seemed to fit the bill.' He smiled broadly at her, 'And I knew even before I met you that you were solo, as the gossip all over the island was about a lovely young widow with two small children who'd arrived to holiday in Nassau Beach Country Club,' he replied.

'Really Colin,' she shook her head. 'Let us get one

thing straight, I don't want or need a holiday romance.'

'I understand.' He gently hooked her little finger around his.

'Friends?'

The warmth and pressure of his little finger was disconcerting. But it roused memories of childhood games.

'Faynights,' she said not knowing whether he recognised the childhood expression.

He did and nodded.

'Truce it is then.' he said.

A busboy arrived and cleared the dirty dishes from the table putting them all onto a large tray before carrying it shoulder high back to the kitchen.

'More coffee?' Colin asked.

Kate shook her head.

'Do you play golf, Colin?'

'I do but really only when I'm here, Andrew loves to play and I play to keep him company mainly. I enjoy it but am not addicted to it like Andrew. My sport is fishing, I love to fish especially deep sea fishing off the coast of Florida and here off the coast of Bimini, not good at the moment but come mid-April through to May you could catch some beautiful tuna and wahoo.'

'My father would love to hear this, he is a champion angler, I mean literally he has won silver cups for his fishing prowess. It is one of his dreams to catch a sailfish.'

'You'll have to tell him, the best place for sailfish is north of Miami at a place called Pensacola on the Gulf of Mexico. I haven't ever caught one yet but have friends who have and they tell me it was the biggest thrill of their lives.'

Ally and Ben had teamed up with some other children and were happily playing together. Colin and Kate's conversation had an ease and synchronicity that leapt from acquaintance into a comfortable friendship. He asked and she talked of Greg's death without feeling she was overwhelming him. In turn he told her that he had lost both his parents in a car crash when he was eight and Karen six. After their parent's death their mother's elder sister and her husband had raised them.

'Their death was devastating and it took us both most of our lives to come to terms with it. Our Aunt and Uncle are wonderful people and simply took over where Mum and Dad left off. The death of someone has such a cascade affect, changing so many lives.'

Kate nodded and sat quietly listening to him, their faces staring ahead beyond the children to the lagoon. She broke the silence by asking quietly 'Do you have someone, I mean a relationship?'

'No, somehow I've made it through to thirty-four without a serious attachment. I suppose it's less risky in my line of work.'

'That is the second time you have told me that, it seems to me that you use your career as an excuse for keeping footloose and fancy free. I feel sorry for all those poor women who fancied you,' Kate teased.

Colin smiled. 'What makes you so perceptive?'

'Ah, I am a very wise woman who sees all.'

He laughed. 'Maybe you are, just maybe you are.'

They ordered more orange juice as the children were

thirsty but once they had their drink they were ready to play again. Kate and Colin walked down to the water's edge with them and cooled their feet in the lagoon water. The children and their friends were sculpting a large sandcastle. Ally patted hard sand onto the walls before sprinkling it with fine dry sand that made it sparkle in the sun. Ben carved out a moat with his spade and stomped the trench down with his feet.

'It's wonderful how kids use their imagination. I qualified as a teacher originally and taught primary school for a few years.'

'That explains it, I was amazed that a single man could handle the kids questions so well.'

'I enjoyed teaching, both my Aunt and Uncle were teachers and so it was a natural for both Karen and myself to follow them. But ever since I was a kid I wanted to be a pilot. Couldn't save enough on my teacher's salary for the training so I took a second job, packing supermarket shelves. It took me a couple of years to get the money together. Now I just love putting my uniform on and going to work,' he said.

'I can understand that, I loved my short but definitely glorious flying career. I sometimes dream I'm flying, but it's so real. With just a kick of my foot and a wave of the arms, I fly. It is so exhilarating and the dream stays with me for hours.'

'I think that's lucid-dreaming, just means you're aware when you're dreaming' he said. Colin picked up a flat stone and skimmed it across the still water. Kate watched it bounce several times before sinking.

'Lucid-dreaming. I like that.'

She too tried to skim a pebble across the water but as it hit the water it sank.

He picked up a flat smooth pebble and gave it to her. 'Here hold it between your thumb and forefinger and visualise it bouncing across the water. Don't try too hard, it's a wrist action.' He said showing her how easy it was as his pebble bounced five times before sinking.

She tried again and this time it bounced twice before it sank.

'See, you are a quick study,'

'God you would have never have said that when I was at school.'

'Perhaps you had the wrong teacher,' he picked up another pebble and handed it to her.

'I've always had a secret longing to do some further education and go to university,' Kate said and with a flick of her wrist she sent the pebble bouncing over the water, one, two, three and then it gracefully submerged.

She surprised herself with this admission. It was even something that she had kept hidden from Greg. She thought of it as a fantasy, something out of her reach and so not worth talking about.

'What did I say you just need the right teacher. I can just see you throwing your mortarboard in the air on graduation day.' Colin said.

When they got back to the table the waiter brought the bill. They squabbled over it, until he put his hand over hers as she tried to take it. His hand was large and she felt warm and protected. But she pulled her hand away and continued the argument.

'Enough is enough I think is the term you use for the children. I am paying the bill,' he said.

It was nearly half past one yet the time together seemed so short but It seemed as though she had known him for most of her life. Kate reluctantly picked up the beach bags.

'Time to go. I think Susan may be home and I want to hear all about her prenatal check.'

Colin nodded 'Perhaps we can go to that beach to-morrow if you are not busy. I'll call you later to see the lay of the land.'

Kate replied 'Thank you that sounds good, but let me see if Susan has planned our day.'

They collected the children from the beach and walked to the car park. 'It was a great breakfast thank you,' she said as she reversed the golf cart. She did not kiss his cheek as on the previous evening, the dynamics of their relationship had shifted to a whole different level. She felt it was safer to have no physical contact. He stood watching her progress down the drive.

Susan encouraged her to go on the beach trip with Colin. 'I am happy to have a lazy day at home. I want to catch up on my plans for the nursery and so the timing is perfect.'

Colin had called mid afternoon and told her that he would pick them up after the swimming lesson and told her not to worry about lunch, he would organise a picnic.

They drove to the far end of the island in his small

rental Jeep. He pulled off the main road onto a dirt track. As they bounced along Colin shouted back to the children that the beach they were going to was always littered with shells at low tide.

'I've got a bucket for each of you to collect them.'

The track turned into a large clearing where he parked the car. They walked the rest of the way, their arms full of picnic and beach paraphernalia. Suddenly through the clearing of palm trees and beach scrub they saw the beach. The sand was fine, almost like talcum powder that crunched under foot when you walked on it. The bleached, almost white sand changed to oatmeal as the beach ran down to meet the foam of the water. The iridescent waters of the ocean beyond shimmered in the morning sun.

'Wow,' Kate exclaimed.

'Yep,' Colin responded and smiled at her.

While Colin set up the beach umbrella, Kate applied zinc to the children's noses and a thick line across their cheekbones.

'You look like red Indians with your war-paint on,' she said as she jammed on their sunhats. She took them down to the water's edge and walked along the beach. As Colin had promised it was alive with shells. Ally and Ben ran ahead picking up the delicate treasures and bringing their finds back to Kate. The pile of shells had grown when Colin, having finished setting up, bought the buckets to them.

'Let's see what you have found,' he said as he carefully picked through the mound of shells. He picked up a couple of large tortoiseshell patterned shells.

'That's good kids, you have found Helmet shells, and people make carved brooches out of these.'

Ally and Ben nodded excitedly, pushing each other for a better view. 'There are different kinds of Helmet shells. I wonder if you could find a Princess Helmet shell, it is all white and more rounded than these,' Colin said.

Ally shouted 'I'll find it first,' as she grabbed her bucket. Ben quietly took his and moved slowly down the beach turning different shells over to inspect their shape looking for any imperfections, casting aside any not meeting his criteria. Colin had laid a beach rug down under the umbrella and they sat watching the children as they explored the shoreline.

'What is it about beachcombing for shells that is so calming?' Kate voiced.

Colin was watching Ben as he picked up a shell and put it to his ear. 'I can hear the sea,' he shouted and waved to them before he trudged on slowly intent on finding more shells.

'I suppose it's meditative because your attention is focused on the bounty of the sea, the more you focus the more you find,' Colin answered her.

'That definitely makes sense, I have started to believe over the last couple of years that what you focus on shapes your life,' she said as Colin turned to listen.

She told him about her illness and how she was convinced that her daily creative projects had healed her.

'Kate that is phenomenal, it just proves the power of the subconscious mind to me. I mean you look bloody fit to me what do the doctors say?'

'When I went back, the specialist found nothing, no symptoms and confirmed that I was perfectly healthy and yet he still hedged his bets by saying I was in remission,'

'Is it professional pride or fear of litigation that makes western medicine so inflexible? I'm always amazed that we see the body as separate to the mind and spirit. How you can heal a patient if you look no further than the presenting symptom. Mind you they would argue that they do with tests and x-rays but holistically?' he said.

He shook his head in exasperation and jumped up. With an easy motion he pulled Kate to her feet. 'I think I need to cool down, how about we take the children in for a swim?'

The water was warm and buoyant and she was able to get Ben to lie flat on his back, arms outstretched to float on his own, without her hand supporting him.

Ally practiced her crawl technique splashing vigorously as she swam the distance between Kate and Colin.

Their bodies still gleamed with oily beads of seawater as they sat eating the picnic of ham and cheese rolls and sweet slices of pineapple gazing out to the ocean. On the horizon was a wisp of smoke and a smudged outline of a ship. 'Wonder where that's going kids?' Colin asked.

Ben shouted 'To Australia.'

'Yes maybe it is, Ben, but it just might be coming here like a lot of cruise ships do and perhaps if Mummy is agreeable we could all go down to the docks one day to see these big ships,' Colin said.

Both children clamoured 'Can we Mummy, can we?' Kate laughed as she shook her head at Colin. 'Okay, okay in the interests of fact finding, I agree.'

Susan and Charles babysat the children one evening so that Colin and Kate could go to the Lagoon Hotel. Tony Bennett was performing and Colin used his contacts at the hotel to get them a front row table. The performance didn't start until late in the evening so they had a drink in the piano bar. The leather armchairs were so stoutly upholstered that when you sat on them they puffed out little breathy sighs. A pianist and bass player were playing Son of a Preacher Man as a waiter took their order.

'Love Dusty Springfield, don't you?' Kate said excitedly to Colin. She was too busy looking around the bar to listen to his reply.

He watched her as round-eyed she took in all the trappings of the hotel bar. She wore a jacaranda blue silk dress and he noticed the thin straps of her dress kept slipping off her shoulders and how in one graceful movement her fingers grazed her skin as she replaced them. Their drinks arrived and the duo struck up the haunting melody of *The Look of Love*.

'Do you know this one?', she asked.

'This is the new Burt Bacharach number he wrote for *Casino Royale* which Dusty sings on the soundtrack,' Colin said.

'It's a beautiful melody. I'd love to hear her sing the lyrics,' Kate replied.

'White soul singer that's what they call her. Did you know she was deported from Cape Town in 1964 because she sang to a mixed audience?' Colin asked.

'I was there in 1964 on my trip to Australia, I saw apartheid first hand and it was frightening. She must have had incredible courage to perform in front of an integrated audience.' Kate said.

They talked of places and experiences, their bodies close before Colin looked at his watch in the light of the candle on their table.

'Time to go,' he said as he took her hand and led her out of the bar into the Lagoon Ballroom for the Tony Bennett cabaret performance.

At one end of the ballroom a large stage had been set up with chairs and music stands already in place. Centre stage was dominated by a gleaming black grand piano. They found their table close to the stage and ordered a supper of conch fritters and Caesar Salad with a bottle of Dom Perignon. Their food arrived as the musicians took their places and tuned their instruments. As Colin took the last fritter and Kate the last piece of romaine lettuce, Tony Bennett walked onto the stage to the strains of *The Good Life*. Kate's eyes widened remembering slow dancing with Fred to the tune. The star was much shorter than Kate had imagined but when he started his first number *Fly me to the Moon* she heard only his voice, his energy wrapping her joyfully. She closed her eyes as his voice vibrated through her. She didn't see Colin looking at her. He reached across and took her hand. Tony Bennett sang all of his most popular numbers finishing with

The Best is Yet to Come.

After the performance as they drove home, the lyrics still playing in Kate's head. 'What a night, I so loved it, thank you Colin it was wonderful.'

He grinned 'I loved it too—it was the best.' He walked her to the back door.

'How about tomorrow?' he asked.

'Yes.' Kate replied.

He kissed her before watching her go in and close the door with a final wave. Their kiss was natural, nothing awkward, just a touch of soft yielding lips. If either wanted more they did not press as both felt what they had between them was too precious to risk.

She checked the children before bed humming softly the best is yet to come and her lips tingling with the soft imprint of his lips.

A week had passed since they had breakfast at the club. The days had sped past with Colin taking them all over the island to explore. Some of the days had spilled into early evening barbecues on the beach or at Andrew and Karen's back garden patio. They all shared a motor cruiser to Rose Island where the snorkelling and the beaches were without parallel. There, in the shallow waters of the Caribbean Sea, Colin and the children found a seahorse; an exquisite creature with a coronet crowned horse's head and curled body. They let it go watching its jerky progress as it propelled away from them through the clear blue water. On the day before Colin left for Miami, Andrew, Karen and Colin were invited for dinner. Kate and Susan stood by the meat counter in the local supermarket trying to decide what to cook. Eventually they decided on chicken and parsley pie for main course. In the kitchen they talked as they diced eschallots finely and cut up the chicken into bite size pieces.

'The children like him,' Susan said.

'And he likes them, he is a natural with small children that's for sure, but…' Kate's voice trailed off.

'But what Kate?

'You know my track record since Greg died, Susan. And it's only in the last year or so that I have really got my myself together. I feel content with who I am and I no longer see the kids as a responsibility I have to shoulder but I see us as a family. They're my priority. To be honest I just don't want risk all that on a relationship that just may simply be a holiday romance.'

'I know he cares about you. Karen says she has never seen her brother like this before. Have you considered that he may want more?

They were both silent as they wrapped the chicken in thin slices of prosciutto and scattered over the eschallots, chopped parsley and a dusting of sweet paprika before layering them into a casserole dish.

'We'll do the pastry later.' Susan said.

Willa Mae had set the table that morning polishing the glassware and silverware with a clean tea towel until it sparkled. Now she was busy making a tropical fruit salad for dessert.

'Take the children for a swim, everything's under

control here. Later we only have to plate up the smoked salmon for starters and finish off the pie. I think I'll have a bit of a cat nap.' Susan said as she covered the pie dish with plastic wrap and put it into the refrigerator.

As Kate sat on the steps at the shallow end watching the children, she thought about Colin and the time they had spent together. Being with him is like playing tennis with a good player she thought, not in a competitive way but he makes me want to stretch myself to match his game.

They had sat on Paradise Island's Cabbage Beach sharing similar childhood histories as they watched the children play. Like her family during the war, he was evacuated, his family to a village in Leicestershire but only for a few weeks as his mother missed her own home. He told her about searching for shrapnel on Richmond golf course and how they had a near miss when a V2 bomb landed three doors down. His parents, like hers, were members of the Conservative party and Winston Churchill supporters long before it was fashionable. With each revelation Kate felt the kinship with him intensify.

She loved that they shared a desire to understand who they were, why they were and what life was all about. He found no point too fine, too little to give a thoughtful consideration. When she told him that she feared some of her dark thoughts in case she made them a reality. He had told her that she should not think of herself on the path to perfection but to an acceptance of who she was, the good and the bad. Then, he said, you can make and give energy to choices from your heart.

She smiled when she remembered his telling of his trip to India where he had stayed in an Ashram for a month.

'I spent the whole four weeks meditating, well four hours a day and running to the john as I had Delhi belly. When I wasn't meditating or shitting I was scrubbing bloody floors and still shitting.' His smile etched the lines around his eyes. 'Must have been good for my soul though,' he said.

Kate laughed 'Bet the brochure didn't say shitting was a prerequisite for the path to enlightenment,' she replied. But what her heart wanted to say was they do say eyes are the windows to the soul and I see clearly that your soul is exquisite.

'Mummy, Mummy watch,' Ben swam half-breaststroke and half-dogpaddle towards her, his face a study in concentration.

'That is excellent, Ben, we'll have to take Nana and Grandpa and your cousins to the swimming baths so you can show them how well you swim.'

In the kitchen Kate rinsed and stacked the dishes and cutlery on the draining board ready for Willa Mae to wash in the morning. Susan and Colin carried in the last of the dessert dishes and Andrew's distinctive guffaws could be heard momentarily as Colin held the kitchen door open for Susan.

'That was a beautiful meal, thank you. How about Kate and I make the coffee and you go and sit down. See if you can keep that rowdy brother-in-law of mine under control,' Colin said

'Thank you Colin, I'll do my best,' Susan untied her apron and left them to it.

'Kate, how about we go for a walk on the beach later?' he said as he put coffee into the cafetière. 'It's a full moon and it will be a sight you won't want to miss, anyway I need to talk to you.'

Kate turned to look at him and he winked at her, diffusing the tension. Kate relaxed.

'Friends, right?' he said and she nodded.

The moon shone a pale luminous path across the ocean to the beach.

'A harvest moon, I think,' Kate said as they walked barefoot along the soft sands of the beach. '*Fly me to the moon and let me play amongst the stars,*' she sang.

'I'm not sure if you know it but singing is not your forté,' Colin said.

'How mean, I thought I might be the next Dusty Springfield.' Kate began to sing again. '*I just don't know what to do with myself.*'

Colin joined in the melody '*Doing everything with you.*'

Kate started to laugh. 'Whatever you do don't give up your day job.'

Their pace slowed as they slowly followed the path of the moon on the foreshore. Colin stopped, turned to her and took her hand and pressed it to his lips.

'Kate we both know what is happening here. I don't want to jeopardise our relationship by taking things too fast, but I know that I don't want it to finish here.'

'Neither do I, but Colin I have just got my life together after five torrid years. I feel centred, I suppose, and at peace with my family and myself. I'm frightened of losing sight of myself, which is my pattern in relationships.'

Colin put his arms around her.'When I first saw you in that bikini with that silly red lace jacket I wanted you. I wanted you as yet another casual but beautiful holiday interlude and you, as the wise woman you are, would know I've had my share of these. But from the very first as we talked so openly and honestly I knew that this was different. You talk of your pattern and you're not alone but I believe we have a relationship that is based on trust and mutual support and that any obstacles that may come up can be worked out together. So far we have got it right, first friends and hopefully lovers.'

Kate's breathing almost stilled as she listened to him.

'We take it take one day at a time until we are all sure, you, me and the children. Sometimes you have to take a risk, a well considered risk to get what your heart wants.'

Kate dashed a kiss at him, his lips warm and salty.

'I just wanted to see if there was any chemistry between us,' she said, in almost a whisper.

'And there I was thinking that you already knew that,' he cupped her face in his hands and kissed her again. She thought—what is it about kisses that are so sweet and give so much joy?

'I knew that from the moment I met you,' she replied.

She smiled 'But if you think I am going to make love on the beach and get sand in my crutch, forget it.' He kissed her again saying 'No sand I promise, when I make love to you it will be in the right place at the right time.'

They stood, arms wrapped tightly around each other. The tide had turned and was lapping at their feet, the cool water reminding her that she had swimming lessons early in the morning. When she got back to the house Susan and Charles were in bed so she locked up and tip-toed to her room. She lay looking out through the window to the night sky repeatedly pressing her forefinger to her lips to capture again the feeling of the fullness of his lips and tenderness of his intent.

She went with Karen and Andrew to the airport to see Colin leave. Willa Mae minded the children. She had not expected to feel so desolate when he went through security to board the small plane to take him to Miami. The three of them waited until the plane took off. Karen stood with her arm around Kate.

'He asked me to give this to you with instructions that you are to open it later on your own,' and handed her a small package in a white paper bag.

They dropped her off at home, Susan was out and Willa Mae was playing with the children. 'Just give me ten minutes, Willa Mae, and I will take over,' she said

'No rush Miss Sinclair they're happy.'

Kate went into her room and opened the paper bag, inside was a forty-five single of Dusty Springfield's *I only want to be with you* as well as a card with a picture of a tropical beach scene on the front. Inside Colin had written the chorus line to the song.

'Cause you started something, Oh can't you see, That ever since we met, You had a hold on me, It happens to be true, I only want to be with you.'

Corny I know but it says it all! Colin x

Kate sat on the bed tears splashing onto her lap. She knew that she loved him and that he loved her and that it would all work out one way or another, all she had to do was hold that knowing.

The last few days of her holiday passed quickly. She took Susan and Charles out to dinner at Café Martinique on Paradise Island the night before they left. They had to take a short boat ride across the water to the restaurant's jetty. Lighted torches led the way along the flagstone path to the restaurant. It was a beautiful evening so they opted to eat outside on the patio. As they sipped their pre-dinner drinks she raised her glass.

'How can I ever thank you for such a holiday, it has been the most incredible time and I'm eternally grateful.'

Charles lifted his glass 'Well here's to the next time we meet, Kate, whether it's another holiday here or in London with you.'

Susan added 'And don't forget you'll have to come out again for the christening as you are the baby's godmother.'

Charles nodded as he rubbed Susan's growing tummy.

The flight home was smooth and the children slept most of the time. Kate lay awake in the gloom of the cabin. She was happy, remembering Colins' touch, the gentleness and companionship of their relationship. There was no comparison to her feelings for Jack, which had been lustful, angular and flinty like grit in a wound. This was measured, respectful, tender and full of trust. She imagined him somewhere over the Atlantic sitting in the First Officer's seat on the flight deck. She had never seen him in uniform. He had phoned before she left to wish them a safe journey and that he would see her in London no date yet, but he would let her know. He finished the call by saying he missed her. She didn't want to sleep as she had little time on her own to enjoy the luxury of thinking over and over about him, but soon sleep crept up on her. Frank and Lucy met them at the airport on the cool April morning.

'You look so well Kate and so do the children, look at you two, how brown you are.' Lucy said.

'Grandpa I can swim,' shouted Ally with Ben adding 'So can I.'

'They had lessons while we were there,' Kate said her mind racing ahead with so much to tell them. 'You should see where they live. It's beautiful and the beaches are incredible, anyway they both can swim now and a darn sight better than my Esther Williams side stroke.'

At home all was ready for the family, the Aga happily spitting and burping and the smell of another casserole in the oven for lunch. She used her spirit and perfume allowance to buy her father a bottle of Glenfiddich Single Malt Whiskey and her mother a bottle of Chanel No. 5 perfume. They sat in the kitchen drinking coffee as she told them about Charles and Susan, their home, their hospitality and the baby due in August. Finally she told them that she had met Colin.

'Colin?', her father asked.

'Colin Hunt or to be exact Colin Warwick Hunt,' she replied

'What does he do?' Lucy asked.

'He's a pilot with Pan Am and at the moment, lives in Miami.' Kate replied.

Her mother groaned. 'So far away, are you sure that this is not just a holiday romance?'

Kate looked at her and saw the frown across her brow, her eyes so anxious and full of doubt. Then Kate remembered Colins' words.

'Yes, Mummy, he is far away but we will work it out. Anyway we all know there is no guarantee of anything in this life. Sometimes you have to take a risk, a considered risk to gain your heart.'

Her mother nodded somehow these words had appeased her. Frank kissed her cheek, 'That's wonderful darling,' he said.

Lucy embraced her, her hand patting her back as she had done when Kate was a child.

'I'm sorry darling, don't mean to be negative, I just want you and the children's happiness.'

When they left that afternoon, she unpacked and sorted the washing and took the piles down to the laundry. She bathed the children early, thankful for the early sunset and got them both into bed before six. She was tired but sat at the kitchen bench to sort through the mail that had come while she was away. The phone rang and she wandered up the hall.

Probably Jane wanting to know all about the holiday and Colin she thought, no doubt Mummy would have rung her by now. The voice at the other end was an operator, 'I have a call for you, please hold,' and the familiar deep voice at the end of the line was singing off key the chorus line of I only want to be with you.

'Colin,' she shouted over the final words, 'I told you not to give up your day job,' she said laughing.

'Ah but I have, I managed to get out of my contract early and the good news is I have just signed a contract with BOAC based in London,' he said, 'and I was wondering whether you could get a babysitter this coming weekend as I will be in London.'

Kate squealed with delight.

'I take that as affirmative,' he said.

'I am only here for the weekend. I fly in Friday evening and back to the States on Sunday afternoon. I have to work out another month with Pan Am and then I'll move from Miami to London to start with BOAC at the end of July, which gives us plenty of time to get to know more about each other.'

Kate could hardly speak.

'That's, that's wonderful,' she spluttered.

'At last I've made you speechless.' Colin said.

'No not quite. I love you, Colin.'

'And precious girl, I love you. You make my heart sing.' He paused delighting in Kate's audible sigh. 'I have booked a room at the Dorchester, are you okay with that?'

'Yes,' Kate murmured.

'Kate don't come out to the airport the traffic is a shambles at peak hour. It will be quicker for me to catch the shuttle in and meet you at the hotel.'

She wandered excitedly through the house, wanting to shout out loud her happiness. She wanted to phone her parents, her sister, Susan and Charles. In the lounge she picked up Greg's picture. It was the black and white profile shot of him smiling and looking into the distance. She kissed the picture and took it into the kitchen. The Aga hissed and coughed as she took out her notepad and wrote.

My dearest Greg,

I hear others who grieve, speak as though their loved ones are close by. Not dead, as I heard some one say but simply in another room. Time stopped when you died and I tried desperately to hang-on to you, to feel that you were simply a room away. Believing I would serve my time, like a prisoner, in my four walls. Seeking diversions to deaden the pain until we could meet again. But as time passed my grief taught me so many things about myself, exposing not only my strengths but laying bare my vulnerabilities. I'm no longer a prisoner of my own making. I have grown into a more compassionate and grounded person. The bitterness and anger has gone.

I look back now with love and thanks for your life. I lost you but I found myself. I feel that grief was your sacred gift to me. I can only write this to you because to others, who have not travelled the same path, it would be untenable to think of grief as a gift and for some who grieve I understand they will never see it as such, but for me this is the way it is. How the children will react when they are adult, I don't know. Their wounds I'm sure will shape their lives. I can only do my best to assuage their loss but if it is not enough it has to be their own journey to wholeness.

I know you would be happy for me that I'm ready to embrace love again. My love for you and your memory will always be a constant in my life but now my dearest it's time for me to let go and move forward.

Katie x

Carefully she removed the pages from the notepad and folded the letter in half. She opened the furnace door of the Aga and threw in the letter watching it curl and ash in the flames.

LOSING YOU

Also by Mary Atkins

A Journey of Creative Healing

I need to put my focus on being creative. I need to create something new each day. It doesn't matter what—I simply need to focus on the planning and joy of creativity.

Mary Atkins was a young mother of two small children when her husband was tragically killed in a light aircraft accident. Her body, already exhibiting signs that something was amiss, bore the brunt of this tragedy and at the age of 27 she was diagnosed with multiple sclerosis. Doctors told her she would be wheelchair-bound within months.

But that's not what happened.

Instead, Mary recovered. Her journey to wellness began when she acted on a powerful intuitive voice that suggested she undertake a strict daily program of creative expression—to plan, create or do something she had never done before. Within twelve months she could once again walk without aids. She has now been in full remission from MS for more than fifty years.

In A Journey of Creative Healing Mary shares her remarkable story—and those of other survivors who have endured equally debilitating emotional and physical shocks—and reveals how listening to your intuitive voice, exploring creativity in all its guises, can deliver recovery from overwhelming grief and profound illness. By following her six steps to healing Mary believes you too can find your way home to health.

Also by Mary Atkins

Finding Your Voice:
Ten Steps to Successful Public Speaking

Have you ever been asked to address an audience? Did the prospect create butterflies in your stomach?

Don't worry—you're not alone! But help is on its way. *Finding Your Voice: Ten Steps to Successful Public Speaking* is the definitive self-help guide to presenting and public speaking. *Finding Your Voice* provides a comprehensive step-by-step approach to becoming an effective speaker, covering a range of public speaking challenges. Learn the importance of sound planning, how to project your voice, manage stage fright, make the most of audio equipment and more. It also includes inspirational advice from some of Australia's leading celebrity speakers.

Organised in two sections, Part One cover the ten confidence-building steps to becoming a successful speaker. Part Two provides practical tips for the ten most common speaking assignments from proposing a toast, the responsibilities of an emcee and presenting a eulogy through to workshop presentations, debates, formal speeches, media presentations and chairing meetings.

No matter what the occasion, *Finding Your Voice: Ten Steps to Successful Public Speaking* will help turn your good ideas into great speeches!